GUIDE US HOME

Visit us at www.boldstrokesbooks.com

By CF Frizzell

Stick McLaughlin: The Prohibition Years
Exchange
Night Voice
Nantucket Rose
Crossing the Line
Measure of Devotion
As Seen on TV!
Guide Us Home

By Jesse J. Thoma

Tales of Lasher, Inc
The Chase
Pedal to the Metal
Data Capture

The Serenity Prayer Series
Serenity
Courage
Wisdom

Romances
Seneca Falls
Hero Complex
The Town That Built Us
Guide Us Home

GUIDE US HOME

by

CF Frizzell & Jesse J. Thoma

2024

GUIDE US HOME
© 2024 By CF Frizzell & Jesse J. Thoma. All Rights Reserved.

ISBN 13: 978-1-63679-533-1

This Trade Paperback Original Is Published By
Bold Strokes Books, Inc.
P.O. Box 249
Valley Falls, NY 12185

First Edition: February 2024

Credits
Editor: Cindy Cresap
Production Design: Susan Ramundo
Cover Design By Tammy Seidick

Acknowledgments

CF Frizzell

The concept of *Guide Us Home*'s parallel stories is Jesse's clever brainchild and I'm grateful she not only asked me to join her on this project, but that the remarkable tale I uncovered begged for a broad audience. I've taken some license with the facts, but the root of Tove and Jonna's story exists in museums and history books throughout Denmark today.

With world affairs currently in turmoil, the irony in the timing here can't be overstated. To the Danes in 1943, their Jewish citizens were—above all—their proud countrymen, and Denmark rose against their oppression. *Rallying as a nation*, Denmark evacuated its Jews to safety and nearly all survived WW II.

Lighthouse tenders like the fictious *Engle* in *Guide Us Home* played vital, dangerous roles in helping the Danish Resistance. I acknowledge the *Engle*'s namesake here, the *Gerda III*, one of three surviving tenders from that effort, and the courageous twenty-two-year-old, Henny Sindig, who led its small crew. Donated to New York's Museum of Jewish Heritage by the Danish Parliament after the war, *Gerda III*, today, is drydocked for restoration at Mystic Seaport Museum in Mystic, Connecticut.

Nearly lost to time, the heroic account of the Danish effort is both staggering and heartening, and I was honored to bring some of it to light.

Jesse J. Thoma

I would be remiss if I did not start my acknowledgments with a hearty thank you to CF Frizzell for joining me on this project. She is generous with her ideas, talent, and time. I'm excited to watch everyone fall in love with Tove and Jonna as I did.

To you, dear reader, I say thank you. Writing for you is a pleasure and I hope you enjoy the stories waiting for you.

Dedication

To Kathy
The most beautiful guiding light.

To Alexis, Goose, Bird, and little Purple Martin
You are the lights of my life.

CHAPTER ONE

The boat rocked precariously under Samantha McMann's foot as she stepped on board. She swung her arms wildly to catch her balance. A two-thousand-dollar power suit and custom-made wingtips were fantastic corporate armor but provided no protection from looking like an inexperienced ass boarding a boat. As Sam looked around at the other passengers and what they'd chosen to wear for their nautical adventure, it was possible the suit and shoes had already pegged her as an ass.

Her boat mates were wearing shorts, cargo pants, T-shirts, lightweight joggers, and windbreakers. The captain of the small water taxi, as he'd called it, was in jeans and a long-sleeved shirt. She was the only one dressed as if they were heading to present at the United Nations. At least she and the clouds on the horizon had coordinated their colors. Charcoal gray was fashionable in any season or weather.

Sam lurched her way to an open seat close to the back of the boat. It was a short walk, but since the damn boat wouldn't stay still long enough for her to pick one foot up and put it back down, she had to move slowly or risk landing on a stranger's lap or worse, going overboard.

"Did you stumble onto the wrong boat?" A woman with fiery red hair and an amused look on her face gave Sam a casual once-over. "This one's heading to the lighthouse. Maybe you're trying to get to Newport?"

Before Sam could answer, the captain pulled away from the dock. Her stomach immediately reconsidered breakfast. She took a few deep breaths. It was a fifteen-minute ride, she could make it. She could do anything for fifteen minutes. *Including puke your guts out in front of this pretty lady.*

"I'm going to the lighthouse too," Sam managed to gasp between waves of nausea. She rested her elbows on her knees and cradled her head.

The redhead leaned forward so Sam could see her face. "My family says I'm too blunt and I don't mean to be rude, but what made you want to buy a lighthouse? You don't look like you've ever been on a boat before. You clearly don't have the stomach." She paused and looked at Sam's feet. "Or the shoes for it, and we're headed to an island. The only way off is another boat ride."

Sam grunted. She didn't have to share her reasons with the competition, and next time she'd take the helicopter. Boat problem solved. Sam's stomach steadied enough that she risked looking up at the woman criticizing her favorite footwear.

Her breath hitched. She'd never seen eyes the color of emeralds. They were stunning. If only the woman they belonged to didn't look so thoroughly unimpressed with Sam. She looked again. Not unimpressed exactly. More amused, pitying.

She'd be more impressed if I had the helicopter.

Sam took a deep breath, gripped the side of her seat with both hands, and sat up. The woman was still evaluating her. There was no way she'd be moved in the least by Sam's helicopter; she didn't look the type. Women were always impressed with the helicopter. *What the hell?*

"I'm Nancy Calhoun. We'll be pulling up soon, but for the ride back, it's better if you focus your attention on a spot off in the distance, something that doesn't move. Then just breathe nice and slow." She extended her hand.

Sam was reticent to unbalance the equilibrium she and her stomach had achieved, but it was rude not to take the offered hand. "Samantha McMann."

Nancy's eyebrows shot up, but she didn't say anything at the mention of Sam's well-known name. "Don't feel bad about puking if you need to. You won't be the first. And there aren't any paparazzi here." She inclined her head toward the front of the boat.

Just the time I want to be recognized.

Sam didn't dare look, but she could hear evidence of stomach upset and pieced together what Nancy meant. She was not going to be joining that group no matter how terrible she felt.

The captain announced their arrival, and Sam heard more than one relieved exclamation. "The motion doesn't bother you?" Sam breathed deeply and looked over Nancy's shoulder as the boat pulled alongside the island's small, well-worn wooden dock.

"Practically born on the water. Haven't had it make my stomach dance yet. You, though, might want to check with the captain about some meds. The forecast and those clouds promise to make an adventurous trip back." With that, Nancy winked and hopped gracefully onto dry land, then hugged someone farther up the dock.

Sam followed with much less grace. Once she was ashore, the wind picked up twofold. Her short hair, which had been styled to look effortlessly windswept, now actually was. For once she didn't immediately try to tame it back into something presentable. Instead, she turned her back against the sand being kicked up. Her stomach was cursing her, she didn't need to be blinded before she climbed the steep stairs to get a look at her prize.

Once up the stairs and on level ground, Sam took a moment to soak in the view. The island was roughly a hundred feet above sea level and provided an uninterrupted panorama of Narragansett Bay. The water squirmed and danced with wind-fueled whitecaps and reflected the darkening, moody sky.

"Beautiful, isn't it?" Nancy indicated the view all around.

"I see a lot that I find beautiful." Sam didn't bother with the scenery anymore. A lighthouse didn't need to be the only thing she captured on this trip.

Nancy rolled her eyes. "Oh please. If you want to 'Samantha McMann' a woman I'm sure you'll have plenty of takers, but it's not going to be me. I'll save you the trouble now. I'm here for one reason and it's not you. No offense."

Ouch.

Sam took a step back. "What do you mean 'Samantha McMann' a woman? Never mind." Sam held up her hand against any answer Nancy might provide. "I'm here for the same purpose you are. I apologize for implying you're beautiful. I didn't mean to make you uncomfortable."

Nancy fixed her with a quick stare. "You can imply whatever you like, you wouldn't be the first, but a compliment with an agenda is hardly a compliment, hmm? We have time to look around the island before the boat takes us back." She started off, away from Sam, before stopping and turning back. "Do you know what that building is?" She pointed to a long low building shaped like a Swiss roll.

Sam considered the building carefully, then walked over for a closer look. The inside was long, perhaps two train cars in length, and the ceiling was concave. Being inside felt like floating in the midpoint of a tube. The lights were dim, and the shape and light made the atmosphere moody and intimate.

"No idea what it was, but can you imagine this place as a pub? It's perfect." The design was materializing before Sam's eyes.

"A pub?" Nancy's voice pitched higher, the annoyance unmistakable. "You don't care about the remarkable history of this building at all? Your plan is to spit on it and build a bar?"

"Yes." Sam felt a small pang of guilt when confronted with Nancy's crossed arms and frown. "I'd put up a plaque of course."

"Ugh. Of course, you would." Nancy pointed at the bridge looming nearly over the island. "Do you know what bridge that is?"

Sam had quickly glanced at a map of Rhode Island before she'd flown from her home on the West Coast and scrambled to remember anything useful now. She shrugged.

Nancy frowned more deeply. "Why do you want this lighthouse, hmm? You live across the country, you clearly don't care about the history, and you get seasick easily."

Given how well her pub idea had landed, Sam wasn't eager to share the rest of her vision for the island. "Why do you want the lighthouse?"

Nancy's expression softened and she relaxed her posture. "This lighthouse is part of Rhode Island's history."

Sam nodded. "And I believe it can be part of its future."

"I guess that's why we have the proposal process. While you were trying not to puke on the boat, I counted four other bidders. One of them wants to turn the entire island into a dance club." Nancy shuddered.

"And now my bar idea isn't looking so bad, right?" Sam raised an eyebrow.

"I can't imagine what would happen to the lighthouse itself if this all became a dance club." Nancy scrunched her nose, clearly disgusted.

"Wouldn't be hard to transform the light into a disco ball." Sam barely kept a straight face.

Nancy laughed. "Even if you're funny, don't expect me to like you."

Sam shook her head. "I should hope not. I'm the competition and I have plans for pubs and other evil things. I'm very unlikeable."

Nancy searched Sam's face longer than Sam was comfortable with. "When you said your proposal made the lighthouse part of Rhode Island's future, who's future did you mean? Would everyone get to take part?"

Sam hesitated. "If this becomes a business venture, then yes, it would be open to the public." Was that vague enough?

"If it becomes a business venture? As opposed to a, what? Private venture?" Nancy's eyes widened. "You're trying to buy this lighthouse and the rest of the island so you can fly across the country and have drinks in there? As opposed to literally any other bar, pub, or fancy club anywhere in the world?" She pointed inside the half dome building. "Have this whole island as your private play place? Doesn't sound like much of a future here for anyone but you. Don't you already have enough? What about the rest of us?"

Sam put her hands up in the universal sign of surrender. "I get it doesn't look good from your perspective, but if we agreed about our proposals we would have teamed up. Let me guess, you're hoping to turn this place into an out of the way, inconvenient museum no one will ever visit? The metaphorical Alcatraz for history?"

Nancy practically growled, confirming Sam's guess.

"We clearly got off on the wrong foot. Let me buy you dinner," Sam said. "We won't talk about lighthouses or either of our proposals. I won't ask you any personal questions and you can choose to ignore who I am too. We can talk about..." She fumbled for a safe topic. "Sports, or Tokyo's conveyor belt sushi restaurants or fashion during the Ming dynasty."

"Do you know anything about any of those topics?" Nancy looked dubious.

"Only one, but you'd have to come to dinner with me to find out which." Sam put on her most winning smile.

Nancy shook her head. Her green eyes had lost some of the earlier softness when they'd been teasing each other. "I told you already, if you want to go full rich playgirl, you do you, but it's not to going to happen with me. We're competitors and I don't swoon at the kinds of things you offer your dates."

Sam huffed. It took work to keep her face neutral. "You don't know anything about me or what I offer."

Nancy shrugged, unapologetic. "You're on the cover of nearly every gossip magazine at every checkout at the supermarket. How could I not know you? And even if I wanted to believe they'd gotten you wrong, you've done nothing here to sway my opinion. Good luck with your proposal. I hope you come visit my museum when it opens." She turned and walked quickly toward the lighthouse.

"I'll comp you a room the first night I open my luxury resort out here. I'll fly you out on my helicopter. We can have drinks at the pub. And I lied, I could have talked to you about all three things. I bet the tabloids didn't tell you that." Somehow Sam managed not to stick out her tongue at Nancy's retreating form. *Very nice, McMann, handled that one like a champ.* Why had she taken the bait and let Nancy rile her up? Maybe more importantly, why had Nancy's words hit such a nerve?

Before Sam could follow, raindrops began dotting the crushed stone pathway. She walked quickly, without another word, for the protection of the lighthouse. She was steps from reaching its shelter when the sky opened into a fierce deluge. She ducked inside but not before she caught sight of the angry water. The boat ride back was going to be hell. This was hardly the introduction Sam had envisioned when she hatched the plan to buy this lighthouse. Today it was hard to picture the exclusive luxury getaway she planned to build here.

Sam looked at Nancy and the others huddled in the main room of the lighthouse, all here to prepare proposals, same as she was. Even though this wasn't a straight bidding process, Sam had money and the McMann name. Apparently, Nancy was a fan of history, but unfortunately for her, history was on Sam's side. She had deep pockets, the right last name, and a winning proposal. It felt too easy. Of course she held the winning hand.

CHAPTER TWO

Nancy stopped stewing about her encounter with Samantha Freaking McMann long enough to give her menu a cursory glance. She and her family came to this seafood shack on the tip of Galilee often enough that she didn't need to look. Maybe one day something new would pop up and surprise her, but that day wasn't today. She ordered her usual fried shrimp.

"She couldn't have been as bad as you're saying, Nan." Kevin, the youngest of Nancy's three older brothers, handed out silverware wrapped in paper napkins.

"If anything, I'm underplaying it. She wants to turn the lighthouse and island into an exclusive luxury resort. If she decides to open it to visitors at all. She might keep it for herself as some kind of vacation island. What do rich people do with whole islands?" She rubbed her temples remembering her sparring session with Samantha.

"Anything they want I would imagine." Sean, the oldest of the five siblings, chimed in.

"Well, hopefully, the committee will see what a joke her idea is. She'll trample all over the history of the island and lighthouse. She wasn't the only one. None of the others there seemed to care how important that place is to Rhode Island's past." Nancy toyed with the paper ring holding the napkin securely around her cutlery.

"If you win, are you going to be able to make ends meet out there? Nonprofits, museums, they have a hard time keeping the lights on, and they're not on islands. Are you confident people will bother making the trip?" Casey, Nancy's middle older brother, looked concerned.

Nancy shot him a look, daring him to say more. "You sound just like *her*."

Casey held up his hands, clearly anticipating her reaction. "All I'm saying is there's a reason it's being offloaded. Maybe the way to make a small fortune off a lighthouse on an island is to start with a very big fortune."

"It would break my heart if she won. You should have seen how little respect she had for anything that came before." She shook her head slowly. "All she could see was how it should be changed."

"Tell them about the part where she hit on you. Twice." Nancy's sister, Eloise, waggled her eyebrows over her water glass.

"She what?" all three brothers choroused.

Nancy rolled her eyes. "Perhaps her biggest offense. Did she think I'd fall for that? I have no interest being her latest plaything on the cover of all the tabloids."

Kevin leaned back against his chair and looked at the ceiling. "One of the richest women in the country, one who's hot as sin in summer by the way, hits on you, and you're offended. There's no hope. I'm revoking my offer of ever being your wingman." He sat up and made a motion of washing his hands of her.

"You never offered in the first place." Nancy rolled her eyes again but couldn't help smiling.

"Well, consider it offered and rescinded." Kevin winked.

"I'm with Kev. I might actually swoon if she hit on me." Casey laughed.

Eloise's eyes went wide. She not so subtly pointed across the restaurant. "Warm up your flirting skills, big brothers, you might get your chance. Look who just walked in."

Nancy and her brothers all turned and gawked in the direction Eloise pointed.

"Very subtle, you four. Everyone okay? No whiplash we need to have checked out on the way home?"

"I wonder how she found this place?" Nancy was more careful when she looked over at Samantha this time.

"The place is packed. She's not going to find a table." Sean surveyed the restaurant. "I'm going to be a gentleman and invite her to join us."

"You will do no such thing." Nancy pointed him back to his seat. He ignored her. She glared at him and tried again to convey how opposed she was to his idiotic plan. He already had his back to her, though, and didn't see. She was faced with accepting her brother's impulsive decision or dragging him back to the table and making a scene. Neither was a good option, but she chose decorum over going viral. It was only one meal. Maybe Samantha would say no.

Before the hope could fully marinate, Sean was pulling over an extra chair and wedging it between his seat and Casey's. "Nancy, you already met Samantha McMann. Everyone else, Samantha McMann."

It was probably her imagination, but Nancy thought Samantha looked a little unbalanced as she gave a half wave to Nancy's siblings and took a seat. Nancy had to admit, without the power suit and looking slightly off her game, Samantha was far more attractive. Not that she'd ever admit that to anyone, out loud, ever.

"Nancy, nice to see you again." Samantha looked like she meant it, which was disarming. "Your brother was insistent I join you. I hope that's not a problem given you don't like me." Samantha smiled, but it didn't look like the megawatt charmer she'd deployed earlier on the island. This one seemed genuine.

Nancy pointed to the empty seat. "You'll never get a table here at this hour. We're your only hope." She smiled. *You'll give her the wrong idea.*

Samantha nodded her thanks and sat.

"So, Nancy says your proposal for the lighthouse is the work of the devil. Tell us about it." Kevin popped a French fry in his mouth and smiled innocently at Samantha.

Nancy kicked him under the table. "Those words never came out of my mouth, Kevin. Samantha's here for dinner, leave her be."

The waitress came by, and Samantha ordered before answering Kevin. "It's okay, Nancy. As I said at the lighthouse, if we saw eye to eye, we would have teamed up. Kevin, your sister and I definitely have a difference of opinion when it comes to the future direction of the lighthouse. But mine doesn't involve pole or line dancing, so I should get credit for that." She looked at Nancy with a crooked smile.

"I never mentioned either of those when I told you about the dance club proposal." Nancy knew she was being baited but swam into the trap anyway. "You were the one who brought up the disco ball."

Samantha raised her eyebrows. "But now my pub in the dome room doesn't seem like the worst thing you heard out there, does it?"

"The 'dome room' is a bomb proof barracks from the eighteen hundreds that was later used to store munitions, including torpedo prototypes during the Second World War," Nancy responded. "The Naval presence in Newport and the islands in Narragansett Bay were almost single-handedly responsible for our Navy's current torpedo capabilities. Did any of you know that?" She looked around the table at five blank faces.

"A pub in a bomb-proof building?" Sean whispered behind his hand to Samantha, but the whole table could hear him. "One that used to hold torpedoes? Think of what you could name the drinks."

"There's already the Depth Charge, the French Seventy-Five..." Eloise started listing drinks.

"Whose side are you all on?" Nancy stabbed her fork at a fried shrimp.

No one paid any attention to her annoyance.

"Isn't there a drink called a Torpedo?" Casey's face lit up.

Samantha nodded. "That one's good, but only if you have a skilled bartender. Your sister's right, though. I didn't know about the history of the building. Would you feel better, Nancy, if I put up more than a small plaque?"

"I'd feel better if you withdrew from the competition and let me build my museum. That building shouldn't be a pub with a cursory nod to history. The history should be celebrated as the main event. Where are you and your guests going to sleep? What are your plans for the other buildings?"

Samantha looked uncomfortable again. "You're not going to like what I have to say and I'm sure you can imagine what's in my proposal given the sour look on your face. I'm not building a hotel on the island, but there needs to be a place to sleep, whether it's for me or private guests. There's no kitchen, so that needs to be built. I'm advertising luxury so no one's going to be using a pit toilet. A spa's not out of the question."

The longer Samantha spoke the more Nancy's stomach churned. Surely this was a joke. How could she be serious?

"I know everything I'm saying boils your blood," Samantha continued. "It's not that I don't respect the history of the place, but I tend to look forward, not back. There's no money to be made living in the past." Samantha must have read the look on Nancy's face because her look bordered on apologetic.

"Some things are more important than profit, hmm?" Nancy concentrated on relaxing her jaw.

"Look, at least with my proposal there will be people still visiting the lighthouse. You can help me put up plaques or write books so anyone who wants to know the history can read about it." Samantha smiled her big, charming smile. Nancy had seen the genuine version, but this one looked faker than fake.

I bet she's used to that smile getting her anything she wants.

"What do you all think about this?" Nancy looked at her siblings who'd been watching the tennis rally back-and-forth.

"If there are going to be yachts, I don't like it. They'll scare the fish away." Kevin nodded decisively at Nancy and crossed his arms. Sean joined him.

"You two don't fish anywhere near there," Casey injected. "If there are yachts count me in. I'm a marine technician and can repair anything on the water. If you ever need maintenance or repair and you're in the area, look me up." He dug in his wallet and handed Samantha a business card. Nancy thought it was funny Casey still carried business cards, but it served him well now.

Samantha took the card with a smile, a real one. She tucked it in the pocket of her jeans and looked to Eloise. "Four out of five. What's your opinion?"

Eloise responded with a prolonged, parental look. "There are two things you need to know about me. The first is that I'm extremely loyal to my sister and if she says your plan is shit, then I agree. The second is I'm a scientist, so Nancy's feelings aside, I don't have enough information to make an informed decision. There are sea birds federally classified as threatened nesting on that island. Have you heard of piping plovers?"

Samantha shook her head.

"Every nesting pair counts in Rhode Island. It's taken decades of work to increase their numbers. I will be personally disappointed in you if you disturb hard won nesting ground." Eloise employed her deadly serious stare which still made Nancy cave to almost anything.

Samantha nodded, mouth slightly ajar. She looked like a child who'd been scolded by her nana.

"I'm not done." Eloise fixed Samantha with another equally powerful gaze. "The waters around the island also need protecting. If you are planning on bringing a flotilla of luxury vessels, you'd better have a plan for protecting the sea life. Your proposal is to buy the lighthouse. You don't own the island residents or the surrounding ocean."

"I suppose not." Samantha looked down at her plate which had arrived while she was being dressed down.

"Leave her be. She got the message." There was no reason to continue banging Samantha over the head with the anti-resort message, and even Nancy was ready to move on. "How about you tell us something interesting about your life? We'll leave the lighthouse talk alone, I promise."

For the rest of dinner, the conversation was light and easy. Samantha was relaxed and charming. Nancy wasn't sure if it was genuine or part of spending time with the famous "Samantha McMann," but it was better than fighting over the best use of a one-hundred-and-fifty-year-old building. And after the committee heard the proposals and she was awarded the lighthouse, she'd never have to see Samantha again. A win-win for her, right?

CHAPTER THREE

Sam squirmed her toes in her shoes and put her hands in her pockets so she could fidget without being seen. She'd never had this kind of reaction to a business presentation before. Unbidden, a thought of Nancy and her furious opposition to everything Sam suggested popped into her head. What the hell did that mean, and more importantly, what if the committee felt similarly?

While she awaited judgment, Sam studied the five members of the lighthouse preservation committee. Mr. Willard Furman, Mr. Spencer Lancaster, Mrs. Katherine Blythe, and Mrs. Grace Coolidge were all businesslike and efficient, but Mrs. Natalie L. Jones was the obvious ringleader. Sam had pegged her straightaway as the one needing to be impressed most, and the problem at the moment was she looked anything but.

"Thank you, Ms. McMann. Please step outside with the others. We'll be out to get all of you shortly." Mr. Furman barely glanced over the glasses dangling precariously at the tip of his nose. It was possible the only thing keeping gravity from doing its work were a few wiry silver hairs poking out of each nostril.

Sam's high hopes were starting to sink. Where had she gone wrong? Was a nightclub or animal sanctuary really a better choice? She shuddered thinking of the island's natural beauty being soiled by porta-potties and poop bags.

"How'd it go in there?"

Sam jumped. She wanted to be upset at Nancy for sneaking up on her, but the truth was she'd been so lost in thought, a marching band could have made an unnoticed approach. "Honestly, no idea. I'd never play those five at poker though. You?"

Nancy looked relieved. "Same. I'm glad to hear you had no better luck with the CIA Five, as we've been calling them out here. No one has a clue how this is going to go."

"My father should hire a couple of them. We have negotiators who make obscene salaries that are easier reads." Sam shook her head with a chuckle.

Nancy studied her. "Do you work for your father?" She asked it as a question, but it seemed like she already had an opinion about the answer. "I see your name listed with your father's when something big happens with the company, but your picture usually circulates for other reasons." Nancy moved a rock around with her toe.

"Are you more interested in my social life now than when we first met?" Sam tried to catch Nancy's eye without success.

Nancy scoffed. "Absolutely not. Only wondering how you have the time to pursue both. If you're as serious about your career as those shoes you wore out here the first time suggested."

Before Sam could think of a witty retort, or decide if she'd been slickly insulted, the door to the lighthouse opened and Mrs. Jones ushered all of the applicants inside.

"Good luck. Here's to the future." Sam offered Nancy a fist bump as they filed toward the door.

"May history be on my side." Nancy gave a sly grin and returned the gesture.

Sam found a spot to stand at the back of the room. She liked keeping everyone in front of her, being able to observe all that was said and the unspoken body language. It was something her father had taught her as a child, and it had always served her well. All she saw now was a room full of tense shoulders and rapt attention.

"First, thank you everyone for your thoughtful, detailed, and heartfelt presentations. It was clear to all of us how much time and energy went into preparing them. This lighthouse means a great deal to each of us which is why we are undertaking this proposal process instead of selling to the highest bidder." Mrs. Jones took the time to make eye contact with each of the individuals who had presented.

There was plenty of shifting and throat clearing from the attendees. Sam wanted Mrs. Jones to get on to the announcement too, but she stayed still. At least no one could see the jitters in her stomach.

"I know you are all anxious to hear our decision, so I'll get right to it. As a committee we've decided we won't be accepting any of the proposals as written."

For a moment, there was silence and then a chorus of questions filled the air. Sam was more interested in hearing from Mrs. Jones than shouting into the din so she stayed quiet. She noticed Nancy was also silent, her eyebrows scrunched in puzzlement.

Mr. Furman put his thumb and index finger on either side of his mouth and whistled loudly. "Don't believe the lady was done speaking. If you will, Nat."

"Thank you, Willard. As I said, we aren't accepting any of the proposals as they are *currently* written. The committee extends its appreciation for your participation. Now, lunch is available on the lawn. Please do enjoy the beautiful view with your meal."

The shuffle to the door was silent. Everyone seemed stunned. Sam knew there were still questions on the tip of everyone's tongue, but Mrs. Jones had made it clear now was not the time.

"Oh, Ms. McMann, Ms. Calhoun, would you mind waiting a moment, please?" Mrs. Jones waved them back in with a small smile.

Sam looked at Nancy. She looked as wary as Sam felt.

"We'll cut to the chase so you don't miss lunch." Mr. Furman ran his fingers along the length of his impressive mustache. "We all like pieces of your proposals but can't green-light either one. Ms. McMann, the exclusivity of your proposal doesn't serve the long-term vision we had for the lighthouse. If you want to buy a lighthouse, there are plenty of others the Coast Guard has for sale. But we do like the idea of the island being open to overnight guests."

The words stung, but Sam could tell arguing would get her nowhere. She glanced at Nancy who wasn't doing a great job hiding her "I told you so" look. Sam didn't want to buy *any* lighthouse. She wanted this one.

"And, Ms. Calhoun. The history of this lighthouse and this island is dear to each of our hearts. However, we didn't feel you made a convincing case that you could sustain a museum out here without another source of income or funding."

Nancy started to argue, but Mr. Furman held up his hand.

"I know you mention donors and grants, but donors are a fickle bunch and grants are never guaranteed. You're a long way from the wealth in Providence, by Rhode Island standards, and the money that arrives in the southern part of the state in the summer will be at the beach."

Sam's gut churned. "You said you couldn't accept any of the proposals as written, but you asked us to stay. Are you giving feedback to everyone, or were we singled out for a reason?"

"A businesswoman, right to the point. I like that." Mrs. Jones crossed her arms and looked intently at Sam and Nancy. "We want you to work together and combine your proposals into something we can accept."

Sam stiffened and felt her eyebrows shoot up. She saw Nancy react similarly.

"No," they said in unison, looking at each other.

"All she cares about is making money." Nancy pointed at Sam.

"She doesn't care if she makes any money." Sam gestured to Nancy.

"She wants to trample all over the history of this place." Nancy sighed.

"If she gets her way, every shrub, rock, and seashell will be designated a historical landmark." Sam looked to the ceiling.

Her focus snapped back down when Mrs. Jones started laughing.

"Are you two quite done? You sound like petulant children not getting your way, but I can also tell that you will be more than okay if you give each other a chance."

"How can you possibly know that?" Sam looked from Mrs. Jones to Nancy. "We don't even like each other."

"Or each other's proposal." Nancy glared at Sam.

Mrs. Jones laughed again. "Because I'm four hundred years old and I've seen some things in my time. Now, you have thirty minutes or as long as it takes us to eat our lunch to decide if you accept our terms."

"What if we say no?" Nancy looked curious now.

"Then we reopen the proposal stage and neither of you are eligible to reapply." Mrs. Jones shrugged and headed for the door with the other four committee members. "I'm rooting for you. Don't let me down."

As soon as the door closed, Sam and Nancy turned to each other. Sam felt like prey on the wide-open savannah. Nancy certainly looked ready to pounce.

"How did you pull that off?" It didn't seem possible, but Nancy's red hair seemed more aflame the angrier she sounded.

Sam pointed to herself. "Me? What makes you think I'd need to pull anything off? You heard them. You'd be bankrupt out here in a matter of months. Sounds like you need me more than I need you."

It looked like Nancy was warring with herself and her better angels. Sam knew all about fighting to keep something desperate to escape locked up tight inside, but she'd never seen the fight play out so plainly on another's face. Or so beautifully.

"We're wasting time arguing. I need a few minutes. Meet back here in five with cooler heads?" Nancy didn't give Sam a chance to answer before ducking into one of the smaller rooms and closing the door.

Sam looked around for somewhere to retreat herself. Nancy had taken the only room with a door aside from the bathroom, so Sam settled into one of the oversized armchairs at the side of the room. She glanced at Nancy's closed door and caught herself wondering what that room was used for. What had Nancy done to her to make her care about something like that?

A book on the end table caught her eye. She flipped it over and read the back cover blurb. She almost set it back down but was taken by its premise: two women struggling to preserve their love for each other *and a lighthouse* amidst the throes of World War II. Too ironic and so fitting for her current moment.

Sam sighed. Although she was happy to give Nancy all the time she needed, Sam already knew the outcome of this standoff. They'd both concede and move forward together. She'd spent enough of her childhood in boardrooms with her father to know when someone had been outmaneuvered and was out of moves. In this case it was checkmate Sam and Nancy.

After five minutes, Nancy emerged, seemingly having come to the same conclusion. "I'm not giving up on my dreams for this place. If that means I have to bring you along with me, I guess we're teaming up. That good with you?"

"I think I should be asking you, since it looks like those words taste like four-day-old fish." Sam winked, which elicited an eye roll and the hint of a smile.

"I have an office we can use for work." Nancy looked less confident. "It's probably not as lavish as you're used to."

Sam wanted to pinch the bridge of her nose and throw something, but she settled for a couple of subtle deep breaths. "Why don't we both let go of what we assume about the other and try to learn a little of the truth? Since we'll be working together now?"

Nancy evaluated her. A smile cracked her impassive facade. "I think that sounds like a good first step. Step two, when would you like to start work?"

Although Sam was used to the fast pace of her family business, she still had the urge to step back from Nancy and ask for another five minutes. This project was supposed to be her carefree pet project, a nice diversion from the real life she didn't want back home. Nancy was certainly diverting, but not at all in the way Sam had intended.

She looked at the book still in her hand. Perhaps Mrs. Jones would allow her to borrow it. Getting lost in the pages of a good book sounded like exactly what she needed. Who knew, maybe the two women and their lighthouse, decades and miles away, would have something to teach her. Nancy certainly believed in the magic of history, time to see what the fuss was all about.

CHAPTER FOUR

October 1943
Nazi-occupied Denmark

"Obviously, it gets a bit lonely out here." Jonna wiped salty mist from her cheeks. She knew Tove couldn't disagree. They leaned on the railing and pondered the Oresund Strait, that vast expanse of open sea surrounding them on the Drogden Lighthouse. Tove's regular visits out here were part of her job, but they meant so much more than that to Jonna.

Tove bumped their shoulders. "Bringing the children now and then livened things up, didn't it?" she countered with a grin. "Everyone enjoyed putting smiles on those faces, you, your father, our whole crew. It brightened everyone's day, made Drogden an exciting, fun place to be."

"Granted. On *those* occasions."

"It's dramatically beautiful here, Jonna, regardless of the weather, really." She cast an eye to the cottony clouds. "Now that you've moved in to help your father, Drogden can't really be a desolate outpost."

Recalling that decision sent a wave of resignation over Jonna. Drogden *was* a desolate outpost, a granite island in the middle of the strait's deep-water shipping lanes, but her heart hadn't given her much choice. And Drogden's occupation by the Nazis a month ago hadn't improved its appeal in the slightest.

"It's just Papa and me, Tove, and he truly loves this place, its purpose, especially nowadays. I couldn't live in the village and just visit him once a week or so, not with him out here by himself, a lighthouse keeper crowded by Nazis." She shook her head. "He was thrilled when I moved in."

"I'm sure. And despite all the soldiers, you're happy to be with him. Here."

Jonna sighed hard. "Well, he's worked Drogden into my blood, it's true. It's part of my upbringing, and being here is important to both of us, no matter how isolated and unforgiving Drogden can be."

"Plus, you have me, don't forget."

Jonna turned to the vivid blue eyes and counted her blessings. The sailor she'd met some three years ago had become a very special member of the crew aboard the *Engel*, the lighthouse tender that regularly maintained Drogden. They had become friends quickly as their occasional meetings grew more relaxed and confidential, and their mutual attraction had deepened.

She rued the day the Nazis arrived, for obvious reasons, but their presence also quashed the quality time, the intimate opportunities she and Tove sought. Jonna knew Tove shared that frustration. She grew to fear an end to their visits, the severing of this miraculous lifeline to Tove.

"You risk far more than I do," she told her, and set her hand atop Tove's on the rail.

"We both risk a great deal. The 'extra work' you do with your father here goes without saying, especially with Nazis everywhere. That anti-aircraft gun they added just scars the majesty of this place and makes them all the more vicious."

"But each night, you gamble your own life and so many others, smuggling our refugees off to safety."

Tove looked down at their hands as she spoke. "There is no alternative to that, Jonna. Sending them off by boat is their only hope, and I'm just one of many helping get them aboard. Thankfully, the *Engel*'s work provides us perfect cover for the operation. We've been lucky to avoid Nazi harassment."

"*I've* been lucky, too." Jonna squeezed her hand. "Having the *Engel* arrive after each trip…Having you here at Drogden brings me more relief, more joy than you know."

❖

Through a sliver of opening in the warehouse door, Tove trained weary eyes on the Nazi sentries pacing to opposite ends of the waterfront. Straining to focus through Copenhagen's pre-dawn darkness should have been second nature after eight consecutive nights, but it wasn't. It would never be. Not until all her Jewish countrymen had been secreted away to safety.

Pressed to the crack in the doorway, she battled the fatigue of frayed nerves, an anxious heart rate, and minimal breathing. The clipped movement of her lungs synchronized with the soldiers' hollow footsteps on the dock, and she relied on that distinct rhythm to time her next escapee.

Blindly, she reached back, tugged the elderly shopkeeper to her side, and felt him tremble. He clutched his wife's hand to his chest, and the woman wiped his tear, kissed his cheek, and inched away.

He turned and stared anxiously at Tove. Her signal could end his life just as quickly as save it. Being caught by the sentries would unleash Hell upon everyone.

She edged him closer to the door and whispered in his ear. "Be strong, Jannick. Think only of good, light footing."

He just nodded and his fearful eyes flickered at the opening in the door.

"The soldiers are far apart now. You can do this," she added, desperate to instill confidence.

"I-I will. I will try, yes."

"Your wife will follow," Tove assured him. "Take a breath now." She placed her hand on his back. "Godspeed." She swung the door wide and pressed him out into the night.

Watching Jannick dart toward the dock, Tove reached back for his wife and readied her at the door. They could only peek through the narrow opening, hold their breath, and pray for him.

Stooped slightly forward, he hustled soundlessly in his worn, soft shoes, across the cobblestones to the wooden dock and directly to the two sailors waiting aboard the *Engel*. They seized Jannick by the arms and hoisted him in a fluid motion over the gunnel and onto the deck, then onto the ladder of the cargo hold. He vanished below in seconds.

At Tove's side, his wife smothered sobs of relief with her hands. They would wait now, as the Nazi sentries pivoted and began their return route toward each other. Their paths crossed near the *Engel*, but once they again had parted a sizeable distance, Tove hurried Jannick's wife to join him.

There was no time to give thanks for their success. The next refugee rushed to her, clamped small arms around her waist. Tove looked down into a teary—familiar—face and her heart lurched.

"Naysa?" The young girl squeezed her eyes shut and buried her face into Tove's jacket. Of the many neighborhood children who frequented the docks, this was Tove's favorite, and the feeling was mutual.

Like Tove, all Danish mariners and fishermen did their best to offer the children happy times during these years of Nazi occupation. And through those times, Naysa had kept her Jewish faith a secret… Until she couldn't. Here now, Tove saw her little friend as one more terrified, endangered Danish Jew running for her life.

"I-I never knew…" Tove stroked the mussed brown hair, hoping to calm her. "Please don't cry. Where is your family?" She peered into the dark warehouse around them and caught the eye of the last refugee, a woman holding an infant. "Taken," was all Tove heard.

"I don't want to go," Naysa sobbed against Tove's side. "Don't make me."

Tove knelt and took Naysa's hands. "It's time for us all to be brave," she whispered in earnest. "We must trust our friends, and you and I, we are friends. Am I right?"

Naysa choked back tears and nodded.

"Then trust in me now." Tove wiped the wet cheeks with her thumbs. "You have other friends, too, and they are waiting for you out there in that boat. Those soldiers simply see the *Engel* as the lighthouse tender it is, just a working boat, but we know it's much more, don't we? Let it take you to safety. You won't be alone."

Watery eyes pleaded for Tove to make all this scariness go away.

Tove kissed her forehead. "Come now. Look through here." She gripped the frail shoulders with all the gentle surety she could muster. "See those sailors? You know my mates, Frans and Vidar. You've sailed with us on the *Engel* how many times this summer? Remember all the fun at Drogden?"

Naysa turned her wide eyes back up to Tove, as if needing to hear more. "But that's where I'd rather go, to the lighthouse again, Tove, not to Sweden."

"Sweden is where there is no danger."

"But the lighthouse is fun. Can't we go there and see Jonna again?"

"There's no fun at Drogden now. Germans are there, things have changed."

"So, are Jonna and her papa in danger out there?"

Tove's heart ached for her. How sad that evil occupied a child's mind. "They are safe because the Germans at Drogden need Jonna and her papa to do lighthouse work." She forced that issue from her mind. Her fear for Jonna couldn't interfere right now.

She bent closer and glanced through the opening in the door. "It's almost time to go. I need you to be brave, my friend."

"You're coming too, right?"

"Yes, to get you and the others across the strait and safely ashore. And there you will have more friends."

Again, Naysa looked at the door. She took a breath and Tove sensed she was as ready as she would ever be.

Pacing toward opposite ends of the docks, the sentries expanded the gap between them, and Tove eased the door farther open.

"Silent as a mouse now—and do not stop. Off you go."

Eager to please as always, Naysa scurried silently across the walkway, then leaned up onto her toes to traverse the wooden dock. Only when Frans and Vidar lifted her aboard did she glance back.

Tove wondered what she saw in that instant and prayed it wouldn't be her last glimpse of her homeland.

Naysa disappeared into the *Engel*'s cargo hold, and Tove knew that if everyone's luck held, they would speak again in Sweden. But then there would be no time for farewells; runs to and from those shores had to be swift. For the *Engel*—the lighthouse tender—it was imperative to arrive at Drogden per the standard work schedule or reasonably close to it. Thankfully, that harrowing daily achievement usually culminated with visiting Jonna.

Tove focused on completing this crucial part of tonight's mission. One refugee remained in the warehouse and Tove drew the woman to her by the shoulder. She glanced at the squirming infant in its mother's arms, saw the young woman struggle to keep tears at bay.

"She should sleep very soon," the mother promised in a hush. The tremulous voice wasn't reassuring.

Worried that the baby might cry out and draw the soldiers' attention, Tove responded almost too harshly. "Did you give her the medicine?" This mother *had* to have followed instructions.

Sedatives had been provided for all children to insure calm and quiet during this lengthy, high-risk ordeal. Secrecy from the Nazis was imperative for the success of this evacuation. The lives of all refugees, the sailors, and all their families and friends depended on quiet. Sometimes, Tove wondered if she, too, would need sedation to sleep once the rescue of her Jewish countrymen was completed.

The woman nodded. "Just a few more minutes and she will be asleep."

Tove looked out again at the soldiers, knowing that a few minutes were a few too many.

"I'll take her," she said, and lifted the baby into her arms. "I'm last. That will give her a bit more time." She tipped her head to the door. "Come. Be ready."

The mother kissed her child's nose and looked up at Tove. "Please…?"

Tove offered a smile. "We'll only be a moment behind you." She shifted the baby into a better position. "Ready now," she whispered, her free hand on the door.

The mother looked back at her child, resigned, and Tove had to urge her out by the shoulder. She held her breath as the woman ran to the dock, a mere shadow flitting across the open ground. Thankfully, she made it aboard and below deck without a sound.

Tove wrapped loose ends of the thin blanket around the baby and tucked the bundle inside her jacket as best she could. Glad the child had finally dozed off, she worked to steady her breathing. All this was only part of the escape process; hours more lay ahead.

The emptiness of the warehouse enveloped her now, and tomorrow night she would repeat this nerve-wracking process with another group of desperate refugees assembled by the Danish Resistance.

Tove checked on the sentries and saw her moment arrive. With both arms round the baby, she traversed the cobblestones with practiced speed and let her mates swoop her aboard the *Engel*. They lowered the child down to its mother and slid the hatch closed.

CHAPTER FIVE

Drogden Lighthouse
Copenhagen, Denmark

Jonna rolled her eyes at her father when the Nazis began buzzing around outside. The *Engel*'s approach had them jumping to alert as if a battleship bore down on the lighthouse. The soldiers had performed this routine almost daily since arriving in August, and now it was October and the ritual had grown old. Ridiculous, in Jonna's opinion.

Barking commands and waving directions, the young German lieutenant sent his soldiers scurrying to the railing that rimmed the island station, their automatic weapons in hand. He followed at a brisk pace.

Sighing, Jonna turned from the window. "He always hurries to be in charge at the stairs as if he's never seen the *Engel* before."

Papa tossed a resigned wave toward the door. "German soldiers get younger by the day. Lieutenant Beck can't be older than you, dear daughter. He needs to prove himself worthy of commanding a dozen men."

"Too bad he's not harmless."

"Oh, I agree, but we're lucky he's not the wisest Nazi they could have stationed here." He finished slicing cheese onto a platter and looked up at her with a toothless grin. It softened his gruff features, tempting Jonna to hug him. He was right, as usual, that a more seasoned officer might already have detected the secret work their father-daughter team produced for the Resistance.

Thankfully, Lt. Gunter Beck was oblivious to—and sometimes overwhelmed by—everything. And that included the hour or so Papa spent relaxing with his friend, the *Engel*'s Captain Holsten. The baby-faced Beck had no idea what passed between the older men as they played cards or chess, no idea that overheard Nazi information or navigational details were being transferred to the Resistance by word of mouth or, on rare occasion, on paper.

Aside from Beck's naivete, Jonna was grateful for his manners. He followed orders in strict fashion, but also displayed courtesy and respect for Papa's experience at Drogden. And those impeccable manners kept him at arm's length from Jonna. He had fumbled his way through compliments after a month sharing the outpost and, when he blushingly suggested more, she had politely but firmly declined.

Jonna retied the bow around her hair and checked that her blouse and skirt were suitable to receive their guests. Usually, she didn't spare much concern for appearances, here among preoccupied soldiers, but she always hoped to please Tove. Hers was a spirit worth nurturing.

She set crackers around the cheese on her father's platter and scanned their common room for tidiness. Such was their minimalist existence, a rectangular, single-story cottage situated at the base of the lighthouse. Nazis had commandeered the same on the opposite side of the tower, and left her and Papa a bedroom housing two beds, and this room to serve as kitchen, parlor, and office. Only a small space remained available to them for storage on the two lower floors, once the soldiers converted those rooms for their own needs.

As coffee percolated atop the little coal stove in the corner, Jonna gave her potato soup a lengthy stir. The *Engel* crew always arrived exhausted and hungry. Not for the first time, she wished she had more to offer instead of the last of their supplies. Lard, dried beef, coffee, and biscuit ingredients were among the staples due today, another partial delivery attributable to the *Engel*'s lack of space. Each trip had Jonna in awe of its success, the clandestine coordination between the crew and the Resistance, the juggling of supplies and refugees, the last-minute "adjusting" of counterfeit cargo paperwork.

She envisioned the *Engel*, now probably only a half-mile out, bouncing on the gray waves, splitting them into spray whiter than the overcast sky. Having delivered its refugees across the strait to neutral Sweden, it now carried a third of its capacity and rode almost too lightly for its speed in the rough water. Jonna sympathized with those who had been aboard since before dawn, how they had endured the impossibly cramped quarters and the heavy slog to safe shores. Hopefully, their relief had overtaken any seasickness.

The *Engel* pressed its luck every day now, constantly avoiding or dodging the ever-increasing Nazi patrols. Jonna knew Captain Holsten always raced across the strait to off-load his precious passengers. He pushed even harder on the return trip, passing out of sight of Drogden before turning back to approach the lighthouse from the east, the direction the Nazis expected. Should soldiers question the extended time, the crafty Holsten always had excuses ready, such as mechanical trouble, weather, buoy maintenance, the discovery of an uncharted wreck.

Holsten owned a special little piece of Jonna's heart, and she readily admitted it. He was, after all, Papa's dearest friend. His tall, beefy stature suited his booming voice, imposing until his devilish smile appeared, and he flashed it often around her.

"Ready to go out?" Papa asked, tugging his knit cap onto his head.

"After you."

The sound of the *Engel*'s horn made Jonna smile, and, swinging into a bulky sweater, she stopped at the little mirror by the door. Tove always said Jonna's smile made her chocolate eyes look "delicious," and Jonna was always too lost in the shimmering blue of Tove's to respond. She adored the ocean-fresh look of her, shaggy blond hair framing that easy, uplifting smile. Tove's ruddy complexion reminded her to pinch her own cheeks for color before following Papa outside.

Cold salt spray whipped her from head to toe and her skirt flapped viciously in the wind. The *Engel* edged closer to the elliptical island's stone base, and Jonna admired the tenacity of the plucky wooden craft. Shielded by rubber tires, it bobbed repeatedly against the granite steps that curled downward against the wall, until lines Papa tossed secured it to the side.

As Jonna cranked the cargo crane over the rim of the island and down to the hatch, two sentries descended the steps and stopped crewman Rolf halfway. He presented the boat's documentation for the day and waited while a soldier took the papers up to Beck. As had become routine, Beck's examination of the documents failed to detect any counterfeit alterations.

Meanwhile, Tove waved from the hatch, grabbed the hook Jonna lowered, and took it down into the hold. Jonna watched with rising anticipation, excited to see her safe and well, buoyed by her athleticism and boundless energy. She couldn't wait to wrap Tove in her arms and be swallowed up by one of those powerful hugs.

Several quick tugs on the line said she could crank up the load Tove had secured, and Jonna concentrated on hoisting crates.

Holsten lumbered up the steps and bellowed a greeting to Beck at the top. "Lieutenant! Rough day, today. All's quiet out here, I hope?"

Beck glared from beneath the brim of his hat. "You are late every day, Holsten." He studied the crew members as they squeezed past his soldiers.

"Join me for a ride, son?" Holsten gestured down to the *Engel*. "A quick lesson about fighting seas like today's." He boldly clapped Beck on the shoulder and walked off. "Ethan! Jonna! Out frolicking in this glorious weather, again, are you?"

Jonna waved to Holsten and trained her smile on Tove, who strode toward her with purpose.

"You," Jonna declared, opening her arms wide, "are a glorious sight!" They swung their arms around each other, and Tove rocked them left and right.

"It's *so* good to see you again," Tove breathed into Jonna ear. "I've missed you."

Jonna couldn't squeeze her close enough. "And we saw each other just yesterday."

"That's too long."

"I agree." Jonna held Tove out by the shoulders and quickly ran her eyes up and down Tove's frame. "You're well?"

"I am." Tove shrugged as she flexed her fingers hungrily into Jonna's sides. "Rough water today, that's all."

Jonna drew her back in and whispered, "Promise me you'll get more sleep. I see more weariness in your eyes with each visit." She pressed her palms to Tove's back, enjoyed the feel of her, even through her thick jacket. "But I thank God you're here now."

Suddenly, Papa added a couple of pats to Tove's shoulder in route to meeting Holsten, and the couple separated a little awkwardly.

"I'm glad to be here," Tove said, and kissed Jonna's cheek quickly. "And you're here, so that makes Drogden my private sanctuary." With a sly grin Jonna treasured beyond reason, Tove led them to the crates and the Nazi inspection underway.

"Oh, now, look!" Jonna tossed her hands in disgust as a soldier pried open another crate and flung the lid aside. He rifled hungrily through its contents, upturning cans and cartons, tearing sacks of produce. "There's no need to make this mess—and they always do."

"This isn't necessary!" Tove waved away a cloud of milled flour caught on the wind. "Enough!" With a sharp yank, she slid the crate away from the soldier, and Jonna took a breath, expecting Tove's impatience to draw severe repercussions.

Immediately, the irate soldier stepped into Tove's space. Jonna braced for trouble because Tove wasn't likely to back down, even if it was prudent.

And, true to form, before the soldier could utter a sound, Tove barked directly into his face. "What's the matter with you? Haven't you seen enough?" She gestured sharply at the torn containers. "You're threatened by flour, lard, and beans?"

Not waiting for him to react, she grabbed an end of the crate, Jonna hurriedly grabbed the other, and they hauled it inside.

"Someday, Tove," Jonna said when they reached the kitchen, "you won't get the last word."

"He was enjoying that too much, tearing things open out there, wrecking everything."

Jonna shook her head. "But just a wave of his hand could—"

"Damn boys showing off."

"Boys with *guns*, Tove." Jonna glanced at the crew members bringing in the other crates and lowered her voice. "I cannot lose you to your temper." She paused long enough for Tove to see the plea in her eyes. Beyond their precious friendship, their intimate attraction had developed permanent roots she wasn't willing to risk. Sometimes, gentle reminders were necessary.

Tove hung her head as she went to the shelves with an armload of goods. "I'm sorry to worry you. I-I promise to be smarter."

Jonna hip-bumped her to restore that smile. "You're already very smart." She turned to the others bustling about the room. "Please pour anything powdery into these jars," she instructed, eyeing the ripped sacks. "Did you bring water on this trip?"

"In those two crates," crewman Vidar answered. "I'll empty a few jugs into your dispenser."

"We should be able to fill your tank with tomorrow's load," Holsten said, and sat with Papa to enjoy the soup Jonna carried to the table.

"Any coal today?" Papa asked. He set a companionable hand atop Holsten's shoulder. "I don't mean to press you. It's just that we have only a few days' supply left, and our *neighbors* don't share."

Holsten turned to Rolf. "Didn't we bring some today?"

"Some—and the tools you listed," Rolf added for Papa's sake. "The coal comes with your lumber, day after tomorrow."

"Well, until then," Tove said, dumping a ripped sack of potatoes into a bin, "both the Friedlers will have plenty to do sorting out *our* mess." She and Jonna surveyed the disarrayed shelves of jars, cans, and cartons.

"It will be our pleasure," Jonna said. "Thank you all." She rounded the table, ladling soup into bowls.

Rolf followed along, pouring coffee. "Do your *neighbors* expect you to share with them?"

Jonna snickered as she set the pot back on the stove. "What do you think?"

Papa shook his head. "It's why we'll hide some of these goods you brought us. Well, hide as best we can. Our *neighbors* can search anytime they want."

Jonna saw Tove's eyes darken with worry.

"It's true, I'm afraid," she said, "and they don't knock."

Heavy silence overtook the room until everyone's focus gradually turned to Jonna's thin but tasty soup. Conversation then veered off to the weather and Papa's plan to wall off a section of the bedroom for her. But Jonna knew Tove's silence said she feared for her, here among the Nazis, and Jonna longed for a private moment to reassure her.

Thankfully, Rolf soon led the crewmen back down to the *Engel*, a gesture both she and Tove appreciated. In addition to allowing Papa and Holsten the privacy to share "men's gossip," it provided the perfect excuse for an intimate little stroll outside.

CHAPTER SIX

Copenhagen, Denmark

As much as she loved the intimacy of this visit to the Friedlers' apartment on the mainland, Tove couldn't stop thinking about someone taking her place at the docks tonight.

"The *Engel* will be overloaded," she said, watching Jonna bring more pork patties and potato salad from the counter. "I hope everyone will be ready on time. Tonight's group might be too large, you know. Some may have to return to hiding and wait another night."

"Trust in your people, Tove," Jonna said. "You need to relax. We *both* need to. We have a rare opportunity here tonight, and we've waited so long for private time together."

Tove couldn't argue with that. Besides, this might be a very special night for them, and *that* roused an entirely different set of nerves.

As Jonna refilled their plates, Tove eyed her more intently than the tasty meal. Jonna's dark hair flowed off her shoulders as she worked, and Tove yearned to lose her fingers in it, feel it drift across her own cheeks. The mellow lamp light cast her perfect, kissable complexion in a warm glow, and there was grace in her every movement, a relaxed comfort in the cozy kitchen.

This moment away from Nazis, the tempest that was the outside world, provided such welcomed relief, not to mention the chance to express feelings at will. Tove worked to keep the concern in her gut from spoiling it all.

"We must have faith," Jonna said suddenly, setting a hand on Tove's.

Tove threaded their fingers together and smiled. "How did you manage to find pork for this delicious karbonader? God. Thank you, Jonna."

"Neighbors. We are like family and always look out for each other. I'm just happy we both could be here tonight."

Tove kissed Jonna's fingers. "A night off in…I don't remember, it's true."

"We must try to set worries aside, at least for now."

"The worries are heavy, Jonna. And I worry about you, too, and Ethan."

"It is hard, with *them* at Drogden now, but it means so much to contribute anything we can. Whenever paper is necessary, it goes right into the stove as quickly as possible. Papa's very strict about that, so you needn't worry."

"None of us on the *Engel* ever speaks about what Ethan and Holsten share." She stroked Jonna's fingers atop the table and worried about the Drogden occupation nonetheless. "I hate having sentries at the beacon looking down at us when we walk. It feels like we're prisoners in a jail yard."

"The first month or so were difficult, but Papa and I grew to ignore them. I do wish we could stroll around the other side of the tower, but the soldiers' cottage has more windows than ours so… well, being watched from above is bad enough."

"I loved going up there with you. We could see forever." She entwined their fingers and squeezed. "Good *will* prevail, Jonna. We'll make more memories there, I just know it. Drogden will always be our special place."

"I tell myself that, too, especially when we hear of things going on here, on the mainland." She slipped her hand free and poked at her food. "Now and then, when a fisherman stops by, we hear horrifying accounts, or we read of them in the secret little newspapers. Those Nazi camps on the continent…Dear God, Tove.

They're killing everyone. Hopefully, this rescue effort will spare our Jewish countrymen. It *is* going well, isn't it?"

"We believe it is, yes, and considering the entire nation mustered practically overnight, it has been amazing." She took another bite and flashed Jonna a mischievous look as she swallowed. "Hitler certainly didn't get the swift round-up he wanted. Everyone rallied to help in some way, everyone with a boat or a truck, and every farmer, shopkeeper, every hospital and church."

"Because no one can be left behind."

"The effort goes on, day after day, night after night, gathering and hiding them until a boat is ready."

"And then there is the crossing," Jonna added with a sigh. "We know some boats don't make it."

"It's true, sadly."

"You still haven't been boarded?"

"No, because, much like you and your father, our work benefits the damn Nazis, too. Ironic, isn't it? Who would have thought a government sanction to tend Drogden and the Oresund itself would help us rescue so many lives?" She shook her head. "We're the luckiest of all boaters. So, we've only been stopped a few times." She rushed to allay Jonna's concern. "Holsten is clever and has spared us from being boarded."

"You are all so brave."

"As are you, Jonna, and your father. What you pass along is vital."

"Do you think there are many left to be rescued?"

"It's so hard to say. Thousands have been saved already, the majority, I think, but, still, there are some we cannot reach, and some, mostly the elderly, who refuse to leave."

"God, I do ache for them. The prospect of exchanging one's entire life in an instant for one in a strange place, Tove, how frightening? They leave everything and go to nothing, know no one, will have no work."

"But they know they have no choice and that the Swedes are generous and welcoming," Tove said. "Our Jewish countrymen are being housed and fed and kept safe."

"Well, I'm proud that we, as Danes, are standing up, caring for each other. It gives one hope, having all faiths, truly a whole nation united against this insanity."

"And thankfully, the children are being well advised. The ones who congregate along our docks seem just aware enough. I can't imagine how they maintain their innocence."

"Remember the summer months," Jonna asked dreamily, "all the sunshine and laughter before the Nazis arrived? When you and the *Engel* brought the children out? Such wonderful days."

"What fun we showed them, ay?" Tove smiled as she slid her empty plate aside. "Remember when you made them drinks from the lemons?"

"And the American chocolate bars! Our bubbly little friend, Naysa, she's crazy about that chocolate."

Tove nodded but couldn't maintain her smile. "The GI candy. I remember when she ate too much and got sick on the boat ride home."

"Tove, why the sad look? Those were fun times."

"I…I think I'm her hero, you know."

"Oh, that's obvious," Jonna said, grinning. "It's not surprising that she worships you. She's a bright child."

"She'd come to the docks almost every day. Occasionally, her companions changed, but she was always there. To her, I guess I was some mighty woman in a man's world."

"What do you mean, 'was'? You definitely are her hero. She chatted about you constantly—and about the two of us being *special* friends. Very perceptive for a ten-year-old."

Tove set her elbows on the table and rubbed her eyes with both hands. "She's an orphan now, Jonna. We took her to Sweden this morning."

"Tove! I had no idea."

"Nor I."

"All those times she visited us at Drogden…the games, the cakes we baked…The binoculars were so big for her." Jonna stared blankly across the room. "How sad. Now that I think back, only once did she mention a mother and father. I think she said the three of them lived above a bank, but she never mentioned her faith."

"Drogden was the place she loved. She lived for every passing ship."

Watching Jonna wipe away a tear raised a lump in Tove's chest. *Is there a limit to how difficult life can become?* The pain of fond memories colliding with the cruelty of war seemed to increase daily.

She could still hear Naysa's delighted squeals each time a vessel greeted Drogden with a blast of its horn. And how she relentlessly begged Tove and Captain Holsten to make a night trip so she could "sail to the light."

"At least," Jonna cleared her throat, "at least they didn't get her, too."

"She's in an orphanage by now, safe."

"I hope they'll let her see Drogden's beacon from her shore."

"I told her to insist, politely, of course, because Drogden symbolizes home, and she should never lose sight of that."

Jonna rested her hand on Tove's arm. "At least she went on the *Engel* with you. I know she will have a future and might even locate relatives someday, but she has no one to come home to."

"But…" Tove's voice broke. "But…maybe that's all right because she intends to become a ship captain—that's what she told me—and captains are seldom home anyway."

Jonna reached out and gently touched Tove's chin. "Let's remind our aching hearts that she had a win-or-lose choice and she won, and wouldn't you guess she'll have more wins in her future?" Her wink made Tove smile. "So, what about Tove Salling, hm? What do I see besides exhaustion in those blue eyes? Don't you aspire to captain your own ship someday?"

"We have to get rid of this war first, then we'll see. Maybe I'll run holiday cruises or something like that."

"And seldom be at home?"

"That depends on who's there." Tove drew Jonna's fingers to her lips and kissed them. "You know, one day you could follow in your father's footsteps at Drogden. No one would be more qualified."

"Oh." Jonna laughed lightly and traced Tove's jaw with a fingertip. "Wouldn't that be exciting? As if the Lighthouse Service would see a woman as capable."

"I disagree!" Tove declared, heartened to see Jonna's face brighten. "The Lighthouse Service knows what you do out there, Jonna. Hell, you're the most capable woman I've ever met. You'd be a fantastic lighthouse keeper."

"Tove, you are so sweet. Thank you, but we both know the odds. I suppose I could make a case for myself, but, at best, they would make me some man's assistant."

"Unacceptable. You need to be in charge."

"You're so good for my spirit." She sat back. "We once had two assistant keepers at Drogden, don't forget. So…I would need company." She eyed her sideways until Tove grinned back.

A brisk rapping at the door startled them and Jonna hurried to answer it. Tove tensed as she followed her, sure Jonna felt just as unnerved by the urgency in that knock.

A small thin man in a tattered jacket tipped his cap and glanced from them to the empty hallway around him. "Jonna Friedler?" At her nod, he jammed his hands into his pockets and shuffled uneasily. "Eh…Captain Merc sent me."

"Who?"

Tove touched Jonna's shoulder. "I know him. Captain of the *Sohest*. A good man."

The stranger nodded quickly. "That's right." He checked the hallway again, then coughed into his fist. "Ah, well…"

Tove squeezed Jonna's arm. "Bring him inside."

They urged him into the apartment, and he wrung his hands as they shut the door. Jonna sent Tove a fearful look.

"The *Sohest* had just come in," he said, now staring down at his hands. "There's bad news…awful news, I'm afraid, from Drogden. Captain Merc sent me to find you."

"Please," Jonna said, a hand to her heart. "What is it? Is it Papa?"

The man finally met Jonna's eyes. "He's been killed, Jonna."

Jonna gasped so deeply she staggered back against Tove. "God, no!" She covered her mouth with her hand and tears erupted.

Tove shivered as icy blood roared through her system. Holding Jonna upright, she scrambled for words. "You're sure? There's no mistake?"

"No mistake. The docks are abuzz with it. The *Sohest* was boarded just outside the channel and the damn Nazis couldn't wait to brag."

"But…" Tove drew Jonna against her chest. "How? W-what happened?"

"They said he resisted arrest—for espionage. They said he had a gun."

Jonna spun to him. "That can't be true!" she blurted through tears. "They just killed him. I know it."

"He wouldn't have fought them," Tove insisted. "To what aim? He was stranded with them on a damn rock! Where was he supposed to go? How?" She ran a hand through her hair.

"I can't believe this," Jonna said, sagging against Tove.

The messenger scruffed at his chin. "The Gestapo were at the docks when I left. They were meeting with the patrol boat to get the details."

Tove shivered again. Not all the Gestapo would race to Drogden to pursue the espionage charge; some would pursue it on land—and Jonna would be next.

Her heart pounding, she turned back to the messenger. "Then… then you must go now. Quickly."

"I-I'm so sorry," he said gently. "Everyone loved Ethan."

Tove grabbed his arm as he turned in the doorway. "Our thanks to the captain. And bless you for coming." He nodded and scurried off.

Tove shut the door and guided Jonna to a chair. She knelt before her and carefully clasped the wet, trembling hands. She had always worried about the intelligence-gathering Ethan and Jonna did at Drogden, and now the nightmare had been realized.

Actually, it had just begun.

CHAPTER SEVEN

Nancy sat heavily in her desk chair and stared at her favorite photograph prominently displayed where she could see it as she went through her workday. It featured Drogden lighthouse in Denmark. The history that beacon had seen was inspiring. Visiting famous lighthouses of Europe was a dream Nancy had held onto for years. She looked back at her desk. Maybe one day there would be time for dreams. For now, her sights were set on a lighthouse much closer to home.

She looked at the clock and her stomach soured. She straightened a ceramic cup on her desk holding pencils, pens, and one oversized cocktail umbrella from a fruity drink she'd gotten at the fanciest bar she'd ever set foot in. She neatened the stack of proposal papers and backup documentation.

Despite her hyperawareness, she still jumped out of her skin when Samantha knocked on the door. Samantha had been away for the past two weeks dealing with business of some sort or another. Based on what had splashed across social media, her trip did not appear to be all work and no play, but now she was here and they had quite a task ahead of them. Merging their two proposals seemed even more impossible with some breathing room from the heat of the moment and Mrs. Jones's intimidating stare.

"Am I in the right place?" Samantha grinned widely, taking in what passed for Nancy's office.

"I'm surprised Casey let you through and didn't insist on taking you out on the water. I think he's doing tours today." Nancy looked out the window toward the docks. She didn't see Casey, but she knew he was around, she'd heard him singing along to the radio earlier. It was a blessing and a curse to have an office in the back of her brother's maritime repair shop.

"He absolutely tried to lure me away. I would pay you a compliment, but I know you don't like them, so I'll say I resisted because we have work to do." Samantha winked.

Despite her deep desire not to, Nancy felt herself blush. If she chose to enjoy Samantha's attention, that was her business. She certainly didn't need to let Samantha in on her secret. Damn traitorous blood vessels.

"We do have work to do. Pull up a seat." Nancy looked around the room. "I'm sure this is not quite the office space you're used to."

Samantha pulled one of the mismatched guest chairs with the stained and fraying cushions to the edge of the desk. "I thought we agreed not to fall into assumptions about each other. I'm not assuming you're from a big, loud, closely-knit Irish family who's already made up its mind about me. Or that you were an introverted, too-smart-for-your-own-good, nerdy kid growing up."

Nancy scowled. "For your impertinence, I'll not share if any of your 'not' assumptions are correct."

"I would expect nothing less, lassie." Samantha laughed at her own joke.

Nancy groaned but couldn't help but smile, too.

"Much better. Now, stop thinking of me as 'Samantha McMann' and stop assuming you know things about me." Samantha made air quotes around her name, and despite the rebuke, her tone was soft and kind.

"You *are* Samantha McMann. It's hard to forget that. Should I start calling you Joe?" Nancy laughed again when Samantha's nose wrinkled in disgust.

"No, thank you. Joe's my uncle and not my favorite one. If, and this is a big if"—Samantha held up her finger in Nancy's direction—"you can stop looking at me like you believe everything you've read in the tabloids, then you may call me Sam."

Nancy sat back and took a fresh look at Sam. She was dressed down today in gray jeans, a dark blue V-neck T-shirt, and sneakers. She looked delicious and a far cry from the pictures splashed across every trashy tabloid Nancy struggled to avoid when purchasing her avocados, Oreos, and coffee milk. Tabloid Samantha always had a new woman on her arm, didn't look like she owned jeans, and her smile never reached her eyes.

"Okay, Sam. You've had time away. Did you come to your senses and the wisdom of my proposal?" It was Nancy's turn to wink.

"You know, I have." Sam paused for a long time. She seemed to enjoy keeping Nancy on the hook and hopeful, even though they both knew she wasn't going to cave that easily. "Not come around to your plan, but maybe I'm starting to understand why you like history so much. Does that get me any points?"

"Afraid not. I grade pass/fail. I can't be bribed or sweet-talked." Annoyingly, Nancy's heart rate kicked up a notch or two. Was this flirting? What was she doing?

"That sounds like a challenge for an ambitious student." Sam started to say something else, but her attention diverted over Nancy's shoulder.

Nancy turned to see what had caught Sam's attention. "You know that lighthouse?" She pointed at the picture of Drogden.

"You don't? Role reversals can be fun in the right situation, but it's going to freak me out if I know more about Drogden Lighthouse than you do." Sam's cheeky grin was enough to let Nancy know she was kidding.

"So, you know nothing about the lighthouse you're trying to buy, but now you're an expert on Danish maritime beacons? And before you give me some cheesy line about being full of surprises or living to keep me guessing, give me the truth, hmm? How the hell do you know anything about Drogden?" Nancy attempted Eloise's stare, hoping even a poor replica would still be serviceable.

"Are you okay?" Sam looked concerned. "Are you hurt?"

Nancy sighed, her impersonation a failure. "My sister has a killer death stare. I was trying to replicate it. Didn't work?"

Sam shifted in her chair. "Might need some more workshopping in the mirror. To answer your question, I'm reading a book. It's a true story of two women who lived in Denmark during World War II. One was the Drogden lighthouse keeper's daughter. I can't get enough. I had to leave them on the run from Nazis to come here."

"Your sacrifice is noted for the record. I'll put it in our final joint proposal." Nancy made a show of writing a note in her stack of papers. "The Danish lighthouse tender crews were heroic during the war." Nancy glanced at the picture of Drogden again.

"One of the women works on a tender. I'm glad I borrowed the book from my lighthouse."

"Our lighthouse." Nancy took the bait and was rewarded with one of Sam's brilliant smiles.

"Right, of course. Anyway, their story is incredible." Sam looked like her mind had wandered back to the book.

Nancy knew that look. If Sam could drift back in time like that, there was hope for her yet. "Are you starting to see why I love history so much? Why celebrating everything that came before is worth the effort?"

Sam shrugged noncommittally. "Not really. Don't get me wrong, I'm loving the book, but it is just another novel. I tell myself it all happened in real life, but history isn't something you can reach out and touch. You have to make it real in your head, and if I'm going to be playing make-believe, I'd rather there be elves."

Nancy was momentarily stunned. "I did not peg you for that kind of nerd." She made another note. "You do realize you're selling my museum idea, right? If you're at the lighthouse, touching and feeling its history, you don't have to make it up."

"I don't think so. How are you going to convince people to take a boat out to see how keepers made bread in a wood burning stove during a hurricane? That's the kind of thing you do to your teenager when she's lost her electronics for a month and you're subtly torturing her in addition to the overt punishment. Unless you're planning on actually firing historically accurate torpedoes, you still haven't won me over."

Nancy stood up and pulled her windbreaker from the hook behind the door. "Just when I was considering liking you. Do you have a car?"

"Excuse me?" Sam stood too. "Are you getting rid of me already?"

"A car. How did you get here?" Nancy waved Sam to follow her as she wound her way through Casey's shop to the front door. "I'm not sending you home. We're playing hooky from work today. I have something I want to show you."

Sam cleared her throat loudly. "I'll have you know just now I swallowed three inappropriate comments that usually work wonders with women, a very nice compliment so as not to offend you, and a reply that would have embarrassed me." Sam wiped at her jeans as if something was stuck to them. It looked more like she was looking for somewhere to focus her attention. "To answer your question, I have a driver. He dropped me off. Would you like me to call him for this mystery venture or should we take your two thousand and four pickup truck?"

Nancy looked behind her at the truck Sam referenced. "Casey picked me up this morning. That's his truck. Mine's a two thousand five. The radio stopped working last week though, so we'd better ask your driver to take us."

Sam nodded seriously. "When you put it like that, the choice is clear." She placed the call.

Ten minutes later, they were tucked into the back seat of the black Town Car and headed south. Nancy hadn't told Sam where they were going and she hadn't asked. Nancy pegged her as an alpha butch, so the apparent lack of concern about their final destination was refreshing.

"You work for your father, right?" She noticed Sam stiffen ever so slightly before relaxing back into the seat again.

Sam nodded but didn't elaborate.

"What do you do for the company?" She worked hard to keep the judgment from their previous interactions out of her voice. She wanted to *know* Sam, not make assumptions based on "Samantha McMann."

"I have the role of heir to the throne." Turning to the window, she added, "I do what my father insists."

Nancy waited for more but none came. "Does that line up with what you want?" Initially, she hadn't given a hoot what Sam cared about or wanted, but surprisingly, now she truly wanted to know. Perhaps it was the business partner effect.

"I knew how to instigate a hostile takeover by the time I was eleven," Sam said. "I'm the firstborn. My destiny was written the moment I took my first breath. In my family, what you want is a secondary, maybe tertiary concern." She looked uncomfortable as soon as the words were out of her mouth.

"Nope." Nancy wagged her finger in Sam's direction. "Not going to work. Still not giving you the lighthouse."

Apparently, Sam hadn't expected that response. She laughed and snapped her fingers. "It was worth a shot."

"If you wanted to use the fact that you're stuck in a job you hate for sympathy points, you shouldn't have gotten photographed with the hottest actress in Hollywood last weekend. You were practically fucking her for the world to see. Hard to feel sorry for you, stud." Did she sound jealous? She couldn't, because she wasn't, so she wouldn't, obviously.

Resorting to feigned shock, Sam slammed her hand to her heart. "We are just friends, I will have you know. You should not believe everything you see on the internet."

Nancy scoffed.

Sam hiked an eyebrow. "You know, for someone who doesn't seem to be all that impressed by me, you care an awful lot about what I'm up to when we're apart."

Nancy rolled her eyes. "You're like a fungus. I think you've disappeared, but I turn around and you've popped back up again."

Sam dropped back against the seat and laughed. "I have been called a lot of things in my life, but never a fungus. Thank you for that." She turned her head and looked directly at Nancy. "I doubt you'll believe me, but I really am only friends with the woman I was photographed with. Her ex, an A-plus asshat by the way, was at the same party that night and had just shoved her into me. I have my hand on her ass because that's where it landed when I caught her." Sam looked frustrated, her thoughts far away.

"You don't owe me an explanation. I'm only teasing you." Nancy picked at the label on her water bottle. "We don't even like each other, remember?" She smiled at that. It was harder to convince herself Sam was as awful as her expectations.

"Well, it seems we're going to have joint custody of a lighthouse. I don't want you to think I'm a cad. Rich, handsome devil is one thing, but I'd never disrespect a woman the way those photos imply." Now, she looked hurt.

Before either of them could figure out what to say next, the driver announced their arrival. As Sam craned her neck to see where they were, Nancy bounced out of the car happily. She sucked in the sea air and let the breeze whip around her.

Sam, on the other hand, made a big production of getting out, groaning and moaning. "You brought me to a museum? I should have known."

Nancy poked her in the shoulder. "Not just any museum. The Mystic Seaport Museum. You said history doesn't come alive? Here it does, literally, since there's a working shipyard. Plus, I have a surprise for you."

Sam took a step back and crossed her arms. "You don't know me well enough to know if I like surprises. And, hypothetically, if I do, how do you know that there's anything in there I'd like?"

Nancy didn't want to notice how full Sam's lips were when she pouted or how her crossed arms accentuated her breasts, but Sam was gorgeous, and Nancy was observant. Sam was hot, Nancy could admit it no matter how annoying it was to do so. Perhaps all she needed to clear her head and stay on track was Sam melting down into a history-induced temper tantrum after they visited half the ships on display.

Nancy considered the alternative. What if Sam enjoyed their time together at the museum? If Sam swooned at Nancy's surprise, as she secretly hoped, Nancy might have to rethink some of the assumptions she'd made about Sam—which seemed very dangerous indeed. History books were full of women who'd lived dangerously...Surely Nancy could be brave enough to tempt Sam with the magic of history come alive. She dragged Sam to the entrance, history and danger lighting her path.

CHAPTER EIGHT

Sam watched, amazed, as the Mystic Seaport volunteer efficiently laid letter after letter in neat rows on the nineteenth century printing press. She leaned toward Nancy. "By today's standard, by the time this guy is done getting the page typeset his story will be four news cycles too old."

Nancy wrinkled her nose like she'd smelled something foul. "I think that says more about our current media consumption than this beauty of a printing press."

The volunteer finished setting his letters and went about the additional work required to actually print whatever message he'd painstakingly spelled out. Sam regarded him and the press carefully. Perhaps Nancy was right about the current media landscape, but she wasn't willing to go so far as pine for the days of the printing press. If there was an emergency, a weather event, or breaking news, a push notification to her phone worked fine for her.

"When do I get to see the surprise you've been teasing me with?" Sam knew she sounded whiny. She'd been cagey about her love of surprises earlier, but she did in fact love them. Patience, however, was not a virtue she possessed in abundance.

"The best things are worth waiting for. We've barely seen anything the seaport has to offer. I want to show you around." Nancy patted her cheek and left the printshop.

Sam followed obediently. They emerged into the replica seaport village, which, Sam learned, contained original buildings from villages of the eighteen hundreds up and down the East Coast, all transported here for visitors' historical enjoyment.

"I want the truth," Nancy said. "You wanted a turn during the demonstration at the cooperage, right?" The sparkle in her eyes, more than her words, told Sam she already knew the answer.

"It looked like fun." Sam shrugged. "Who wouldn't want a barrel they could say they made themselves?"

Nancy cocked her head. "I'd say a lot of people wouldn't care much about that, but I'm glad you do. I'm bringing you over to the dark side. I'll have you under my spell by the end of the day."

"If that was the goal, you didn't need to bring me here. Lunch in your office, driving up and down the highway, arguing about our lighthouse, I doubt you'd need to try very hard." Sam clapped her hand over her mouth then lowered it enough so she could speak. "Please forgive me the insult of paying you a compliment. I know how you hate that. I'm finding that, despite not liking you, I'm starting to like you, even though you brought me to a museum. It's damn inconvenient and entirely your fault."

Red crept up the sides of Nancy's neck and tinted the tops of her ears. "Come on, sweet talker. You can test your spellbinding theory because lunch is next on our agenda."

Nancy set off quickly toward the open-air café. Sam felt a small measure of guilt that she'd made Nancy uncomfortable, but Nancy was the most interesting woman she'd ever spent time with and she was gorgeous on top of it all. From time to time, those truths snuck out.

"We don't have time for lunch. There are three hundred old boats to look at before this place closes." She hurried to catch up.

"Comments like that aren't going to get me to reciprocate by liking you." Nancy walked backwards, facing Sam. "There are less than twenty and only a select few I want to show you. I'm not going to push my luck or your attention span and take you on a tour of all of them."

Sam gasped. "Words wound. I will follow wherever you lead." She held out her arm for Nancy.

Nancy took it. "First, I'll lead us to lunch. Historic vessels after a full belly. We have a whaling ship to explore."

"A what?" Sam abruptly pulled them both to a stop.

"Whaling ship. It's the last remaining wooden whaling ship in the world." She looked confused.

"Why would I want to know how whales were hunted and killed?" Sam was far less hungry than a moment ago.

"History isn't always sunshine and roses, but that doesn't mean it's not important. The whaling industry was a huge driving force of our economy during its heyday. It provided oil for lighting, for lubricating new machines being used in factories when all that was fairly new." Nancy looked over Sam's shoulder toward the waterfront. "Do you see that ship down there, the one with the tallest masts?"

Reluctantly, Sam looked where Nancy pointed as if she might see a whale hunt playing out before her eyes. She scrutinized what she could see of the ship Nancy indicated.

"That ship first put to sea in the eighteen hundreds and sailed all over the world hunting whales. You told me history doesn't come alive for you. Well, when we step onto that ship and look around, I dare you not to feel what it must have been like to live on board for years at a time, doing one of the most dangerous jobs in the world." Nancy turned back toward the café and waved Sam to follow her.

Sam hustled to catch up. "So, the whales got a few sailors too?"

Nancy nodded solemnly. "Sailors and ships. There were a lot more ways to die whaling than there were to make a catch and earn money."

"I should probably feel worse about that than I do, but we've already established history is dead to me." Sam grinned.

Nancy just sighed as they ordered.

They picnicked on the large lawn in front of the café. It offered an expansive view of the harbor and the historic vessels on display. Sam closed her eyes and turned her face to the sky. "Thank you for bringing me here today. I never would have stumbled upon this place myself, but I'm glad to experience it."

"A point for history? Oh, my. You haven't even seen my surprise yet."

Sam opened her eyes and furrowed her brow. "About that. I don't like to be kept waiting this long."

Nancy laughed. "I do apologize, Your Majesty. Next time you can plan the day and make sure there are no surprises."

Sam grumbled but didn't take the bait.

After lunch, they visited the whaling ship and Nancy proved to be right. Standing below deck, seeing the cramped sleeping arrangement for the crew, it was impossible not to feel surrounded by flickers of the past. Not that Sam was quick to concede any points, even if doing so would make Nancy's eyes sparkle brighter than the sun playing off the water.

As they disembarked, Sam looked to the top of the towering masts. She pictured crew members perched high above the deck, around the clock, scouring the ocean for signs of a whale spout. She rubbed her eyes. For a second, she could have sworn she saw the hazy image of a sailor outlined above the sails. All this history and education was making her hallucinate. Great. She didn't think Nancy meant history was literally supposed to come alive.

She followed Nancy along the water toward yet more boats. Although she was loathe to admit it, she was content to wander the seaport, read plaques, look at old things, and listen. The last part was the major draw, of course. Nancy's enthusiasm and knowledge about everything here was impressive and watching someone fully immersed in something they loved was sexy as hell. Not that she was overly concerned with that of course. They were uneasy business partners, at best.

"Why isn't anyone taking pictures of you or following you around?" Nancy asked. She looked amused, which was concerning.

"No one here cares about me." Sam glanced at their fellow history buffs and subtly pointed at various groups. "That dad has his hands full with two grumpy kids, probably sad that their history tour isn't scheduled to continue for another four hours. That tour group just looks hungry. Two of those three families look thrilled to be here and the other looks like each member has spent the past hour reevaluating all the miserable life choices that led them to this moment. That older couple only have eyes for each other. I doubt any of them even know who I am."

Nancy considered the couple on the bench. "Has anyone ever looked at you the way those two are looking at each other?"

Hating to stare, Sam managed a good long look. "No. I think that comes with a love so deep it's etched into their bones."

"Maybe someday." Nancy took another look at the couple before she set off again. "But you didn't really answer my question. Why wouldn't people here care about you when it seems there are cameras in your face all the time on the West Coast?"

Sam didn't squirm outwardly, but her insides compensated. "Can I plead the Fifth? There's no way to answer without you thinking I'm a privileged, wealthy diva."

"You wore wingtips on a water taxi to visit my lighthouse and you want to turn the whole island into a private resort or your own personal vacation home. I *know* you're a privileged, wealthy diva. Now spill." Nancy's grin diffused any sting her words might have had.

"Well, when you put it like that." Sam dusted off a shoulder dramatically. "They take pictures because they know I'll let them and because of who I'm with." She exhaled wearily. She'd killed the vibe. "They don't care about me except that I'm rich and I'll get them a good enough picture to sell their stories."

Nancy looked horrified. "Why would you *let* them take pictures of you?"

Sam shook her head. Would Nancy understand? "I don't let them take pictures of *me*. They take pictures of 'Samantha McMann.' She's the only version of me the world gets to see. As a bonus, it pisses off my father. I love him, don't get me wrong, but his ideas about a lot of things would seem more at home riding the waves with the men on that whaling ship back there." Sam pointed over her shoulder.

"I like Sam better."

"Ah-ha. I knew you liked me." Sam pumped her fist triumphantly.

"I don't think that's what I said." Nancy adopted a very serious expression. "I said I like Sam better. That's not the same as liking. I like soccer more than football but I still couldn't tell you the difference between offside and pass interference or why anyone would watch either."

"Nope, no take-backsies. You like me, you admitted it." Sam did a little jig down the path in front of Nancy. "Besides, the only penalty you really need to know is backfield in motion." Sam added a butt wiggle to her dance.

What are you doing, McMann? Don't let her see so much of who you are.

"You're lucky I don't take out my camera and show the world whoever this is. Samantha McMann has nothing on you. A fact I rather like, by the way." Nancy stopped in front of the boat they were passing and motioned for Sam to come closer. "Fortunately for you, there isn't time for photography. We've arrived at your surprise."

Sam spread her arms to the side and gestured to the small, unassuming boat. "You brought me to a seaport, showed me tons of boats and other things related to boats, so that you could surprise me with, another boat? You know how to show a girl a good time." She didn't try to hide her smile or even pretend to be annoyed.

In truth, Nancy could have reneged on the surprise promise and Sam still would have had a great day. Nancy was fun. Sam's chest filled with unexpected warmth when she thought of spending more time with her.

"For your sass," Nancy said, her head cocked, "you can read about this little beauty on your own. Off you go, I'll wait." She shooed Sam toward the large sign near the bow.

Sam had had her fill of signs, plaques, and historical tidbits, but she didn't want to disappoint Nancy. Three sentences in, her stomach jolted in the way reserved for momentous, emotional experiences. She quickly read more.

Nancy joined her, clearly unable to wait for Sam to finish. "What do you think?"

Sam looked from the boat, named the *Gerda III*, to Nancy. "This little boat actually…? In real life? Back then?" She stared at the *Gerda*. "For real? It's not a replica?"

Nancy put her hand on Sam's shoulder and squeezed. "Not a replica. This brave lighthouse tender rescued Jewish Danes and smuggled them to neutral Sweden exactly how you've been reading in that book of yours. This boat alone rescued three hundred people."

"You're incredible, *Gerda*." Sam couldn't stop staring at the vessel and imagining the danger it had seen. "Can we go on board?"

"Not this one. It's not open to the public." Nancy sounded as disappointed as Sam felt.

Sam looked from Nancy to the *Gerda III*. "Then, let's not be the public." She flagged down a Seaport worker selling tickets for a sail on yet another piece of history. "What size donation would I need to make for you to let me and my friend here spend a few minutes aboard the *Gerda III*?"

"We can't buy our way onboard." Nancy looked annoyed. "History is for everyone, not only for those who can afford it."

"No one is hiding the *Gerda*'s contributions to the world. Why shouldn't we be able to pay for more? You can't tell me the museum wouldn't be happy for the money. How do you think they attract large donors to places like this? Special perks always open wallets." Sam tried to hide her own annoyance. This was the lighthouse argument all over again.

"I guess one day of fun isn't enough to forget you and I have very different plans for my lighthouse, hmm?" Nancy grimaced "Truce for now? I guess we have some people to bribe."

"I prefer to think of it as incentivizing. Bribery sounds gauche."

Nancy smiled at that.

Sam liked the way the corners of Nancy's eyes crinkled when she smiled. Agreeing to a truce so she could see more was all the motivation she needed.

One very confused walkie-talkie call later, and the executive director of the seaport and two security guards joined Sam and Nancy at the *Gerda III*. And, after one very large donation transfer, they were led onto the boat.

The moment Sam set foot on the deck, she felt an inexplicable energy crackle around her. She felt connected to this vessel. She thought about Jonna and Tove, the two women from her book. Had one of them walked across the deck where she now stood? Had the *Gerda* and Tove's boat, the *Engel*, been sister ships? Had they crossed paths on daring runs to Sweden?

Their tour guide showed them the cargo hold. It was smaller than Sam had envisioned, even though, given the *Gerda's* size, she shouldn't have been surprised.

"Ten to fifteen people sandwiched down here must have been suffocating." Nancy crouched next to Sam, both of them avoiding the low ceiling.

"I don't know how long the journey took, but it must have been the most terrifying time of their lives." Sam felt the walls closing in on her. Her heart rate increased, and perspiration erupted on her neck and along her hairline. "Can you imagine uprooting your entire life overnight and boarding this boat for a frantic trip, your only chance at survival?" Reading about the dash to freedom from the perspective of the ship's crew had not prepared her for the feeling of being here, now.

Nancy shook her head sadly and took Sam's hand. It didn't seem as though she realized what she'd done, but Sam enjoyed the feeling, their connection through mutual appreciation and respect.

"Thank you for my surprise. This is the nicest thing anyone's ever done for me. I mean that sincerely. You're right, seeing the *Gerda*, coming aboard, being down here, it's real to me now when it wasn't before." Sam squeezed Nancy's hand then slowly pulled away.

They disembarked and made their way to the exit in contemplative silence. Nancy was the first to break the quiet between them. "You saw the transformative power of touchable, accessible history. Do you see where I'm coming from for my lighthouse museum?"

Sam hesitated. "Yes, I have a better understanding of why you're so passionate about it now. But, I still don't think it will work." Before Nancy killed her with her glare alone, Sam rushed to explain. "Mystic is a whole community. There is the seaport museum, but there are a lot of other things to do here too. If my lighthouse is only a museum, people have to choose to go out there for no other reason than to visit."

"That argument doesn't hold water. There are plenty of things to do in Newport and other towns near my lighthouse. Why is buying a ticket to this museum any different than buying a ticket to mine? Bonus with mine, you get to ride a water taxi, which is an adventure all on its own."

"You made my point. That's the problem. There's so much to do in Newport, why would someone go out of their way to ride a water taxi, *not always an enjoyable adventure*, to a lighthouse museum their kids are going to complain about the whole time? Hypothetically, of course." Sam held up her hands innocently.

Nancy's shoulders sagged. "You're not giving much credit to the next generation, but let's set this aside for our next working day. I told you we were playing hooky and I for one enjoyed the day off. I don't want to end it arguing with you."

"You're right. If we schedule a sparring session for tomorrow, we can prepare our material tonight. Should make for a livelier bout. I'll come prepared." Sam shadowboxed around Nancy.

"I can't tell if I think you're cute or not." Nancy looked bemused. "But you are definitely nothing like I expected from your tabloid persona and that is gratifying."

Sam half bowed and fell into step next to her. "I aim to please."

They were both quiet on the ride back. It was a companionable silence despite the high hurdles they faced in completing the joint lighthouse proposal.

Nancy fell asleep halfway back to her office so Sam had a chance to steal more than a glance without fear of being caught.

She was beautiful, something Sam had noticed immediately, even in the midst of her seasickness. It was Nancy's mind, however, that was particularly attractive. She wasn't anything like the women Sam usually found surrounding her. Those women used Sam and she used them, for pleasure, for exposure, for a friendly face to spend time with. None of them could have provided the kind of meaningful surprise Nancy pulled off despite barely knowing her.

Sam marveled at Nancy's surety in her love of history. There wasn't anything Sam loved like that. The only thing she felt similarly passionate about was something she didn't love, which was the life she was destined for as the head of her father's company. How would history judge her contributions to society, running a company she hated that provided no measurable good to the world? The first line on her tombstone would read "CEO." How pathetic.

She thought about the *Gerda III* and the crew that had risked so much to help their neighbors. Her heart ached for those forced to flee their homes, their jobs, their lives, all because of the most hideous expression of human cruelty. Suddenly, Sam found herself desperate for more of her book. She'd left Tove and Jonna in danger and needed to see them to safety. So many lives had been cut short, destroyed, and forever changed because of the war, but maybe there was some solace to be found in the story of two women who found a happily ever after.

Nancy stirred, catching Sam's attention. The light shone off her hair, dancing against the red like a crackling campfire. Before today, Sam never would have guessed a step into the past would be so harrowing and emotional. She still saw problems with Nancy's proposal, but she could admit to herself, if not yet to Nancy, that there was potential in leveraging the history of the lighthouse.

But they'd never make progress if Sam kept thinking of where she might sweep them off to next, instead of buckling down on the work ahead and what surprises she could hold in reserve for Nancy. That line of thinking needed to stop immediately. No sweeping, no surprises, no more playing hooky. Tomorrow it was serious business only, no matter what Nancy had to say about it. Tonight though, was reserved for her book and memories of the day. Her mind was free to wander.

CHAPTER NINE

Copenhagen

Tove leaned upward from her knees, pulled Jonna into a hug, and let the tears soak her shoulder.

"We…we've always been so careful, Tove. Papa drove me mad, harping about secrecy. I-I can't believe they discovered anything. I can't."

"We may never know what really happened, my sweet Jonna. Beck and those boys would make up anything to look like heroes. For an achievement like catching a spy?" She rubbed Jonna's back, wishing she could soften this blow. All the while, however, a looming fear grew larger by the minute. Somehow, they had to set sorrow and shock aside.

Tove smoothed Jonna's hair back tenderly as her mind raced. Even the implication of spying for the Resistance brought deadly repercussions, and the Gestapo most likely were on their way.

"You know you can't stay here, Jonna," she whispered, trying not to panic. "Grab a few things in a satchel. We must go. Right away."

Jonna saw little through her tears, but she glanced vacantly around the apartment, imprinting images she might never see again. Tove was right: Gestapo certainly would come for her, would use every measure in their power to learn what she and her father did for the Resistance and what they knew about it. She shuddered as she swallowed more tears and let Tove help her stand.

Sniffling, Jonna moved as if in a fog. She collected several photographs, a little money from a jar by the stove, and a block of cheese. Suddenly, she was just as desperate for rescue as the thousands of her Jewish countrymen. The sympathy she felt for their plight turned to blinding fear for herself, fear of capture and death. *Oh, Papa!* Forcing back tears made her gag. Her legs shook. She battled to think clearly.

She gripped Tove's arm. "I can't ask for refuge. I-I won't put a neighbor in jeopardy."

"I understand," Tove said, holding her by the shoulders. "We know they'll search here, your neighbors—"

Tove's words were clipped. She fought back her own tears, Jonna could see that much, and knew this heartbreak was mutual. But there was a defiance in Tove's beseeching look that made Jonna swallow hard. Thank God, Tove had strength to spare, and Jonna willed herself to accept all she could.

"I-I know I must go—"

"*We* will go."

Jonna searched Tove's face. As if reading her mind, she could think of only one sanctuary, but Tove needn't risk involving herself. "You…They've seen us together at Drogden, Tove. You mustn't stay with me. They will question you."

"I can play innocent. I have sailors who'll lie for me if necessary. But it's not me I'm worried about."

Jonna pressed her hands to her eyes. She had to stop the tears. The common sense she sorely needed seemed impossible to grasp.

"Okay. Okay, now I…My God, this is so hard." She peered at Tove through blurry eyes. "I-I know what you're thinking," she managed, somehow able to broach the subject Tove probably dreaded mentioning herself. "There really is only one place to go, isn't there?" The prospect of Swedish exile overloaded her senses.

Tove took Jonna's hand and pressed it to her breast. "My heart's aching for you. I want you safe. We h-have so much to look forward to, a future. Do you agree?"

Jonna nodded and tears began again. "I do, my precious Tove." She closed her eyes. "I don't want to lose you, too."

"Nor I, you. W-we must be strong."

Jonna rested her cheek against Tove's. "Somehow, I always thought Papa and I would avoid this. How foolish of me." She leaned back, sniffled, and fought for composure. "It's…it's Sweden, then."

"There's no choice," Tove whispered. "Take my heart with you."

Jonna squeezed her as tightly as she could. Soft lips kissed her eyes, tenderly erased tears, and Jonna desperately wished they would erase the impossible images that refused to abate.

"I'm so scared."

Tove held her at arm's length and tried to convey the strength she knew each of them needed. "I am too, my love, but we *have* to go. *Now*, if we hope to find a boat with room."

With the door and Jonna's life closed behind her, Tove led them along Copenhagen's narrow dark alleys in violation of Nazi curfew. They darted into shady doorways and storefronts to avoid patrolling sentries, which only delayed their arrival at the docks. A slim chance remained to locate a reliable boat with room still available. Space not previously allocated disappeared in seconds.

Tove kept them in the shadows as they ran along the storefronts— until a pair of soldiers appeared on the upcoming corner. She pulled Jonna into a doorway just before they were spotted. The soldiers' conversation grew louder.

"Here," Tove whispered, and gestured to the broken glass door. She reached through the opening and twisted the doorknob from within. They ducked inside and eased the door shut just as the soldiers passed.

Jonna pointed to the street and Tove nodded. Yes, the sentries could still be heard nearby, and the scent of their cigarette smoke wafted on the breeze. Tove fought the edginess in her feet. They had to keep moving. But the soldiers stood talking and smoking for too long. Waiting ate away precious time, was undoubtedly costing them space on a boat.

By the time they reached the docks, Tove's hope had nearly vanished. With Jonna hidden nearby, she adopted the air of a working sailor and openly strolled to her last choice among the many innocent-looking craft. But inquiries proved fruitless. Workers aboard the four boats she approached anxiously shared the news of the evening, that soldiers had killed the Drogden keeper and Gestapo now hunted his daughter.

When she returned to Jonna, huddled in the back of an abandoned truck, she found it impossible to hide her disappointment.

Jonna cupped Tove's cheek. "You did your best," she whispered, and wiped strands of disarrayed hair off Tove's forehead. "I-I've been thinking and, well, there *is* one last option—if we have enough bravery to share."

Jonna had no idea where she'd found the courage to even contemplate such a far-fetched suggestion. Desperation, she figured, and saw the acknowledgement in Tove's widening eyes. There *was* a boat—a dinghy—that would demand every ounce of their collective will.

"You mean—"

"I know," Jonna agreed, sniffling. "It's as…as unappealing as it is promising."

"You're not serious. You can't be thinking of the Salthoven dinghy. Jonna…You're willing to *row across the strait*?"

"Well, haven't many already gone even farther in their own little boats?"

"Yes, but—"

"And, well, the weather tonight is calm, isn't it?"

Tove's eyes grew rounder. Obviously, Jonna's daring shocked Tove as much as it did her.

"W-well, yes, it is a relatively warm night," Tove conceded, "and…and the waters out there are flat and there's no wind, but…" She sat back and stared at her. "You're serious, aren't you?"

"I am unless…Don't you think we could make it?"

"Sure, I do, but that dinghy on Salthoven Island is tied on the far side, the strait side."

"Yes, for sailors in distress. I'm as aware of it as you."

"Because boats just wreck themselves there, Jonna. It's just a huge pile of rocks. No one ever goes to Salthoven." Tove took her hands. "And don't forget that, first, we would, well, somehow, we'd have to cross the channel to get there."

Jonna's fragile enthusiasm faltered. "I know." She didn't have a solution to that problem.

"Jonna, listen. If…if you're really willing, and I mean *really willing,* then we'll find a way." Tove looked away, thoughtfully, then quickly turned back, her eyes brighter. "There is a man, an old friend of my father's." She ran her thumbs over Jonna's hands. "Mikkel Andersen has fished these waters forever and the Nazis know he goes out every night—in fact, right about now. We might be able to convince him to bring us to Salthoven's near shore."

"Can we get to him in time?" Jonna snickered at herself. "Listen to me, casting all fear aside." She clutched Tove's hands tightly. "We *can* do this, can't we? Tell me again that we can."

"Yes, I know we can." A spark of daring broke through the concern in Tove's eyes and Jonna felt it lift weight from her shoulders. "I do, indeed," Tove added, "especially when the alternative is running between hiding spots until the damn Nazis leave Denmark."

Again, Tove sensed time ticking away from them. She watched Jonna think hard about everything and couldn't imagine coping with this much stress. *How she and her father managed at Drogden was courageous. Surrounded by Nazis since August? And now losing her father, her home, and running for her life—and rowing across the Oresund?* Tove couldn't give Jonna enough credit for such bravery. She hoped their private memories of Drogden shined brightly through these times.

At last, Jonna met her eyes. "I've become no different than the other refugees, Tove. I have to face the inevitable."

They wound their way across the city to Andersen's boat and scampered aboard when the coast was clear. Hunkered down outside the wheelhouse, they knocked on the weathered wooden door.

When it swung open, the old man squinted down at them in the dim light, his wire-rimmed spectacles balanced at the end of his nose.

Tove removed her cap as they peered up at him. "Mikkel. It's me, Tove Salling."

His haggard jowls lifted in a grin. "Tove? Good heavens!" Surprise tilted his wooly eyebrows upward. "What are…" He looked to Jonna and back. "Come. Get inside, quick."

Crossing the channel an hour later, he still disapproved of their plan and assured them for the third time that all this was against his better judgment. For good measure, and probably in a last attempt to dissuade them, he predicted that Tove's father would roll in his grave.

He powered the engine down until the boat crept in among the island's dangerous outcroppings. The protruding rock fingers threatened all who approached, and the old craft creaked nervously as it bobbed in the darkness. Andersen had risked plenty with this favor and coming so close to Salthoven's unforgiving coastline bordered on foolhardy.

"Eh, I'm an old man," he mumbled as they hugged him good-bye. "Been through trickier maneuvers. And don't you worry about those animals getting any information out of Mikkel Andersen. If this damn sea hasn't taken me after all these years, they're not going to."

Tove and Jonna slid into the water as slowly as they could to keep their heads above it, gasping uncontrollably, their bodies recoiling, clenching. October's brisk temperature had taken on a severe chill out in the channel but didn't compare to this bone-numbing sensation.

Treading water with one hand to remain upright, Jonna labored to keep her satchel out of the water with the other. Andersen carefully lowered a duffle with blankets and matches to Tove's raised hand. He shook his head as they swam with one arm the several yards to the rocky shore.

Jonna matched Tove's long strides upward and onto the slippery, rocky ground. "Do you think we should wait and dry off tonight?"

Beyond Tove, she watched Andersen's boat disappear into the night. Utter solitude amplified this dark and foreboding place, and the heavy reality of her predicament threatened to crush her. She struggled to keep misgivings at bay.

"I'd love to wait," Tove finally answered, "and I know he gave us matches, but we'll be safer crossing the strait at night. The rowboat should be right over the next rise."

Jonna tried not to think about the warmth of a fire, or the growing list of things she shouldn't be thinking about. Every one that didn't scare her threatened to make her cry. She decided to focus on warmth after all, eager to huddle in one of those old wool blankets. "Thank God this decrepit place is so small."

"Walking hard and fast like this keeps our blood hot," Tove said, and took her hand. "We'll use the blankets once we're under way."

Atop the knoll, they paused and scanned the gradual slope ahead to the water's edge. Tove slipped an arm around her shoulders and Jonna appreciated the warmth. She tried not to shiver in her dripping clothes.

"Not too long of a hike, was it?" Tove asked and pointed to the southwest horizon. "See that?"

Jonna blotted away tears with her sleeve and spotted the speck of Drogden's intermittent light. "Do you think they've taken Papa ashore by now?"

"He's at the Lighthouse Service headquarters, I'm sure. They'll honor him, Jonna."

She sniffled and shook her head. "He should be watching us from out there."

Tove hugged her close. "He knows Drogden will be there for you, will guide you home."

"Oh, but he should be there." She pressed her face against Tove's wet jacket. "He is gone forever now."

"Dear Jonna. He'd hate to see you so sad. Think of what would please him. Think of his pride in Drogden, that it remains defiant in its promise, the strongest, most patriotic of all Danes." She gestured to the horizon. "Think of our adventure now, how proud he would be of our determination to persevere."

"To row far beyond that light…I really haven't had time to think of what's ahead." Jonna gazed across the open water. "Thankfully."

"We have many countrymen at those Swedish villages over there, remember. And you will be coming home the very second it's safe. I promise to bring you home myself."

"How will I manage without you?" Jonna cupped Tove's cheek, cold and wet with mist. "I will miss you so."

Tove ducked her head and swiped at her eyes. "W—we can't think about that now, Jonna. My heart—" She cut herself off. "Come."

They walked hand-in-hand over rocks of all shapes and sizes, until Tove stopped and pointed to the largest one. Jonna nearly cheered the welcomed sight, the weather-worn rowboat lashed to a heavy stone.

"Thank God." Stooping to inspect the boat's interior, she wasn't especially impressed. "It's seaworthy?"

Tove tossed their bags inside and began unwinding the rope from the rock.

"Everyone who sails these waters knows it is, that it's always been." At the bow, she set her feet and lifted with a push, sliding the craft backwards down the slope, closer to the lapping waves.

"Papa often talked about the unwritten rule on Salthoven. 'Always return the boat properly, ready for the next sailor in need.' And you're a sailor, so you qualify."

Hands on her hips, Tove surveyed the boat, ready for a final push into the strait. "I do." She lent Jonna a grin. "And you are my 'Mistress of Drogden,' so you do, too."

Jonna chuckled at the title. "Honestly, Tove? I really can't believe we're doing this."

❖

"Not just at Malmo or Linhamn or Klangshamn," Tove explained as they rowed steadily across the rolling current. "All the little fishing villages between them—from Helsingborg all the way down to Skanor—they have taken in refugees as well, by the dozen, so many in some places that Danish enclaves are being established. The Swedes have been amazingly generous." She prayed that Jonna would learn this immediately upon walking ashore.

"I'll be happy just to be warm," Jonna said. The blankets they wore over their wet clothes were a godsend, but hardly sufficient on this vast open sea. "At least working this hard helps."

Tove agreed, relieved to know Jonna saw the added benefit of this strenuous effort. Currently rowing backwards to face Tove, Jonna displayed every ounce of the determination Tove had hoped to see, and a natural rhythm in sync with hers as if they did this together every day.

Such coordination made for swift travel and Tove guessed they had been under way for about twenty minutes already. She was optimistic about reaching Sweden within two hours, although unhappy to hear Drogden's foghorn cut into the silence. She exchanged an anxious look with Jonna, who obviously was well acquainted with the signal.

A fog bank threatened from the south, diminishing Drogden's beacon, and Tove began to doubt that the light breeze would keep trouble at a reasonable distance.

"It's going to overtake us, isn't it?" Jonna said, having caught Tove eyeing the fog.

Tove stared into the thickening haze and could no longer see the beacon. She nodded solemnly, all too aware they lacked a compass or guiding light. Approaching the middle of the strait was not a place to be aimlessly adrift. Boats and ships of all sizes relied on this deep water.

Mist grew heavy as the fog arrived, wafting over them like trails of smoke. Tove wiped droplets from her eyelashes, saw Jonna brush her face with the blanket.

"Keep the pace even and steady," she advised, her chest tightening. "It's all we can do now. If we don't change anything about each stroke, we might stay pretty much on course."

"How long before it passes?"

Tove wished she knew. "It got here fairly quickly, so maybe it will move on just as fast."

"I can't see Drogden anymore."

"Me neither." Losing Drogden's guidance felt like dropping off a cliff.

A flash of light suddenly slashed through the fog ahead of them, then behind them. The beam bounced from left to right and back, seeking, leading some unknown craft.

"I can't make out what it is," Tove said as they rowed on blindly, mechanically in unison.

The beam of light skimmed the dinghy's bow, then snapped back to it.

"Halt! You in the boat!"

The German words were all Tove needed to hear. She stabbed an oar into the water and held it in place, providing a pivot point around which Jonna's rowing turned them from the light.

"Don't stop!" Tove blurted in a hush, rowing hard. "We can dodge them."

"Halt! Prepare to surrender your boat!"

Like a monster from the deep, the Nazi patrol boat emerged from the fog less than twenty yards away. They both gasped.

Tove rowed furiously away from it. "Faster!" she whispered severely. "Deeper into the fog!"

She could hear the patrol boat change gears, motor into a different direction, and knew it was trying to follow. She dipped an oar, pivoted the dinghy again, and returned to rowing in sync with Jonna, avoiding the beacon that darted around them.

"Tove. We can't keep this up much longer."

A machine gun sprayed the water behind them, the noise ear-shattering over the drone of the Nazi engine.

"Tove!" Jonna's forceful whisper was almost too loud.

"Shh! Keep hiding, into the fog," Tove said as quietly as she could. "Bend down. Try to stay low, but row. Hard."

"Turn us again! The fog is shifting."

Tove dipped her oar for several seconds and they rowed off in another direction, keeping to the fog. The beacon searched far to their right now, but the staccato spray of bullets seemed to go everywhere.

"Damn you," Tove growled.

Another spray of bullets swept through the search light, through the fog, and through the rowboat.

"Jesus, Tove!"

"Are you hit?"

"No, but…now the water—look!"

"Don't stop, Jonna. They don't know the boat's been hit."

Water flowed around their feet as they struggled to row deeper into the fog. It covered their ankles, and its increasing weight slowed their progress. Tove shook her head as it rose toward their shins. Within minutes, rowing became impossible, and they were forced to let the boat drift. Her heart pounded mercilessly as she calculated their time left afloat.

We'll only be able to tread this water for so long.

Then, the patrol boat engine revved again but this time miraculously faded away.

"My God," Jonna whispered. "They're leaving?"

"Not worth their eff—"

The rowboat lurched sideways.

"Tove!"

"Hang on!"

They both grabbed their seats to stay aboard.

A violent wave sent the bow knifing upward, clear of the water, almost throwing them overboard, and then suddenly fell away. The boat dropped onto rock, the flimsy decking shattered, and they went under.

CHAPTER TEN

Salthoven Island
Denmark

Totally spent, Jonna practically collapsed onto the space she'd cleared with her shoe. It was a patch of dirt-caked cement she hoped was now free of the broken bricks and mortar and God-knows what else she couldn't see in the dark. She was too wet and cold and traumatized to care. She was fairly certain they were back on Salthoven but had no doubt they were stranded.

Tove plopped down beside her and assumed the same position, cross-legged and scrunched forward, arms tightly folded across her breasts, equally desperate for warmth.

"My father cursed the government for letting this place go," Tove said, peering through the darkness at the rubble around them. "Even back then, this old lighthouse was a relic, but keeping it running would have been a smart compliment to Drogden. Nobody wanted the mariners' opinions."

Jonna nodded. Papa likewise had opposed decommissioning this old lighthouse, once Salthoven's only structure. But now recalling anything about him hurt. It made this present dilemma seem so petty.

"At least there's this," she managed, "or what's left of it."

What had once been Salthoven's cement block lighthouse currently stood half as tall, a crumbling, open-topped ruin, littered with its own rusted and broken debris. But they were grateful for any shelter from the wind.

"Now we need that fire," Tove grumbled, rubbing her upper arms.

Jonna agreed wholeheartedly and longed to see more of her surroundings. What remained of the lighthouse's circular walls reached only one story high, open at the top to a sky of crisp, sparkling stars. Along with a broken metal stairway and glass-less windows, the upper floors had long since collapsed. She imagined collecting scraps of that wood framing to burn for heat, then remembered losing the matches. She shivered, glad when Tove edged closer.

"I never thought we'd end up back where we started," Jonna said on a sigh. "I mean, yes, I feared we'd meet trouble on the strait, but never this." Jonna stopped short of voicing the obvious. Salthoven offered no prospects for a fire—or rescue.

"At least Nazis won't come here," Tove said with a snicker. "I guess we can be grateful for that. They must have known they were dangerously close and turned away." She pointed toward the gaping opening that once had been a doorway. "Look to the horizon."

Jonna studied the blackness ahead and found it difficult to discern inside from outside. Until a flash of light caught her eye.

"Drogden!" The discovery brought a surge of comfort. "Yes, I see it."

"It's telling us not to lose hope. We'll come up with some kind of signal, attract a boat, a fisherman. I know nobody sails close to this place, but we'll get someone."

"At first light."

"Yeah." Tove took both Jonna's hands in hers. "We might be a little warmer if we enclosed ourselves more, piled up these blocks and other junk."

Jonna stood and drew Tove up with her. "Then, better to be moving than shivering to death." Her voice shook with the cold and, when Tove cupped her face with both hands, she trembled again.

"We are together," Tove whispered. "We'll make it through this." She lowered her mouth to Jonna's and kissed her slowly, carefully.

Jonna's body hummed at the first real warmth and surety she'd felt in hours. Previous kisses paled in comparison. This conveyed passion and desire, need, and she yearned to make it last.

She couldn't imagine surviving this nightmare with anyone but Tove. Their connection seemed predestined. Their actions coordinated so automatically, their thoughts often emerged in identical words, and their hearts… Jonna found her self-assessment so wonderous, she shook her head. She'd been right about this blond sailor from the very start, and no matter how or when this particular nightmare ended, they would be together.

They stumbled through the darkness for the next two hours, gathering planks, blocks, remnants of furniture, enough to encase themselves in a space barely big enough for two.

"I'll lay these planks across the top," Tove said, "unless you think it's too much like a coffin."

Jonna could see the impish grin through the dimness. "At this point, I'm for anything that helps." She watched Tove pick her way gingerly through debris to reach their small enclosure. The intrepid sailor in her was showing and Jonna liked the look of it very much.

Tove aligned the boards across the top of the low structure and straightened to look for Jonna's opinion. Her hair swung across her face, and she swiped it back, seemingly irritated when it interrupted their eye contact. It was then that Jonna realized how much her visibility had improved. Darkness was giving way to predawn light.

"I think that's just fine, the finishing touch," she said, "considering the sun will be up in an hour or so."

"Then drop what you've got and let's get inside."

Jonna ducked and crawled in between the gritty floor and ceiling, settling onto her side to make room for Tove. The boards around her smelled of wood rot and salt water, and, although their damp clothing would collect all the aging dust, these conditions were welcomed.

"A little cramped, but…"

Tove worked her way in beside her. "Like being stashed in a cupboard."

"But rather a perfect fit for two, I'd say."

"Just us."

Jonna welcomed Tove with an arm across her back, excited and grateful when Tove hooked her waist and drew them together. The intimacy made the chill of their damp clothing bearable.

"You're shivering so hard," Tove whispered before kissing Jonna's nose. "We're not close enough." She tucked Jonna's arm between them and wrapped her arms around her tightly. "This is better."

"Your hair smells like the sea."

Tove laughed. "We *both* smell like the sea, and I don't care." She ran her palms heavily along Jonna's back, pressing her closer. "I've dreamed of this, you know—"

"Shipwrecked?"

"Yeah, right." Tove gave her a squeeze. "Lying with you in my arms."

"In *my* dreams, we enjoyed a soft, warm bed."

"Mine, too."

"And nothing between us."

"Like wet clothes."

Jonna leaned back slightly. "You believe we will have that someday?"

"We were meant to be together, that's what I believe."

Jonna returned her cheek to Tove's shoulder. "And, I agree, you know. Honestly. It's just...well, it's just so hard to see through all that's ahead. Getting off this rock is one problem and then there is Sweden." She leaned away again. "No home, no means, no Papa, and...no you. It's hard to look forward, Tove."

"But you must. For your sake, for ours. You *are* that strong, Jonna, stronger than any Nazi effort to sweep you from this world, and Sweden will help you." She brushed Jonna's hair from her face and set their foreheads together. "I will do everything I can to help. You *will* come home to me."

Jonna thrust an arm around Tove's waist and kissed her desperately. She no longer knew where home would be, at Drogden or the village apartment or someplace new or if she would have *any* home, but right now Tove and her vow were everything.

Tove kissed her onto her back, and her weight, the trail of heated kisses along Jonna's neck had Jonna escaping into blissful euphoria. She clutched Tove to her with both hands, a leg, relishing every bit of contact. She drove her fingers into Tove's hair and brought their mouths together for a long, penetrating kiss that left each of them breathless.

Tove set delicate kisses to Jonna's cheek, her eyes. "No tears, my sweet Jonna."

"I can't help it. There are so many emotions. I'm afraid and sad and…" she palmed the side of Tove's face, "and I am so in love with you. I can't be without you."

Tove felt her heart skip. She had yearned to hear those words, share such feelings for so long. She refused to let this setting quell the joy rising inside.

"You have my heart, every ounce of my love," she whispered, kissing Jonna's lips softly. "Neither will ever let you down. I want them to guide us, to guide you, now, like…like Drogden, strong and constant. I promise we will have our day."

Jonna drew her down into a fierce hug. "I need to feel you with me now, not someday. I've waited forever for 'someday' and we both know it might never come."

"But it will."

"You don't know that, Tove. You could be captured on any trip you make on the *Engel* and now they'll be hunting for you. Aiding the Resistance in any way could take you from me—and I'll be helpless in Sweden. I'll never know if—"

Tove knew Jonna was right, but dwelling on the negative only heightened their most private fears.

She rose on her elbows and kissed Jonna again. "Shh. Stop. Let's not think the worst. When we get off this damn rock—and we will, we have so much to look forward to, the war ending, a return to peaceful living, making a home together."

Jonna sniffled and, as dawn approached, it was easy for Tove to see the tears trickling from those scared brown eyes. She ached for something reassuring to say, but thinking through all this emotion was difficult.

She knew they needed sleep, at least a little before tackling the matter of signaling for rescue. Fleetingly, she wondered if the boat that ultimately plucked them from this island would agree to bring Jonna to Sweden. It would be a lot to ask of a well-meaning, unsuspecting mariner.

She kissed Jonna again and lowered her head onto her chest, snuggled beneath her chin. She could rest like this for eternity, she thought, bound within Jonna's arms, Jonna's leg over hers possessively. This bit of contentment felt like home in a unique way, if only sleep would allow it.

❖

Equipped with broken steps and pieces of pipe railing, Tove sat on a plank in the sunshine, watching for passing vessels. The two German warships that passed hours earlier didn't count. And the Danish freighter, now almost out of sight, had been too far away to hear the noise she was prepared to make.

"A trawler is headed south," Jonna reported, returning to Tove after relieving herself near the lighthouse. "Coming along our west side."

"Maybe we'll get lucky. Let's get ready."

They hefted the pieces of metal stairs and railing, prepared to bang a sizeable commotion out over the waves.

"Lovely day to make a racket," Jonna quipped, optimism shining in her eyes.

The unseasonably warm temperature and gentle breeze actually made for a lovely day, serene on the calm sea, and Tove had to marvel as much at Jonna's spirit as their good fortune. They'd awakened in late morning, warm and in dried clothes, if a bit stiff from the salt, and reluctant to leave each other's arms. But desperate to resolve their crisis, they aimed their hopes at attracting rescue with these pieces of lighthouse debris.

The trawler finally came into view, and they began pounding metal-on-metal, waving their arms, jumping, yelling, although the latter was more instinctive than practical. A half-mile out and abreast of their position on the island, the trawler showed no sign of hearing them. They intensified their effort, but the boat maintained course, seemingly oblivious.

Tove sat again and tried not to let her disappointment add to Jonna's concerns.

"I guess we could pretend we're on a sandy beach, hot in the August sun."

"Not a care in the world," Jonna added. "We *could* but that's really hard."

"How about strolling past that café near your apartment, smelling coffee and hot bread?"

"You're being cruel."

"How about that flower shop? Do you like roses?"

"Actually, I love all flowers. It's been a long time."

"First chance I get, I'll bring you some."

"And I'll bake you bread, once I have an oven. A kitchen."

"In a cottage by the sea."

Jonna turned to her sharply. "You would like that?"

"A cottage for two by the sea? I can't wait."

"I'm surprised that the adventurer in you would care to settle in a cottage."

"Well, Drogden could be our cottage, once the Lighthouse Service puts you in charge."

"I see. And you'll be off, sailing passengers to who-knows where." Jonna shook her head as she looked back to the empty horizon.

"I would only sail for the day, come home every night. I'd never sail far from you." Tove leaned against her and kissed her cheek. "You're my home."

"Wherever we are will be our home, Tove, but not Drogden. It's only a workplace now. It can no longer be a home."

"Why not? We'll paint the red stripes back over the Nazi whitewash, empty the place of Nazi dirt, and reorganize it properly. We'll redecorate it into cozy quarters for ourselves. A workplace *and* a home. It…it deserves to be."

Jonna heard the hesitation in Tove's voice, knew they both recalled the happy times when Drogden actually was home.

"I am reminded of Papa, Tove. Every time I see Drogden's light, I see the smile in his eyes, how Drogden fulfilled him, brought him purpose after Mama died."

"And you were always his pride and joy, Jonna. He couldn't hide how proud he was that you chose to stay there with him. *You* made Drogden a home."

Jonna shrugged. "It will forever remind me of him, that beacon reaching out."

"Never lose sight of it, though. People have no concept of a lighthouse's power, its true value. And, as we've learned, even a lighthouse broken by age is a noble treasure."

"But Drogden just brings back so much. It always will. I don't know if I will ever *not* feel his presence there."

She let Tove tug her close and rested her head on her shoulder. Although she knew it unlikely she would succeed Papa as Drogden's keeper, the concept still warmed her heart. And the fantasy of making it her home with Tove provided relief from this present, sad reality.

Tove squeezed her closer. "You need to see things the other way around. You *should* always feel your father there, Jonna, because he will always be with you, whether Drogden carries on as a workplace, a home, or both. Through Drogden, he will always look out for you."

Jonna closed her eyes and let Tove's uplifting message settle deeply inside. Despite everything, fate had blessed her. Love she had once thought unimaginable now embraced her. She had a companion she would cherish for life and dared to hope for happiness.

"You know," she began softly, "sometimes I think the sea has cast a magical spell over you, Tove Salling. Your strength, your energy, they're remarkable, but your heart is so powerful, sometimes it takes my breath away."

Tove kissed her lightly, her lips lingering as she whispered, "It's called love, my sweet Jonna." She deepened their kiss, drew all foreign thoughts away, made room for passion, the singular joy of them together.

Jonna threaded her arms around her neck and returned the kiss with just as much yearning. "I've wanted to be free to kiss you like this for so long," she whispered, kissing Tove's cheek and jaw. She pressed against Tove's chest, kissed her firmly, urged her down onto the board beneath them.

Tove locked both arms around her to hold her in place. "Sometimes dreams come true," she said, stroking her back, squeezing. "You've been my dream for just as long." She kissed Jonna's cheek before finding her lips again.

Suddenly, Tove turned her face aside. "Shh!"

Jonna heard the hum of the distant motor and sat up quickly.

Tove joined her, shifting onto her knees. "Those two big rocks," she said, pointing behind them. "Let's get back to them. But don't stand, just keep very low."

They half-crawled back toward the lighthouse ruin and huddled behind the boulders. Jonna didn't want to think the worst, but it was hard to ignore, considering how life had shifted in little more than a day.

"Tell me they haven't come back to search for us," she said as they peered over the rocks to the sea.

Spotting the Nazi boat sent an unwelcomed chill along Jonna's spine. Dark gray and about the size of the *Engel*, it appeared just as threatening in the late afternoon sun as it had last night in the fog. Probably because they were a far easier target now.

"They can't know we survived," Jonna said, afraid to take her eyes off the craft.

"As long as they don't see us, trying to land around here won't be worth it to them." Jonna liked that logic, but she appreciated Tove taking her hand. "As we well know," Tove continued, "you don't come ashore on Salthoven unless you feel like swimming."

The patrol boat turned and crept along the shoreline again.

Tove's nerves began to tense. She cursed under her breath, wishing the Nazis would give up the search. "They're taking a second look." What concerned her most was the long reach of German binoculars and weaponry.

"Thank God for these big rocks," Jonna said.

"True, but the Nazis will focus on the big things, like these rocks and our hulk of a lighthouse. Where else would somebody hide?" Jonna sent her a blank look, as if her faith had just been stripped away, and Tove regretted being so frank. "We'll just stay here, hidden, and listen. I think that's the smartest thing to do."

Jonna sat and leaned against the boulder. "It's the *only* thing to do."

Time dragged as they waited, wondering how many times the Nazis would cruise the shoreline. Sitting on the rocky turf for another half-hour led to sore bottoms and stiff legs, and Tove feared they wouldn't be very mobile if the need arose.

She jumped when Jonna grabbed her arm.

"Hear that? The engine changed. Maybe they're leaving."

The boat's motor shifted gears and, to their immense relief, the sound of it slowly faded. Tove leaned out from behind the boulder, caught a glimpse of the departing patrol, and sat back with an exhausted sigh.

"Finally."

Jonna took a peek as well. "I think they should be out of sight before we stand up."

"Definitely. Never trust them."

"I'm just happy they left."

Tove couldn't have agreed more. *Took our minds off your father, the life-altering trip to Sweden, and how we're getting off this damn island.*

CHAPTER ELEVEN

Salthoven Island
Denmark

"What are you up to?" Tove turned where she sat to watch Jonna rummage through debris in the lighthouse ruin. "I thought we were going to sit here in the doorway for a while."

She didn't know what Jonna was doing but enjoyed the sight of her and her vigorous effort, the tossing of that silky hair. Just as much as the sweet, fun-loving Jonna she adored, this was a sturdy, industrious Jonna she honestly loved. The pounding of her heart told her so.

"I'm making us an enclosure to sit in." Jonna grunted as she pulled a plank from beneath a pile of bricks. "Like the place where we slept."

"You're building another coffin?"

"No, silly, a windbreak. I want us to sit there past sunset, so we'll need something to block the breeze." She added the board to a pile at Tove's side, then left to find more. "I want to watch Drogden."

"Ah."

Flipping her hair over her shoulder, Jonna turned back and set her hands on her slender hips. "And what are *you* watching?"

Tove made a point to show her. She took her time surveying Jonna's lithe form, her disheveled appearance, the rise and fall of her full breasts as her breathing steadied. Jacket, blouse, and trousers were as worn as the woman herself, yet she simmered with a cocked eyebrow and an allure that tripped Tove's heart.

"I'm watching a beautiful woman on a mission."

"Careful. Flirting might jeopardize that mission." Jonna spun back to her work.

"Is that so?"

"You could add your muscle to the cause, you know."

Tove hurried to her feet. "Oh, I'm in. Hopefully, it won't be as cold tonight."

"Hey, we can use this."

Jonna held up a large shard of window glass.

Immediately, Tove faulted herself for not thinking of it sooner. "To flash a signal. Damn, of course!"

Staging one last board atop chunks of cement, Jonna exhaled with satisfaction. She took Tove's hand and sat within the three walls, tugging her down with her.

"I do say," and she slipped an arm through Tove's, "this works perfectly." She pointed through the old doorway to the horizon. "If the temperature doesn't drop too low, we'll be okay."

Tove saw her nod at her own statement. She wrapped an arm around Jonna's shoulders. "Yes, we'll be okay." She set a long kiss into her hair. "Please tell me, my special lady, why did it take us this long?"

Jonna turned within Tove's arm and rubbed their noses together. "It doesn't matter anymore. Even when I—*we*—have to part ways, we'll be so much closer." Tove's eyes blurred with tears when Jonna cupped her cheek. "Tove, you are what I've always wanted. No amount of time away from you in Sweden will change that."

She leaned in and delivered a slow, promising kiss, and they clung to each other as it deepened.

Tove returned Jonna's kiss with profound longing. Tears inched down her cheek. Actually, she couldn't tell whose they were. Although the impending separation saddened each of them, these were joyful tears worth sharing.

She kissed Jonna onto her back, cushioning her head atop her arm, and laid a trail of gentle kisses across her cheek, to her ear, along her neck. Jonna's hands stroking her back, squeezing her closer made Tove's blood thrum. Her heart hammered as she reveled in the satin texture of Jonna's throat.

"We've waited so long, Jonna," she whispered between kisses, "we will not lose each other now." She raised her head and met the dark eyes. Slim, firm fingers combed through her hair and Tove nearly swooned. There were only a few select words she could muster. "I love you truly."

"Oh, and I love you so." Jonna slid both hands beneath Tove's jacket and tugged her closer as they kissed. She urged them onto their sides, slipped a hand upward and onto Tove's breast and made Tove's breath catch. "I love the feel of you, Tove. When I touch you, when you touch me, there's such softness and strength and I need them both so much. I need all of you."

Tove lowered her head to Jonna's neck and tasted the sensitive, salty skin along her shoulder, untying the thin bow that clasped her blouse closed. She sought all of Jonna's softness at that moment and kissed downward from her throat. Competing sensation fired from deep within as her own chest was exposed with each button Jonna unfastened.

Tove opened Jonna's blouse and cupped her breast, took the stimulated nipple between thumb and forefinger, and made Jonna inhale deeply.

"Tove, yes."

"I knew you would be beautiful everywhere." In awe of what she was about to do, Tove slowly nuzzled into the plush breast, lost herself in the warmth and velvety sensation against her face. Stroking the hardened nipple with her tongue turned Jonna's sigh to a wanton gasp, made her squirm as Tove nursed it deeper into her mouth.

She clasped Jonna's waist in both hands, massaged her ribs, held her in place as she kissed her way to the opposite breast. To Tove's endless delight, Jonna welcomed her, gripped her shoulders, and encouraged her with a guiding hand on the back of her head.

Tove eased her palm into Jonna's trousers, as lost in the softness of her skin as in the magnitude of her own action. It took Jonna unbuttoning them for Tove to awaken to her own boldness, and she sought approval with a string of kisses all the way back to Jonna's lips. Lacing her arms around Tove's neck, Jonna delivered the perfect response, a deep moan that sent Tove's fingers on a most reverent mission.

"Tove."

"I only want to please you."

"God, Tove. This feels like nothing else, ever." Her hips shifted as Tove explored deeper.

"Dearest Jonna." Tove stopped and cupped her sex, kissed her abdomen. "The greatest pleasure of my life. You honor me." She squeezed and watched Jonna writhe beneath her.

She claimed a nipple between her teeth and nuzzled into Jonna's breast, consumed by a desire for more. Delighting in the salt of her skin, she stroked her to a roiling climax until Jonna hung quivering from her shoulders, moaning deeply.

The throaty sound heightened Tove's own arousal, pushed her hunger beyond any previous experience. When she felt Jonna's hand between her own legs, Tove nearly exploded.

"Now, I-I have you, too," Jonna managed on a ragged breath.

The sensation forced Tove from Jonna's breast. She groaned hard and lurched higher upon her, unconsciously freeing Jonna to slip even deeper inside. In that instant, she realized what she sought for Jonna mirrored her own desperate need, and, at long last, this spectacular moment was happening.

Tove kissed her firmly, felt herself grow rigid against Jonna's trembling body. Jonna cried out as they shuddered into each other, suspended in that treasured moment.

Jonna woke to the sounds of seagulls in an uproar, cawing and flapping just outside the broken doorway. Despite the ruckus, she smiled at the fluffy blond hair on her shoulder. Memories of last night would last a lifetime and, right now, they warmed her against the cool morning air. Or maybe the pleasant sensation came from Tove's body covering hers.

She tightened her arms around her and stared up at the puffy clouds passing overhead. It was a sunny, blue-sky day, and had to be a sign of good things to come. Unfortunately, optimism toward leaving this desolate place dimmed when she thought about where she would end up. Tove and moments like this, snuggled together, glorious moments like last night's, would all be left behind.

She blinked away tears as she luxuriated in the feel of Tove's muscled back. Separation simply must not last forever. *I just won't allow it. I can't. And Tove won't either.*

Tove lifted her head and sleepy eyes opened to dreamy, azure pools.

Jonna fought back more tears. "Good morning," she said and kissed Tove's forehead.

Tove inched upward and kissed her lips. "Waking up like this, it can only be good." She kissed her again before looking toward the doorway. "Those birds must be feasting, with all that racket."

Suddenly, Tove thrust herself up to her knees. "Did you hear that?"

"What? Another motor?"

"No, a voice! I'm sure of it!" She lunged to her feet, pulled Jonna up with her.

"A voice?"

"Hurry!" They fumbled madly with their disarrayed clothing and ran to the doorway, scanned the rocky terrain. "I could have sworn I heard someone."

Jonna rubbed her eyes in the bright light. "Might have just been those damn bir—"

Then they both heard it. A man's distant call. Tove flashed her an amazed look and took a quick step.

"Wait!" Jonna grabbed her. "Careful, Tove."

They hurried toward the southern shore, hunched as low as hurrying would allow. Tove whispered forcefully, "I can't imagine someone's on this island, but..."

"A boat wouldn't come this close."

The voice sounded again, louder, and she couldn't believe what she heard: *her name*. A man's voice called. There was no doubt.

Peeking over a boulder, both women jerked upright in shock. The *Engel* bobbed several yards from the rocks.

"Oh, my God!" Tove waved frantically with both arms. "Here! We're here!"

"It's Rolf!" Jonna exclaimed, spotting him yelling from the bow. "Do you believe this?"

"I should have known," Tove said and seized her by the shoulders. "When I didn't show up last night, they had to wonder."

Jonna almost lost her breath when Tove crushed her in a hug. "You think Andersen went to them? Your father's friend, the old fisherman?"

"He must have." They rushed to the shore, the rocky ground slowing their progress. "The *Engel* can't sit there for long," Tove said, huffing.

"They must be on their way back from Drogden." Jonna couldn't believe that the *Engel*, of all boats, had appeared out of nowhere to rescue them. Maybe fate had sent it directly from the lighthouse.

Now, Frans, Vidar, and Rolf lined the gunnel, urging them to hurry. Captain Holsten looked on from the wheelhouse, careful to keep the *Engel* off the rocks.

At the water's edge, Tove stopped and surprised Jonna by abruptly cupping her cheek.

"My sweet love. I'm sure the way we woke up is preferable to an October swim in the Oresund, but—"

Jonna held Tove's hand in place. "Nothing can spoil what we shared."

"Hey!" Rolf yelled. "Keep moving!"

Holsten shook his fist at them from the doorway. "Don't have all damn day!"

Hand-in-hand, they waded into the sea and Jonna shivered so hard, they lost contact.

"My God, this is so c-cold!"

"Warmth, Jonna. Just think about warmth."

Jonna prayed that her desperation would prevail over the onrushing physical shock. She took a deep breath and dove in. The cold contracted her muscles, her lungs, but she counted strokes as they swam for all they were worth. Netting splashed just ahead, and they grabbed it in unison and were hauled aboard. Immediately, blankets cocooned them, and the crew ushered the pair below as the boat sped off.

While Tove fielded questions and comments from her mates, Jonna sat beside her on the bunk, numb, trying to absorb all that had and was about to happen. The heavy drone of the engine told her the *Engel* was barreling cross the strait. *If we don't get stopped, I'll be in Sweden in less than an hour. It's happening.*

As Frans returned to the deck and Vidar poured coffee, Rolf crouched before them. "Second time around the island, Frans spotted the debris from the dinghy."

"We just knew you wouldn't go down without a fight," Vidar added. "Not you."

"Not an easy adventure," Tove said, "and very little of it we'd want to repeat."

Jonna appreciated Tove clasping her hand beneath their blankets. There *were* a few moments worth repeating.

Rolf set his hands on their shoulders. "I'm going topside to relieve Holsten. He wants to speak to both of you." He gave them a squeeze and left.

Tove leaned against her and whispered. "Are you okay?"

"Considering, yes." She struggled to look into those eyes. "Thank God for the *Engel*, Tove. Thank God we…" she lowered her head, "we had last night."

Tove inched closer until they were pressed together and spoke against her cheek. "The most beautiful moment, Jonna, and we will have more. I promise you." She looked up as Vidar turned from the stove with their drinks. "Beware of Vidar's coffee. It's terrible but will warm us up." He swore at Tove as he offered the mugs. "He means well," she added with a wink.

Jonna's coffee shimmered more from her own shaking than the boat's motion. She brought a second hand out from the blanket to secure the cup. "As long as it banishes the chill in my bones."

The cabin ladder creaked as Captain Holsten descended. He took two steps in and slammed his hands to his hips. "Damn you, Salling! Even your father would have you keel-hauled! You realize that, don't you?"

Jonna didn't bother looking up. His paternal tone reminded her too much of her own father, angry yet relieved, grateful for their well-being. Besides, he obviously wasn't finished scolding Tove.

"Did you simply forget that those Nazi patrols were increased a few days ago? Why else would you attempt something so damn reckless? I know you're a skilled sailor, so I'm left to assume you had to run from them. You did, didn't you? Why didn't you at least time it better, wait for their shifts to change, like now, when it's safer? What were you thinking?"

He paced across the little room, not waiting for Tove's reply. Jonna tried to formulate a response for her. *It was all because of me.*

Arms across his barrel chest, he turned to Jonna and exhaled with finality. He knelt on one knee before her and gently covered her hands around the mug with both of his weathered paws. "I'm so, so sorry about your father, Jonna. I'm sorry for all of this."

She nodded toward their hands. "Thank you. It's so hard to think of him now, to think of what happened. None of this seems real."

"He was a great man, Jonna, a brave man who performed vital work. He dedicated himself to serving others through Drogden and, if I had my way, we'd rename that place Friedler Light. We all mourn him deeply. The Lighthouse Service will honor him. We'll make sure of that."

"You're very kind, Captain Holsten. I'm glad you two were good friends."

"For many years. From before you were born." He gestured to Tove. "John Salling and I, we could never beat him at cards, you know."

Jonna sipped her coffee and smiled at the memory. "He talked of those games so much. Those were some of his favorite times." She glanced at Tove, wondering about her memories of their fathers together. "But please don't be angry at Tove, Captain. This was my—"

"Oh, hell," he said with a sigh. "You're both fine, that's what matters. Scared the hell out of us, but..." He surprised her with a chuckle. "I, well...I guess I might have done the same thing."

Jonna was relieved to hear that. Tove nudged her with an elbow.

"Now, eh..." He stood and looked around awkwardly. "There's bound to be enough shirts and trousers here, so you both get out of those wet clothes." He forced a grin at Jonna, then turned a foreboding look on Tove. "Half hour if our luck holds. We'll talk after that." He fidgeted with his cap and left. Vidar followed him out.

Gloom settled back in. Jonna didn't want to think what would happen in a half hour. She had thirty minutes left with Tove, with friends, before everything changed. *Should I start a totally new life? What will I face in Sweden? And Tove, what will she face?*

With a fingertip, Tove turned her chin to face her. "At least you'll have no need to fear. You'll be safe. Sad, I'm sure, but..." She quickly wiped away an errant tear. "Without fear, we can cope with sadness. That's what I'm telling myself."

Jonna combed Tove's hair back from her face. "And have you convinced yourself? I haven't."

"We'll figure out a way to communicate, Jonna." Tove set their mugs on the floor so she could hold her hands. "The *Engel* may not take me to your port very often, but I'll send word whenever I can't get there."

Jonna dipped her head. Exchanging words through someone else would be far from adequate. It was all Tove could offer and Jonna certainly didn't want to dash Tove's hopes, but... *How long will we be forced to live this way?*

"Just think, Jonna. No Nazis. That burden will be lifted."

"But not for you." Jonna couldn't help herself. "You will still be—"

A light, quick kiss stopped her words, and Tove's forehead settled against hers. Jonna wanted to keep her within kissing distance forever, feel the warmth of her skin and let the tenderness sweep her away like it had last night.

Tove's breath stroked her cheeks as she spoke. "The Resistance will advise me, Jonna. I'll do whatever they suggest is wise. Please take heart in that."

"Promise me you won't take chances?"

"And risk a future with you?"

❖

Tove could hardly speak as they held each other on the dock. She squeezed her eyes as tightly closed as she squeezed Jonna to her chest and held her breath to hold back tears. Her eyes already burned from them, anyway. This embrace mustn't convey "the end," but her heart drowned out such common sense. Besides, her brain couldn't be sure. She sniffled as she rubbed Jonna's back, feeling her sob against her shoulder.

"I-I'll be back whenever possible. Don't forget that. And keep an ear to other enclaves along these shores because I'll send word with any boat I can."

Jonna straightened in her arms. "Don't forget you promised to behave yourself, not take chances or…or do dangerous things."

Tove almost laughed. She'd been taking chances for months already. "I intend to keep that promise."

"I'm going to be at this dock every day, Tove." She took Tove's face in her hands. "I will study the horizon just as I used to at Drogden, watching for you."

"Neither of us will be able to see beyond Drogden, my sweetheart, but we can use each blink of that beacon to connect, to touch us like this. It's where our love began."

"And holds strong."

"Because we *are* strong, Jonna." Tove swallowed hard. She forced the words out, past the thudding heartbeat in her throat.

"We're going to carry on, do what we must, and believe in each other. We'll be apart but we'll make our way through this together."

"God, I can't let you go. I know the captain's waiting, but… Oh, please, please take care of yourself for me. I love you, Tove."

"And I love you. With all my heart." With more tenderness than she'd ever felt, she kissed Jonna's lips, knew hers trembled just as much. Their tears intermingled.

She drew Jonna's head down, kissed her eyes, her cheek and ear, caressed her neck beneath the old work shirt collar. She would remember them like this here for as long as she lived. And she hoped that would be forever.

Footsteps sounded behind her, and a man cleared his throat to announce his presence. Rolf. It was time.

She smoothed her fingertips along Jonna's cheek before turning away in tears.

Blurry-eyed, Jonna kept her sights on Tove at the gunnel. Their penetrating eye contact delivered kisses, promises, farewell gestures, and more. She hugged herself for strength and warmth as the *Engel* backed away from the dock. *I will not see this as a final farewell.*

She returned Tove's wave, followed her every move, the hurried stride to the stern to keep each other in sight. Tove was a mere speck and the *Engel* a tiny craft on the horizon before Jonna gave up watching.

CHAPTER TWELVE

Nancy crumpled up the tenth attempt at outlining a new proposal and tossed it at Sam. It bounced off her forehead and landed next to all the others that came before. "I thought you liked the *Gerda III*."

Sam's eyes lit up. "I loved it. Can we put it in our proposal?"

Despite her frustration, Nancy allowed a small smile. "We can put it in, but it has as much chance of success as your hot sauna."

"It's just sauna. They're hot by definition and I don't know what you have against them. Have you ever been in one?" Sam raised an eyebrow.

Nancy crossed her arms, not liking the challenge. "I have nothing against saunas in theory but I have a great deal against them on the island holding my lighthouse." Where had the easy, fun conversation from Mystic gone? Nancy missed it.

"Why don't we each make a list of the components of our proposals. That way we can see where we might be able to compromise." Sam slid another piece of paper across the desk to Nancy. "Or at least you'll have more ammunition to fling at me." She pointed between her eyes and dramatically fell back in her chair as if knocked unconscious.

"Hey, we have work to do. Quit goofing off or I'll report you to Mrs. Jones." Nancy shook her pen in Sam's direction.

"Oh shit. Don't do that." Sam quickly put pen to paper and started writing.

Nancy tapped the pen to her chin, considering her proposal and how best to capture the crucial aspects that would transform the lighthouse into her dream scenario. She jotted down her list.

Main building: first floor general history of island and keepers, upstairs history of lamp and lens technology

Bunker building: military history of island

Building by water: marine and maritime history of the island and bay

Nature walks

Bird watching

Picnicking

Kids nature activities?

Conservation group activities?

She peeked at Sam's list, but Sam put her arm around her paper protectively.

"I'll show you mine if you show me yours," she tried.

They exchanged lists. As expected, Sam's looked very different from hers.

Bar

Sauna

Spa

Overnight accommodations (high end)

Restaurant/food (top trained chef)

Bathrooms

Activities & transportation

"We both use the word 'activities.' That's a step in the right direction." Sam's mouth twisted to half smile, half frown.

"I also forgot to put bathrooms on my list, so we finally agree on something." Nancy retrieved her list and added *bathrooms*.

"I think we're ready to turn this in. We have agreed to build bathrooms on the island." Sam threw her hands up as if declaring a touchdown.

"You laugh." Nancy pulled out a third piece of paper, titled it *Agreed upon*, then wrote *bathrooms*. "This is now our binding document. Once it goes on the list, we can't take it back. Sign next to bathrooms."

Sam looked amused, but she did as she was told. Nancy signed next to her.

While Nancy signed, Sam evaluated the lists. "There *is* a way to make this work."

"So says Mrs. Jones." Nancy shoved their sole source of agreement to the center of the desk and blew out a breath. "Tell me what you're thinking."

Sam smiled in a way that made Nancy shiver. She wasn't sure if she should be good or bad nervous under that mischievous grin. It made Sam look roguish and handsome and got Nancy thinking of things other than their proposal. Maybe she could get Sam to agree to a few more things in writing if she kept looking at her like that.

"I'd rather show you. Can you take a few days off and do you have a passport?"

"Passport? What are you talking about, Sam?" Nancy couldn't tell if Sam was messing with her or asking serious questions.

"I'm asking you to imagine something I'm guessing you've never experienced. I want you to see it for yourself. You gave me the *Gerda III* and Mystic. Now it's my turn."

Nancy crossed her arms and countered Sam's self-assured grin with a stern look. "Are you trying to bribe me with some luxury linens and a trip to a spa, Ms. McMann?"

Sam looked aghast. "You're un-bribable, I am sure. Your character is clearly unimpeachable. Perhaps I should reconsider and bring one of your siblings. Maybe your sister is a scalawag and can be bought for the right price."

Nancy exploded from her seat and pointed at Sam angrily. "Don't you dare live up to the worst of your reputation. And leave my family out of it."

"Hey, I'm joking." Sam came around the desk and tentatively put her hands on Nancy's arms. "I'm sorry. It was a stupid joke. I didn't mean to imply what you clearly think I did."

Nancy couldn't let Sam off the hook for that. Or could she? She wasn't sure. She was too distracted by the way her arms tingled where Sam's hands still rested. Was there a lot of static electricity in the air today? And why did she have to smell so good? She looked up at her, which was a mistake. Concern swirled in those beautiful eyes, and an inviting softness that contrasted perfectly with those handsome, chiseled features.

"I shouldn't have jumped to conclusions." Nancy took a step back when she wanted to step forward, further into Sam's arms. What would they feel like wrapped around her waist, holding her tightly? Nancy nearly fled the room at a tiny clench of excitement in her abdomen. That was quite enough of that. "Where are we going and when did you want to leave?"

Sam smiled. "How about tonight and I'll let you know once we're airborne. I need to finalize our accommodations as soon as you say yes." She sat back down and put her feet on the desk.

Nancy pushed Sam's feet off and perched against the edge. "What's your angle, McMann?"

Sam schooled her face into maximum outrage. "Ma'am, you doubt my intentions? I thought you knew we play for the same team."

Nancy leaned forward and stage-whispered. "I didn't need confirmation of that. You and your lady friends are regularly photographed, remember? Speaking of which, will that happen to me if we go wherever it is we're going? I don't want to be photographed as the next latest thing on your arm."

Sam sat up straighter and took Nancy's hand, then seemed to reconsider. She looked reluctant as she let Nancy's hand fall from her grasp, but she quickly recovered and met Nancy's eyes. "I'd never let that happen to you. This will crush your soul to hear, but I might be starting to think of you as a friend."

Nancy dramatically rolled her eyes. "I should have known you wouldn't be able to handle the *Gerda*. Now look what's happening. Suddenly we're friends? What have I done?"

"Oh, you secretly love it. Look what you get in return." Sam made a show of moving her hand in front of her body from head to toe.

Nancy was looking and that was problematic. Even more vexing was how much she enjoyed the damn view.

"Hey, *friend*, are we going or not? I have phone calls to make and you need to pack." Sam wiggled her phone in the air for Nancy's benefit.

"Go make your calls. I'll clear my schedule." Nancy didn't pretend to consider it any longer. Of course, she was going to say yes. "Thank you."

"You're welcome." Sam kissed Nancy's cheek as she headed for the door. "I'll see you soon. Oh." She doubled back and picked up the paper with their signed agreement. She folded it neatly and tucked it into Nancy's back jeans pocket. "I think you should bring this. After a couple of days where we're going, I think you'll come around to my way of thinking."

Nancy wanted to tell Sam she needn't be so careful, touching her ass, but that was out of bounds. Instead, she settled for calling after her retreating form. "You are impossibly arrogant, you know that?"

Sam gave her a thumbs up over her shoulder but didn't turn around. Nancy smiled. Arrogant, but somehow not obnoxious. It was a fine line to walk, but Sam seemed to thrive on the high wire.

"Welcome to Ireland, Ms. McMann. I hope you enjoy your stay." The captain of the private jet shook Sam's hand as they deplaned onto the tarmac and were ushered toward the waiting SUV.

Sam slid in next to Nancy and was immediately aware of her presence in a very unsettling way. Since their jaunt to Mystic, she'd started paying attention to where Nancy was, how often she tucked an unruly strand of hair behind her ear, or how she smelled like lavender and sea air. From the first time in the boat, she'd noticed how beautiful Nancy was, but how had she not *seen* how stunning she was? Now, it was all she could think when she looked at her.

Despite the reputation she'd developed as a bit of a libertine, Sam didn't mix business and pleasure. Fixating on how the sound of Nancy's laugh made her feel wasn't going to get their proposal finalized.

"Are you okay?" Nancy leaned close enough so only Sam could hear her, despite the driver not paying them any attention. "You look like you're regretting this trip, or is it having this massive gas-guzzling SUV for just the two of us?" Her breath tickled Sam's ear and made her shiver as heat shot through her.

"No regrets, not even the car." She didn't dare look at Nancy now. "If you look out the window, our accommodations are coming into view." Sam pointed to one of her favorite places to stay when she was in Europe.

"Is that a castle?" Nancy's voice was full of reverence.

Sam finally did look at Nancy as she answered. "What better way to understand the merging of history and modern luxury than staying at an eight-hundred-year-old castle?"

When they arrived, Nancy looked like her head was on a swivel. She couldn't seem to take in each detail swiftly enough.

"Ms. McMann, Ms. Calhoun, if you'll follow me, I'll show you to the presidential suite." The young man picked up their bags and set off down the hall. "Ms. McMann, I want to assure you, you and your guest can expect the utmost privacy and discretion during your stay."

Sam tensed but made sure not to let her discomfort show. "Seamus, I appreciate your discretion. Despite how frequently I end up in the tabloids, I do not want this trip to be paparazzi fodder. We chose your location because of its reputation for privacy and service." She slipped into her rich playgirl persona so easily she almost didn't recognize she'd done it.

Nancy made a funny half cough, half choking sound behind her, and Sam knew she'd have some explaining to do when they got up to the suite.

It turned out she didn't have a chance. No sooner had the young man shown them the suite and left, than Nancy let the questions fly.

"Why are we sharing a suite, Sam or are you back to Samantha now? Why did you let that guy think I was one of your conquests? What are we doing here? I told you the first time we met if you try to 'Samantha McMann' me, you're barking up the wrong tree. It's still true, even if I think you're cuter now than I did then." Nancy had her hands on her hips and her brow furrowed.

"You think I'm cute?" Sam perched on the arm of what was surely an armchair of historical significance. Nancy would probably tell her to move her butt soon.

"That's not what you were supposed to hone in on, Sam. Answer my questions." Nancy shooed Sam off the armchair as expected.

"We're sharing a suite because I called them ten hours ago and this is all they could offer me that didn't suck. I'll take one of the other rooms they have, though, if you'd rather not share with me. I thought we might be able to work a little if we were in close proximity. I should have asked if you were comfortable with the arrangement. I have no ulterior motive." Sam held up her hands in innocence. "I would never try to 'Samantha McMann' someone who claims to not like me."

"I don't like you." Nancy's scowl wasn't terribly convincing. "You think a restored castle catering to the super rich is honoring history, so how could I like someone so horribly misguided? And what the hell happened to sweet Sam back there?"

Sam wasn't put off by Nancy's stubborn refusal to see the historical and modern complementing each other all around them. "Sweet Sam is the mirage. That version of me is the one I've been raised to be. You should know that before you decide to like me."

Nancy shook her head. "I'm not buying that for a second. You get to decide who you want to be, not anyone else. Someone also raised you to be this version of yourself or maybe this is who you are deep down. You get to decide. Don't sell yourself short. As for the history of this place, you have some convincing to do." Nancy ran her hand along the back of the ornate couch.

"This place is dripping with history. They don't have to put up wall plaques and wave their hands around like we do in America. Look around, this place was built four hundred years before the United States became a thing." Sam stood and pointed out the window. "Besides, they have falconry and we're going to try it. And the historic boat tour, the garden tour, and the spa. You're going to love it."

"And what if I'm not interested in any of those activities?"

Against her better judgment, Sam took a step closer. "Then you can choose different ones."

"And what if I choose different company for my activities?"

"Then I would be disappointed, but I'm a grown-up, I'll only cry for a short time." Sam thought Nancy moved ever so slightly her way, but she couldn't be sure it wasn't wishful thinking.

"Well, discretion would be hard to maintain if you were blubbering at the bar the whole trip. Even those trained to look the other way notice someone pining for hours. I guess we should choose some activities." This time Nancy did move closer to Sam. She put her hand on Sam's shoulder and let it drift down her arm as she moved past. "I'm going to change. You get first pick."

"I didn't say I'd be pining."

It was pointless. Nancy was already closing the door to her room. Sam looked around the suite and then back to Nancy's closed door. She startled when Nancy opened the door again abruptly.

"You're right about the castle. It's incredible. I can't believe I get to sleep in a place that's seen so many centuries. Thank you for bringing me here."

Sam resisted the urge to high five herself or do a dramatic fist pump celebration in case Nancy opened the door again and caught her. After Mystic, she'd wanted to show Nancy more of her own vision, but somewhere along the line, it had become equally important to her that Nancy have a good time.

Sam had shared hotel rooms with others before, but she'd never felt this comfortable with the arrangement. It had only been a couple of months since she'd first laid seasick eyes on her, but Sam was more comfortable around Nancy than some people she'd known for years. She'd have to give some thought to why at a later time. Now, she had to prepare for falconry.

That evening, after a full day taking advantage of all the castle had to offer, from the adventurous to the luxurious, Sam was pleasantly exhausted. She flopped on the sofa in the suite's living room and spread her arms to the side along the back. She tilted her head and rested it against the cushions and closed her eyes.

"Mind if I join you?"

"Of course not." Sam didn't open her eyes, enjoying how the sound of Nancy's voice floated over her.

Instead of sitting next to her as Sam expected, Nancy crashed onto her lap with a curse. Sam started upright and instinctively wrapped her arms around Nancy who was now fully ensconced on Sam's lap looking disheveled and beautiful.

"I'm so sorry, Sam! I caught my foot on the edge of the damn table." Nancy swiped the hair out of her face.

"Are you okay?" It wasn't lost on Sam how close they were together and what Nancy's breath on her cheek was doing to her heart rate. Nancy's ass against her crotch was also having an impact she was trying to ignore.

"I'm fine. *I* landed on *you*. Are you okay?" Nancy made no move to get up.

"Me, yes, fine." Sam licked her lips. She saw Nancy follow the action.

"Sam, you should let me go now." Nancy brushed her fingers tentatively along Sam's cheek. "I don't think this is what Mrs. Jones had in mind for us."

"How do you know? What if she did?"

Nancy looked wistful. "I still think you should let me go."

Sam dropped her arms to her sides and leaned back dramatically. Nancy stood and repositioned farther down the couch. She looked like she missed the connection as acutely as Sam.

"History is dangerous," Sam said. "Look at that table. It's probably three hundred years old and it tried to kill you. Good thing I was here to save you. Then this magical castle put a spell on us and made us do, you know." Sam indicated between the two of them. "I can't believe you want to fill a whole island full of historical nonsense. Imagine all the trouble it would cause."

Nancy mirrored Sam's position on the couch and looked at her. "You are nothing like I expected you to be. I'm so glad. I'll never admit to saying this, but you're wonderful."

Sam puffed out her chest and preened for Nancy's benefit. Nancy groaned, playing her part.

"So, was there enough historical representation and honoring during our day of fun?" Sam tried to keep a smile at bay.

"Historical judginess isn't the only thing I'm good at you know." Nancy scowled.

"No, you're an above average falcon flyer too. You should put that on your resume."

Nancy's face lit up. "That was so much fun. Maybe I will. And I know I'm going to regret saying this, but despite my initial misgivings, this place does a good job steeping everything in the history of the castle and the area."

Sam raised her arms in victory. "Castle and Sam for the win. History and luxury aren't mutually exclusive."

Nancy shook her finger in Sam's direction. "No, no, no. You are not building a castle next to my lighthouse and calling it historical."

Sam tried her best pouty face. "But it already has a moat."

"It's an island and that's the bay, not a moat. No castles. I won't sign if that goes on the list." Nancy's smile danced all the way to her eyes making them sparkle with delight and something so alluring Sam was scared to put a name to it.

"Spoilsport." Sam made the mature decision to stick out her tongue, but it was short-lived as they quickly dissolved into a fit of laughter.

They each scooted closer together but kept enough space that they were not touching. As if by silent agreement Sam handed Nancy the TV remote and she scrolled until she found a movie.

Sam didn't care what they watched. She was content to sit next to Nancy for the rest of the night. The feeling of comfort was back, but it was more than that. She craved her presence. That had never happened before.

And she thought about her father's company and the life that awaited her when he retired. Hell, the life that she'd return to when this personal project was over. This lighthouse was the first thing she'd allowed herself, her true self, to want in years. The rest of her life was scripted with other people's expectations. How cruel that Nancy was a part of this labor of love which could never occupy more than the smallest slice of her life.

CHAPTER THIRTEEN

Nancy looked out the window of the private jet carrying them farther from Ireland. She couldn't see the ocean stretched beneath the sea of clouds, but knew that was all that would stretch below them for hours.

"You spoiled me with that exquisite escape and now I don't want to return to reality." She caught Sam studying her.

"Then let's put it off a little while longer." Although there was a question in Sam's voice, there was hope in her eyes.

Nancy tried to remember her schedule over the next few days. She couldn't think of anything pressing. Even if there had been, she would have worked hard to rearrange. Soaking up more time with Sam was worth nearly any logistical inconvenience.

"What did you have in mind?" Nancy quirked an eyebrow and waited for a response.

Sam's face flushed dark for a moment and her eyes flashed with what Nancy swore was desire, but it was gone before she had a chance for a second look. "I was thinking something a little closer to home this time, unless you have a specific destination you'd like to visit and then we'll go there."

"You knocked it out of the park with Ireland." Nancy hesitated before plowing ahead. "I wouldn't have said this a few days ago, but I had a great time with you. So, I am confident that wherever we go, if you are there, I will enjoy it."

"Be still my beating heart." Sam dramatically fake fainted against the leather seat. "Just when I thought all hope of you ever seeing any of my many virtues was lost."

"You didn't seem very virtuous when you held me captive on your lap."

"Oh no, no, no." Sam raised a finger to emphasize her point. "I was being a gentleman after you stumbled and fell. It would have been rude to not assure your well-being."

She stood and started toward the front of the plane and the flight crew but stopped when Nancy rose as well. Sam looked frozen in place as Nancy approached.

Nancy's fingers and lips tingled with the desire to take a handful of Sam's shirt, pull her into a kiss, but that was probably a bad idea. Bad or no, Nancy hadn't been able to extinguish thoughts of Sam's arms around her since she'd fallen onto her lap. She feared her thoughts were telegraphed across her face, but Sam seemed none the wiser.

Instead of kissing her, Nancy passed by, much closer than was strictly necessary, and kissed Sam on the cheek. She let her hand slide across Sam's abdomen as she passed, and that backfired on her. The teasing feel of Sam's body generated a rousing surge of want. So much for that smooth move.

"I'm going to use the lavatory. When I come back you can tell me about the next leg in our adventure." She took a deep breath as she walked to the bathroom, trying to still her racing heart.

When she returned, Sam was sitting, looking out the window, on the phone. She tried not to eavesdrop, but they were on a small plane and they were the only two passengers.

"Is he okay?" Sam sounded concerned. She listened for a long time before speaking again. "You've made your opinion clear, Philip. It doesn't sound like there's anything I can do there that I can't do from here. If that changes, I'll be wheels up immediately."

Nancy could hear a frustrated sounding male voice on the other end of the phone. Sam glanced over with what appeared to be an apologetic look. She held up a finger indicating another minute.

"I'm not CEO yet. Hopefully not for years to come. I'm not coming back until I've finished my project which you conveniently forget anytime you want something from me." Sam's voice softened. "Philip, this is important to me."

Nancy strained to hear the other side of the conversation while making sure to look like she wasn't trying to do so. She couldn't hear anything and didn't know if her acting would win her any awards.

"Little brother, do you tell our father what to do as much as you do me?" Sam was smiling now. "Please keep me updated. I want to be your first call if something changes with him. I love you."

Sam hung up and tossed her phone on the seat beside her. She frowned, her brow creased deeply.

"Is everything okay?" Nancy fought the urge to move to Sam's side. They didn't have the kind of relationship, or any kind of relationship, where that would be expected.

Sam didn't seem to feel the same hesitation. She relocated next to Nancy, sitting closer than she needed on a plane with plenty of seating for the two of them. All the same, Nancy inched closer. Their thighs brushed together and Nancy shivered. She was supposed to be focusing on Sam's phone call, not how sexy she was.

"That was my brother. My father's in the hospital. It seems like he's fine. They're doing some tests and keeping him for observation." Despite her upbeat tone, Sam looked worried. "Philip wants me to fly home."

"I'd be happy to finish up our proposal while you were gone." Nancy pushed her leg playfully against Sam's.

"Taking advantage of me in a moment of weakness is unsporting, Ms. Calhoun." Sam turned more fully toward Nancy. Her eyes were filled with emotions Nancy couldn't pinpoint, but they sent her stomach cartwheeling all the same. "Besides, you heard me refuse. I promised you another adventurous date."

Nancy held Sam's gaze. "Date. Is that what this is?"

Sam's ears pinked. "Would you say no if I said yes?"

"I wouldn't say no." Nancy's heart beat so loudly it sounded like a caffeinated bass beat in her ears. "But family comes first if you need to go back." *Please say no. Please say no.*

"What happened to being repulsed by Samantha McMann?" Sam's lazy smile was hot as hell.

Nancy hesitated. "She's still not my type, but I don't think she's you. Despite myself, I like Sam quite a lot."

"I, on the other hand, have never been cagey about my admiration for you." Sam leaned against the back of the bench seat and rested her head on her hand. "I hope our next destination wins me a few more points."

Nancy's stomach clenched, but this time not from lust or excitement. "We come from such different worlds, Sam. I can't give you any of this." She abstractly waved around the plane.

Sam took Nancy's hand and kissed it. "I already have all this. Why would I need more? I don't even need what I have. Besides, we're not committing to marriage. All I want is to spend more time with you and not have to hide it when I'm checking out your ass."

"My ass is behind me. I'd have a hard time catching you checking it out." Nancy put one of her hands on each of her breasts. "Pretty hard to hide if you were taking a long hard look at these, though."

"I'm dead. You killed me." Sam flopped dramatically on her back on the seat. "Why would you do that to me?"

Nancy leaned over Sam. "Because now I know I can." She laughed when Sam groaned. "Revive yourself, stud. It feels like we're descending."

Landing and deplaning were uneventful except for the two Smart Cars waiting for them on the tarmac. "I didn't want to offend you with another gas guzzling SUV so I found these two used toy cars." Sam laughed at Nancy's hands-on-hips attempt at disapproval. "But that's offset partially because we needed two. One for us and one for our things. I knew they were small, but wow."

Nancy appreciated the moment of levity. It gave them each a chance to collect themselves. The flirting had been fun, but she wasn't ready for more than that. It was hard to wrap her head around the fact that they had arrived where they currently were.

She was with Samantha Freakin' McMann, after all, even if Nancy wasn't keen on admitting it. If she did, she'd have to face the fact that Sam was destined for a life literally and figuratively a world away from hers which didn't leave much room for anything more than flirting and what she assumed would be amazing sex. If that was even a road she wanted to go down. Casual sex wasn't something she did often, and she wasn't sure how casual things were between them.

Nancy shook herself out of her musings. The time in Ireland had been wonderful, but tossing up barriers to a relationship, or whatever this was, that hadn't even begun was foolish.

"You okay? You're not having second thoughts, are you?" Sam looked concerned.

"Not at all." *If only she knew.*

"Good, because we're here." Sam jogged around to the passenger side and helped Nancy unfold from the tiny car.

Nancy surveyed the classic seaside inn, nestled comfortably among the boats and restaurants of a picturesque New England marina. It looked like it hosted an exclusive clientele while trying not to advertise that overtly. It was lovely but somehow, after staying in a castle, it felt like a bit of a letdown.

Nancy was careful not to show it. "Bring me to the water and you know I'll be happy."

"I'm not only bringing you to the water." Sam grinned and ushered Nancy inside.

"I draw the line at sleeping on a submarine if that's what's waiting for me." Nancy slowed her pace, but Sam urged her on.

While Sam checked in, Nancy wandered the lobby, taking in the art and photographs of the local landscape. Sam hadn't said, but Nancy was fairly certain they were back in Connecticut. She'd been up and down the coast on the family boats enough times to have a feel for the architecture and the different states' waterfronts. She lingered over a photograph of a lighthouse jutting away from the marina, a mega yacht, and a small fishing boat captured in the background.

"Of the three, where would you rather spend the night?" Nancy jumped when Sam spoke next to her.

"In a dream world, the lighthouse." Nancy gazed at the photo again. "But the fishing boat seems more realistic."

"You know, in the book I've been reading, the two women end up shipwrecked and spend the night in an abandoned, crumbled lighthouse. Should we see if we can do better?" Sam tentatively took Nancy's hand and gave a gentle tug.

They walked hand-in-hand through the lobby and out a set of French doors onto a flower- and tree-lined patio. Nancy had plenty of questions about where they were going, but they were superceded by the feel of Sam's hand in hers. If there had been something in her past that made her as happy as she felt now, she couldn't remember it. Why was the simple joining of hands having such an effect?

Nancy stole a glance at Sam who looked like she was actually strutting. "Proud of yourself? You look like a peacock."

Sam quickly looked behind her. "Shh, don't talk so loud. The woman I'm holding hands with is a little jumpy around *Samantha McMann*." Sam whispered her own name. "I don't want her to realize she might be here and let go."

"I do not get jumpy." Nancy started to pull away but thought better of it. She could defend her honor and keep her hand in Sam's. She was a multitasker.

Sam gave Nancy's hand a little tug and pulled them to a stop. Nancy turned and stumbled as she did and ended up in Sam's arms, again. Instinctively, she let go of Sam's hand and wrapped both of hers around Sam's waist to steady herself. That brought their faces only inches apart. Their hitched breathing came together like the ebb and flow of waves crashing wildly ashore.

"Now I feel jumpy." Nancy kept her hands on Sam's waist but took a step back. Kissing her definitely appealed to those body parts now humming with rushing blood and tingling nerves, but her brain hadn't been *completely* overwhelmed by lust. Yet. So, distance it was. "But it's a one-time phenomenon."

"I certainly hope not." Sam stroked the side of Nancy's face, then down her neck, and across her collarbone to her shoulder.

"Stop that." Nancy slapped Sam's hand away. "You made me promises about this place that you had better be prepared to keep.

And you made me promises about places my face would never end up, like the tabloids. So, hands off, lust eyes off, clothes on. Where were we going?"

Sam tipped her head back toward the sky but held out her arm indicating their direction of travel.

When Nancy turned the corner, the excitement of a kid on Christmas morning fluttered wildly in her chest. "Sam! It's the lighthouse from the photo. Did you know it was back here?" Nancy looked at Sam's lazy, knowing smile. "Of course, you did. Now, I'm not sure whether I should hug you or go back to not liking you for keeping this from me."

"I'm voting for hugging. If you're still on the fence though, maybe I sweeten the deal. Shall we go inside?" Sam pulled a set of keys from her pocket and jangled them.

Nancy swiped the keys and took off toward the lighthouse door. She was up the steps and nearly there before Sam caught her. As soon as Sam wrapped her arms around her from behind, all hope Nancy had of being able to unlock any door or operate any doorknob was gone. She leaned back into Sam's embrace and let her take over key operation.

She felt wanton and free, exactly how couples looked in the cheesy commercials for expensive resorts. Living in a different world, in Sam's world, or at least a piece of it, was intoxicating. Being with Sam jumbled her senses. She didn't care if they were playing make-believe or if it continued after they got home. All that mattered now was the way Sam's touch set her skin aflame and set her heart leaping.

As soon as the door was open, Sam released her, and Nancy took in the lighthouse interior. "I don't know what I expected, but this isn't it. This looks like a beautiful beach cottage ready for guests."

Directly in the door was a small living room, dining room, kitchen combination. A loveseat was tucked into a nook just the right size and faced a large television mounted over an inviting fireplace. Further into the space were two closed doors, the first she discovered led to the bathroom, the other to a spacious bedroom with a king bed. Off the bedroom she could see a deck facing the water.

"Do you like it?" Sam sounded shy.

Nancy almost melted at the shyness in Sam's voice, the hint of nervous energy in her posture, those keys in her hand. Taking a breath, she looked around the lighthouse again.

"Is this where we're staying?" She could hear the excited squeak in her voice but who cared? Was she going to stay overnight in an actual, honest to goodness, lighthouse?

Sam nodded, still looking uncertain. "Only if you want to. It seemed like a good idea, but maybe it's a letdown after a castle."

"Samantha...what's your middle name?" Nancy waited.

"Phillippa"

"Isn't your brother named Philip?" Nancy waved away her own question. "Never mind. Samantha Phillippa McMann, you could not have picked a more perfect place. This is as good or better than any castle, even an Irish one. Thank you."

"This probably isn't the time, but that made me want to do something naughty so you keep scolding me. I like hearing my name on your lips."

"I think I'll like you on my lips, too." Nancy wet her lips slowly, thrilling at how raptly Sam followed her actions. "For now, though, you'll have to settle for talking to me." Nancy sat on the loveseat and patted the cushion next to her. She caught the look on Sam's face. "Not like that. Get your mind out of my bra. Tell me about this place."

Sam flopped on the loveseat and Nancy pulled her down to rest Sam's head on her lap.

"I don't know anything about it," Sam admitted, gazing up at her. She dangled her long legs over the loveseat arm. "We can ask back at the inn what the history is."

"That won't do. If you can't tell me about this place, what about your book? Will you read me the part about the shipwreck and the lighthouse?"

Resetting herself into a more comfortable position, Nancy had to grin as Sam rushed to retrieve the book from her suitcase and hurried back to her repose.

While Sam read, Nancy related to the two women making shelter from a crumbling shell of history and honoring what was once there. She considered the lighthouse where the pair stayed and the tragic failure to acknowledge its place in history. How could those two realities be bridged?

Nancy sat up so abruptly she caused Sam to drop her book and nearly dumped her on the floor. "Earthquake warning next time, please." Sam sounded grumpy as she leaned down and picked up the book.

"No, get up. I know how to finish our proposal." Nancy skipped across the room to her backpack and rummaged until she found their official compromise document, their two proposals, and a few blank pages. Ideas were darting so quickly through her mind she wished she had a net to grab them all and cage them. Hopefully, they stayed close, and she'd be able to give each its due. And most importantly, she needed to convince Sam she'd struck on the answer to their impasse.

CHAPTER FOURTEEN

Strandhem, Sweden

Jonna cleared her eyes with her sleeve and assessed her surroundings, a wooded settlement of tiny cottages and shops that now comprised her home. She was surprised to find a trio of villagers, a rabbi, and two women, possibly a mother and daughter, standing silently nearby. She wondered how long they had been there, if they had witnessed the heartbreaking scene at the dock.

The rabbi was elderly, no doubt as prim as manageable in his long, threadbare coat, and he ambled toward her with a severe limp. The older woman gathered her knitted shawl around her shoulders and hushed her daughter about something, probably the young woman's work trousers. Jonna glanced down at herself, dressed in a seaman's ill-fitting shirt and trousers, and sympathized. *And what do you do for work? What will* I *do?*

"By any chance, are you Ethan Friedler's daughter?" The rabbi's tone was tired and breathy. "Jonna, isn't it?"

"It is, yes."

He took her hands reverently. "You are welcome here in Strandhem, Jonna. My name is Isak Speiser, rabbi for this village and several others, and this is Hedda Lofgren and her daughter, Elin." Jonna shook their hands as he continued. "They are among the many Lutherans here, but we are all one family caring for one another."

Hedda poked loose strands of blond hair back beneath her kerchief and quickly placed her hand to her ample bosom. "We are so sorry about your father, dear. He was a very sweet man."

"You knew him?"

"Oh, my, yes. He visited us many times in recent years before you began staying with him. I think his visits helped him pass the time, taking a break from Drogden."

"But when he came," Elin added enthusiastically, "that place was his favorite topic."

"He did love Drogden," Jonna said, "although I always worried about him out there on his own."

Hedda patted Jonna's shoulder. "It's what good daughters do."

"He loved visiting the village councilmen and sharing news," Elin said. "Actually, I think we spoiled him with our cooking. And he had a knack with cards, didn't he?"

"A *sly* knack, yes," Jonna admitted with a conciliatory tilt of her head. She sniffled and fought back a shiver. She liked all three of these villagers, but Elin's perceptions of Papa actually brought a hint of comfort.

"That's enough for now." Speiser set them all walking toward the village. "Our newcomer needs to warm up. Perhaps she could use a solid meal as well."

"Thank you for welcoming me. I confess, food and warmth sound wonderful right now."

"Then, that's what you shall have," Hedda stated. "Our place is right up the road, that one with the yellow window boxes next to the livery. We are several dozen Swedish families here in Strandhem, and, I dare say, most have taken in at least one Dane like yourself. So many are in need of refuge."

To Jonna's eye, the wooden house they approached was not unlike the others, single-storied and compact with shuttered windows and thin, stone chimneys, all currently in use. Aside from attics beneath the peaked roofs, there couldn't be much room to spare for refugees, which made her appreciate all this hospitality even more.

"We'll introduce you around as soon as you feel up to it," Elin added. "You may know some of the newcomers—and, if not in Strandhem, then maybe others staying in our neighboring villages."

"We believe nurturing togetherness is a necessity for those forced from their homeland," Speiser said.

"Strandhem's church is over there." Elin pointed to the white-washed building at the far end of the village. "A Lutheran church, but Rabbi Speiser shares the back rooms. He runs the orphanage there."

The concept of an orphanage took Jonna aback. She'd forgotten about the orphanages in these little coastal settlements. As Hedda opened her front door, Jonna turned on the walkway.

"Are there many children?" she asked Elin.

"Yes, sadly. There are several orphanages along the shore. We never know, from one day to the next, if more will arrive by boat or be sent to us from other villages."

"Here in Strandhem," Speiser said, "the young orphans are fortunate, because there is little hope of adoption for the older ones, I'm afraid. Families seek the toddlers, the youngsters."

Jonna turned to him. "How do you ever manage?"

"People here open their hearts when they can and volunteer their time."

"Come inside," Hedda said. "Let's get you settled, and we can talk more."

Jonna sat at the small wooden table as invited and absorbed the warmth of the kitchen. Famished, she found it hard to be polite eating Hedda's soup and bread. In no time, Hedda refilled the bowl and set the entire loaf in front of her.

"You are my size," Elin said brightly, appearing from a back room. "I can lend you these until we see what the town seamstress has available." She held out trousers and a blouse. "I-I'm sorry if you prefer lady's wear. I work next door at the livery, so my clothes are…well…"

"That's so kind. You—all of you—are beyond generous. I prefer working clothes, too, Elin. Thank you."

Elin set the clothes aside and eagerly seated herself beside Jonna. "What is it like, living at Drogden?"

"Elin." Hedda stopped slicing bread to glare at her daughter. "It is a sad place for Jonna. Mind your manners."

"I'm sorry, Jonna. I didn't mean—"

"Drogden holds all sorts of memories. Some are painful, but all are meaningful. Papa and I enjoyed our time there. The work seemed secondary, more like fun, until the Nazis came."

Elin leaned closer, her blue eyes wide with excitement. "And did you really spy on them for the Resistance as the rumors claim?"

"Elin! Enough." Hedda sighed at Jonna. "Please forgive a sixteen-year-old who has *nothing better to do than gossip.*"

Jonna wasn't about to reveal the Resistance work she and Papa had done. Trusting strangers with such information wasn't wise, even if they gave you food, shelter, and clothes. But as Elin sat back, duly chastised, Jonna felt obligated to share something.

"Perhaps, in time, talking about our life there won't be as hard." Elin nodded. "A large part of my heart is still at Drogden and always will be."

"Your…friend," Elin began cautiously, "the sailor who left on the *Engel*, she…"

Jonna stared into her empty bowl and saw Tove waving good-bye from the gunnel. "Heartbreak is difficult to put into words."

"Elin," Hedda injected, "pour us all coffee, please." She sat opposite Jonna. "There will be plenty of time for reflection, my dear, but, for now, I'm afraid you must begin considering what lies ahead."

"She doesn't have to sleep in the attic, Mama," Elin stated, pouring for Speiser. "I'll arrange space in my room."

"No, no," Jonna objected. "I am not inconveniencing such a kind family. No. I will go wherever I'll be the least bother."

Hedda tipped her head at Elin. "Well, if that one can *find room in her realm* for you…" she bent toward Jonna and whispered, "which normally would require the king's decree," she rolled her eyes, "then you two are welcome to settle things between you."

"Good!" Elin rushed to her bedroom.

Jonna laughed as Hedda shook her head.

"From the moment news of your father reached the village, Elin's been hoping you would come and stay with us. The Friedlers of Drogden have been celebrities for some time—and now they are heroes, so I apologize in advance for her—"

"Oh, I don't know about being heroes, Hedda. And please, don't worry about Elin. She is a wonderful young lady. You should be very proud of her."

"Well, we all are proud of you and your father, and we're honored to have you."

"Everyone is so thoughtful. You obviously work hard, keeping a home...for just you two? There is no...?"

"My husband passed right before the war. We've learned to manage on what Elin earns at the livery and my baking for the village store." She raised her cup but paused in mid-sip. "An independent woman such as yourself will soon be eager for employment, I'm sure. Then you can find housing of your own, maybe a nice little apartment in one of our fishing villages or market towns, huh?"

Jonna tried to appear enthused instead of overwhelmed, exhausted, and heartbroken. *But how lucky am I to meet these people? Good does still exist in this world.*

"You're giving me hope." Smiling, she clinked her coffee cup to Hedda's. "I haven't had much of that lately."

Speiser tapped a bony finger to the table. "Hope, dear girl, is... hope is everything. It is the most important offering we have for all of you. No one can say when this war will end, and even though Hitler is having difficulties these days, so many still must flee. A hard, painful reality. But, because of hope, the refuge is temporary." His small gray eyes cast downward. "The Jews and those with Christian families, the Resistance fighters and supporters, even soldiers and sailors and our wounded allies, they all come and lean on hopes of returning to their homeland someday. As you will return in time. Life will be different for you, of course, without your papa now, but you must not lose hope."

Jonna took his frail hand and squeezed it fondly. "You are an inspiration, Rabbi Speiser. Thank you. I will do my best."

Setting her losses aside would never come easily, but making something of this new life, this blank slate, *had* to take priority. She began scrambling through her past, searching for skills she'd always taken for granted, hoping she could handle whatever challenge awaited her. A room of her own or possibly even an apartment was paramount but would require some savings, so she did have to start right away.

"It's a lot, I know," Hedda said, "and at a time when your life has been upended."

"I-I'm sorry, Hedda. I was just thinking about money. I intend to earn my keep here, please be assured. But as time goes on, you're right, I have to…I will do whatever it takes to stand on my own as soon as possible."

"Oh, I'm sure you will, dear. Everything will work out. You just have to get situated and weather the storm."

"But it's quite the storm."

"That it is," Speiser added, sitting back with a worn smile.

"Now, when you're ready," Hedda began, "I know of some opportunities for employment here in Strandhem and nearby villages. Wagons travel the roads every day, so it is possible to work a distance away."

It was a lot to consider, living in this house, this village, beginning a new job, maybe traveling for it. She just wished she had Tove's opinion. The longing rose now stronger than ever.

"I think it's best to start immediately."

Her practicality surprised her. Working would keep her mind occupied. She couldn't allow loss or heartache to overwhelm her, regardless of how long she'd have to carry them. She promised herself—and Tove—that she'd stay strong.

Within minutes, Hedda and Speiser were compiling a list of potential employers, but Jonna's thoughts drifted. She imagined Tove back in Copenhagen, eating or sleeping or valiantly preparing for another daring, early-morning send-off of refugees. *But what if the* Engel *never reached the docks? Were the Gestapo waiting for her? Has she been arrested?* Jonna's stomach turned. *How or when will I ever know?*

CHAPTER FIFTEEN

Copenhagen, Denmark

The ancient stone floor made the grungy little room feel like a cave. It smelled of beer and cigarettes, and three kerosene lamps created eerie shadows around Tove at the table. Concern for Jonna and lack of sleep left her feeling weaker than she preferred, certainly too jittery for an encounter like this.

Captain Holsten had briefed her on what to expect and what she'd missed during her "stay" on Salthoven, how the Gestapo had begun a rabid search for Jonna and anyone who dealt with the Friedlers or Drogden. Thankfully, the Resistance had responded swiftly and coached the *Engel* crew about dealing with the Nazi investigation. And, because the Gestapo still searched for her, the Resistance had provided an "interception."

Tove had never made it to Copenhagen aboard the *Engel*. Instead, prior to reaching the city's canal, a two-man rowboat had stolen her away from Gestapo waiting at the docks. Here, now, in the basement of a warehouse on the opposite side of the city, she awaited instructions from people she'd never met but trusted with her life.

"Seaman Tove."

She looked toward the deep voice and a tall, thin man emerged from the darkness, his hand extended. Completing the handshake, she noted the pistol in his waistband.

"They call me Max," he said, sitting opposite her. "You're the hottest commodity in all Denmark right now."

Tell me something I don't know.

Three other people, similarly dressed, stepped out of the shadows and sat. Two of them laid rifles across their laps. Tove wondered who else lurked around her, but reminded herself that she was safe.

Oddly, Max's little grin made her relax, or maybe it was the clever glint in his eyes. She guessed he was about forty, and suspected his calloused hands, weathered skin, the hint of gray in his black stubble said he was no stranger to strenuous activity.

He kept his coal-black eyes trained on her. "You're aware of the situation you're in?"

"I believe so, but...I honestly don't have anything the Gestapo need. I never knew any details of what went on at Drogden."

"The only thing that matters to them is what they suspect. You and Jonna disappeared instantly, so they read a lot into that—and they hate looking like incompetent fools. You did remarkably courageous work, getting her to Sweden."

"I-I got us shot at and wrecked on Salthoven. That's no great accomplish—"

"You're wrong. Moving as quickly as you did saved her, saved both of you." He scratched his head through his wool cap. "And now, here you are. The more time and effort the Gestapo spend searching for you, the madder they get, and the less likely you are to survive should they arrest you. You know that I hope."

"I do. But the more determined I become against them."

He grinned again and his associates nodded.

"You're going to need that spirit." He glanced at the others and sighed. "It pains me to say this, Tove, but I have to emphasize that you cannot go home. Nor can you go to Jonna's apartment, or to the *Engel* or any crewman's or friend's home. And your days tending Drogden are over as well. There's great risk now every place you know."

To her right, a bearded middle-aged man folded his hands on the table. "If any one of us is arrested and held for more than a couple of hours, our entire operation becomes jeopardized. We have to assume the Gestapo is extracting critical information about us, leaving us precious little time to protect ourselves."

"So, keeping you out of their hands is imperative," Max added, "for our sake as well as yours."

"Well, where does that leave me?"

From the start, she had avoided the issue and thought only of Jonna, not herself, during those worrisome hours on Salthoven, but very real fear had begun creeping in during that sail home from Sweden. Of course, the Gestapo would seek to arrest her. Jonna had been right to worry.

"I spent every breath I had, trying to boost Jonna's spirit, give her faith that she'd survive all this. That meant more to me than my own troubles."

A woman at Tove's left shifted in her seat. "You are lovers?"

Tove straightened and felt her heart skip with pride. "Yes."

The woman nodded. "We've heard that the Gestapo assume this. It is why they suspect you know more than most."

"Well, I don't. I'm surprised Captain Holsten hasn't been arrested. He and Ethan were long-time friends."

"He was arrested that very night," said the bearded man, "but after an hour of interrogation, he was released. The Lighthouse Service commander spoke on his behalf, said Holsten's work was absolutely critical. He emphasized how much the German navy relies on Holsten and the *Engel*."

"Good to hear. No one said much on the ride home."

"Your mates were arrested, as well," Max told her. "Like you, they knew very little, only that Holsten and Friedler liked rum and playing cards and chess. They were all released when their stories matched, but I'm sure the Gestapo had doubts."

"But you," the woman said, "what you might know is different. Claiming to know nothing won't stop them from making you say things you normally wouldn't, just to spare yourself pain."

Tove groaned toward the ceiling. "I hate them with every ounce of my being. I'd never say anything that would help them. Never!" She slapped the table. "I'd die first."

Max cocked an eyebrow. "Oh, they'd gladly see to it."

Tove knew that. Every Danish citizen did. So did all of Europe.

"So, what happens now?" she asked, anger and frustration flaring. "Looks like it's up to you, where I go, what I do." She met each set of eyes around the table. "I want to continue servicing Drogden. It's what I've always done. I...I *need* to be out there." She paused and reconsidered. "But...now, I probably shouldn't."

"There's no 'probably' about it," Max stated. "It's out of the question."

"So?" She flipped her hands in the air. "I can't just sit in some cellar somewhere doing nothing. Can't I be of service?"

Max leaned forward again. "Absolutely, you can. Your drive, ingenuity, and courage, your willingness to fight back are exactly what we need. In fact, we need more of you, especially now." He stood and meandered around the table. "Now that we have nearly completed the evacuation of our Jewish countrymen, we must focus harder on the enemy in our midst. We're done with the 'sly maneuvering' of the past, the timely disruptions, and scattered robberies. It's time for us, as a group, to rise and confront the increasing terrors being inflicted upon us all."

Tove sensed where this speech was headed. It was true the Nazis were tightening their grip on daily life like never before. Resistance subterfuge to date, while helpful and timely, seemed only to stall the inevitable. And now having volunteered, she couldn't imagine what she might be called upon to do.

"Some might say we're too small to make a difference," Max continued, "but I disagree." He clenched a fist. "We are just one of many cells across this country and there are far more in our group than you see here tonight. Together, our dissension will be felt to a degree not yet seen. We *will* make a difference. The tide will turn on this occupation and you will help us push it forward."

❖

Jonna hauled the last armload of netting aboard and folded it into a till at the stern. She straightened and stretched her back, stiff, lately, from work she'd never done so regularly.

"How goes it, Jonna?"

She looked to the wheelhouse and smiled at Leo, the captain of this fishing boat.

"All set. I think you'll be pleased."

He joined her astern and opened the till to check her work. "You even packed it the right way. I didn't think you had that much of a fisherman in you."

She grinned at him. "Living at Drogden, fishermen were our only neighbors, remember, and now and then, they needed our help. So, I'm quite familiar."

"Well, I appreciate you delivering this heavy load. My thanks to you and the shop for such fast repair work."

Glad to be finished for the day, she managed to hop onto the dock. Some muscle soreness wasn't much of a price to pay for a job she enjoyed, a job that often involved boats and the sea. But now this visit to the docks, like two before it, had passed without any sailor bearing word from Tove.

Gathering her jacket closed against the rising breeze, she hiked up to the nearby promontory to watch the colors change on the water. The late-afternoon sun disappeared so early, faded as fast as these October days. Seven had come and gone since her arrival, since she'd felt arms around her and tender, reassuring kisses.

"I miss you so, Tove. What are you up to over there?" She sniffled and shrank deeper into her jacket. "Are you safe? That's the most important thing."

The last of the water's orange glow shrank into a fiery streak along the horizon, uninterrupted by fishing boats, freighters, or German ships. She sat mesmerized, taking in the serene setting. From the northeast, a flicker of white light greeted her like a wave from an old friend.

Her breath still caught, no matter how familiar the source. She stared at the spot, heartbeats thumping in her chest as she waited for another flash. Anxious, she bit her lower lip. Then, Drogden's beacon flickered again.

Jonna lowered her face to her hands and wiped away the onset of tears. At least she hadn't dissolved into uncontrolled sobbing like the previous few days. Could she be learning to cope with all this? Drogden meant Tove, Papa, love, safety, home, so many things she had thought she couldn't live without. *Being strong is so damn hard.*

As she watched the lighthouse repeat its signal, she recited a silent prayer for peace. It was a ritual she'd begun at her first viewing from Strandhem, and still, as then, she hoped Tove was connecting in similar fashion. Before turning away, she blew a kiss to Drogden and everyone and everything it represented.

Elin appeared to be waiting at the front door for Jonna to catch up. Her usual enthusiasm seemed tempered.

"A long day for us both," she said, opening the door for them. "Any word?" She frowned when Jonna shook her head. "Well, she must be very busy, Jonna. I'm sure she'll send something along as soon as she can. Have faith."

Faith, hope, strength. If only I could purchase some at a shop.

Later that night, Jonna settled onto her bedding in the corner of Elin's room and read her writings from the previous night. Once she had money, a journal would be her first purchase.

Elin stared from across the room. "Are you keeping a diary?"

"Not exactly." Jonna turned the page to begin adding to her work. "More like letters I wish I could send."

"Why?" Elin popped up on an elbow. "That sounds too sad."

"Well, yes, at first it was, but not really anymore. I'm…telling a story. It helps, you know? So much has changed and…It just helps."

"I think I understand. Your papa and your Tove."

Jonna nodded. "Everything."

"Life out there at Drogden must have been so exciting and now you're in a shop, sewing. I'd hate it."

"I miss everything about Drogden. There was always an adventure, although the Nazis took over and made us nervous about every little thing. They didn't need any provocation to throw their weight around."

"What did you do there for fun?"

Jonna set her pencil and paper down and laid back, gazing at the ceiling. "We played lots of board games, lots of cards. Papa could play through the night. We'd redecorate, rearrange our furniture, build things. We had a little radio we kept hidden and when we were sure it was safe, we'd listen to shows or war news. Most importantly, the *Engel* came practically every day, and we'd chat endlessly, enjoy meals with the crew."

"That's how you met her?"

"It is. Thank God." She smiled at the memory. "It was back when the atrocities of war were only rumors to us. I remember being shocked to see a young woman among the crew, just as energetic and strong at those chores. Her father had been the *Engel*'s first mate for years and she grew to be an expert sailor, fit right into the crew." Jonna tilted her head to see Elin. "We became good friends quickly and I so looked forward to the *Engel*'s visits. Could hardly wait."

"I'm sure she brightened your days."

"Last spring, she convinced Captain Holsten to bring children on outings to Drogden—before the Nazis took over, of course. They came almost once a week, and that was great fun for everyone."

"I bet they loved it. The children living at our orphanage would love outings like that."

"Tove and I took a particular liking to one girl, an adventurous ten-year-old who ended up crossing the Oresund."

"So, she's in Sweden now? An orphan?"

"Yes. One of the last evacuations Tove made, in fact."

"Ah. Ten years old, you say. That's a shame. Rabbi Speiser says there's not much hope of the older orphans getting adopted."

"That's so unfair. They've lost everything, too." Jonna could relate.

"You should visit them," Elin stated, sitting up. "There's no work tomorrow, so you should go."

Jonna had planned to spend the next two free days seeking out weekend work. She needed that distraction. Visiting an orphanage required a bright spirit, and Jonna doubted she could muster one to lend any decent support to orphans.

"No, Elin. I don't think I—"

"But who has more in common?"

There's no disputing that.

"And, Jonna…" Elin sent her a sideways look. "Wouldn't your Tove do it?"

Now, that's reaching pretty deep.

"Well," Jonna said, "maybe in time I will. I need to concentrate on finding more work first." Elin's bright expression dimmed as she lay back down, and Jonna knew she'd disappointed her. "Let me gain a little more stability, Elin, then I'll go, okay? I suppose I could offer something."

CHAPTER SIXTEEN

Alborg, Denmark

Tove ran like hell. Counting the seconds, she dodged trees, hurdled fallen logs, and ducked branches while her two associates disappeared on their own routes through the woods. All were desperate to vacate the perimeter of the Nazi complex before their bombs exploded.

At last, the road appeared, and Tove huddled among several spruces, eternally grateful to see the canvas-covered truck slow to a rolling stop. She darted to the street, grabbed the back flap, and swung herself inside. A quarter-mile on, her associates did the same and the truck whisked them away.

The gray-haired man inside with them nodded at his watch. "You three are fast. Excellent time."

Deafening explosions buffeted the truck. Five of them sounded in succession, enough to destroy the massive fuel depot and dozens of trucks, troop carriers, and officers' cars. The Nazi complex was only one of several across Denmark's western waters, but this mission made a significant statement.

Tove dropped her head back and exhaled deliberately, relieved to have succeeded unharmed. She'd never been more nervous, avoiding sentries and search lights, sneaking around the grounds to wire bombs and set timers. She held out her hands and watched them shake. Her heart felt just as tremulous and would probably take hours to calm.

She had taken quickly to all the training the Resistance provided, but that had been a whirlwind of a week. From the introductory meeting, she had been shipped immediately across inland waters to Jutland, Denmark's distant reaches, and had her body and mind inundated with survival and attack skills.

Workouts left her completely spent each night and sleep passed too quickly. Dreams of Jonna were always cut short, spoiled now by images of guns, disguises, and explosives. She found it difficult to take comfort in warm, romantic memories when surrounded by so much anxiety and risk of capture. That she could excel in such an environment came as a personal surprise, however, and provided a significant confidence boost. Being a fast learner, she had earned her first mission after only seven days.

The Nazi garage complex came a week later, and she couldn't believe that her heart hadn't exploded right along with all that German equipment. But the gray-haired man whose name no one needed to know slapped her shoulder with congratulations.

"Sailors are a quick and nimble sort, aren't they?" he said, grinning. "We should have more of your kind."

"We work hard." She wondered if he knew her name, considering he knew her profession. "But nothing we do blows up."

He laughed. "No, they just drown."

The associates chuckled at her, and she had to join them. They were her age, she figured, innocent-looking young men who could have been playing football or delivering someone's new sofa just moments ago. *Look at us. How did we come to this?*

An hour of circuitous driving extracted them from danger, and Tove experienced an empty twinge of longing as they distanced themselves from the shore and the closer proximity to home. She'd glimpsed Denmark's huge island of Zealand during the mission, seen the lights, the silhouette of buildings she knew, and seen herself back there in Copenhagen. She yearned to be on familiar ground, to receive Drogden's signal again, to reconnect.

But now they returned to the old farmstead, the Resistance camp deep in the Jutland hills. The house and large barn emerged after a considerable ride through dense woods, and she was so exhausted, she was relieved to see it.

Tove climbed to her bedding in the loft and flopped onto her back. She didn't want to hear about bombs or trucks or Nazis for at least several hours. Her arms and legs felt rubbery from all that running.

Apparently, the mission had succeeded beyond the leaders' wildest hopes. But, although proud of her performance and delighted to have damaged even a bit of the Nazi war machine, Tove had no desire to repeat the adventure any time soon. *There are at least twelve others here. It's someone else's turn.*

Below her, two women entered the barn and Tove leaned over the side to watch them arrange stools and boxes for seating, a large pot and bowls on a bench for the group meal. The Resistance had established a system as organized as the military, from drills and lessons to accommodations and meals. Tove had been tempted to salute more than once during these past two weeks.

The older of the two women called everyone to eat, but Tove's body resisted. And equally reluctant, her mind was elsewhere. Prone on the hay like this was where she wanted to stay. With her nerves settled, thoughts reached for the one person on Earth who mattered more than anything.

You wouldn't believe all this, Jonna. I hope your new life isn't too strange. Hope it's similar to what you were used to, a welcoming household, maybe a job that's challenging, enjoyable. Can you see our beacon from your shore? I'd give anything to share that with you.

Once again, Tove returned to the dilemma she pondered during every free moment, every night: how to communicate with Jonna. So far removed from Copenhagen and the docks, she had no means to transport word. Writing endangered not only the person caught carrying it, but herself and the entire Resistance operation. Still, she thought, there had to be someone she could speak to, someone who could convey her message. Two weeks were too long to go without connecting.

Please don't give up hoping for some word. I know I promised you better and I will find a way. Can you at least look to Drogden?

During a break in shooting practice the next day, as Tove helped unload a delivery truck at the farmhouse, she seized the opportunity to get news of home from the driver. He was a hefty fellow with a jolly personality, and chatting with him helped her forget the work itself.

"They say the evacuation should be finished next week," he said, passing her another crate off the truck. "Damn proud of that effort, I say."

"Do you get into Copenhagen much, the docks?"

"Oh, no. Too far. I get loads *from* there. *That* driver has to deal with all those patrols and roadblocks, not me. We're lucky to have him 'cause I'm not that clever."

Tove paused before leaving for the house and adjusted the heavy box of produce in her arms. "So…that driver might visit the docks?"

"What's this about the docks? You homesick, maybe?"

She caught herself before revealing too much. The less they knew about each other, the less Nazis could extract.

"Well, I have friends there," she said, "and I'd really like to know how they're getting on, somehow let them know I'm okay."

He nodded as he set another crate at the edge of the truck bed. "I'm sure you would, but you know how it is."

"Any chance you could ask that trucker to pass along word?"

"Me? Remember something like that?" He laughed and his belly jiggled. "God, woman. Sometimes I forget the names of my children."

"You could rig something to remind yourself, couldn't you? Like…like a string on your truck's gear shif—"

"Hey, I don't know if he even goes to the Copenhagen docks. He might connect with somebody else who does. Besides, it'll be some time before I see him again." He shook his head. "Sorry, but no."

"I'd like to pay you for your trouble."

"Oh, would you?" He appeared to grow irritated by her persistence. "You don't have any money. Nobody does." He eyed her for so long, she thought he might throw his crate down at her. Instead, he sighed as he squatted at the edge of the truck. "Okay, look. If you make it brief, I'll try to remember."

With a satchel of basic medical supplies hanging from her shoulder, Jonna followed Elin around to the back of the church and into the orphanage. After landing a job last week assisting the village doctor, she discovered helping him and fellow villagers to be remarkably gratifying. Added to her daily chores at the seamstress shop, the doctor's minor weekend assignments left her little time to dwell on heartache. Almost a month without word from or about Tove threatened to break her whenever memories crept to mind.

Entering the orphanage, Jonna braced herself. She had so much in common with these orphaned Danish children, and summoned all the resolve she could against feelings of isolation and loss.

But high-pitched chatter and laughter struck her immediately, and she was warmed by the lively mood in the large space. Children's drawings decorated the plank walls and toys lay scattered on layers of mismatched rugs. Youngsters scurried about, an older girl of about twelve stoked the little wood stove, and a boy Jonna guessed to be in his early teens sat reading atop a very tiny table.

Elin nodded toward a woman who was explaining a wooden toy to a toddler. When she straightened and Elin introduced Jonna, the woman's eyes grew wide.

"Jonna Friedler? My goodness!" She pumped Jonna's hand enthusiastically. "I know who you are. Welcome."

"Jonna, this amazing woman is Birta," Elin said. "Volunteers supervise the overnights but she's in charge here during the day. She's a Dane from Copenhagen like you."

"I'm so glad to meet you, Birta. Bless you for your hard work here."

"We must be strong, Jonna, for ourselves and our country, but, most of all, for the children." Her eyes went to the small boy hurrying toward them and she leaned to Jonna, whispering. "Thankfully, this little one and his sister were not at home when the Gestapo came. Their parents had been hiding a Jewish couple."

The child looked up at Jonna and tugged on her jacket. "My name is Peder Christensen. Who are you?"

Jonna crouched and shook his small hand. "My name is Jonna Friedler and I am very pleased to meet you, Peder. How old are you?"

"I am six." He turned and pointed across the room. "Teresa is painting a picture of our house."

"I see." She spotted the young artist at the easel and hoped the rendered memory would serve them well in life. "She is your sister?"

Nodding, he stated, "She's eight. You want to come, see her picture?"

Birta bent down to him. "Maybe later, Peder. Jonna has work to do."

His expectant eyes flicked from Birta to Jonna. "Are you a doctor?"

"No, but I'm helping because he's very busy. Today, I'm just checking to see how everyone's feeling."

"She needs to meet all the children," Birta told him.

"I don't know anyone," Jonna explained and looked up from her crouch. "Perhaps, I'll need someone to help me?"

"I know everyone," Peder declared, "and I'm a good helper."

Jonna glanced up at Birta again, but Peder didn't wait for permission. He took Jonna's hand and led her away.

"Nice meeting you, Birta." Jonna winked over her shoulder. "Elin. You don't have to wait. This might take a while."

"This is Teresa," Peder said, his arm outstretched. "She's not sick."

The little artist eyed Jonna curiously. "I *was* sick but I'm better now. Are you the new doctor?"

"She's just helping," Peder injected, "and I'm helping her."

"My name's Jonna, Teresa." She pulled paperwork from her satchel and hurriedly scanned it for Teresa's name. "I see you were sick a few days ago. Did you stay in bed as you were told?"

"She did," Peder said. "I got to eat her dessert. We had strudel."

Teresa scowled at him. "I couldn't eat it, remember?" She sighed at Jonna. "He doesn't know everything."

Jonna bit back a grin. "Let me check a few things, okay? Like your temperature."

She had a highly attentive audience as she opened a small case and prepared the thermometer. Peder squatted at her satchel, studying the contents.

"Don't touch anything," Teresa told him as Jonna coaxed the girl's attention back to her. "He's nosey," Teresa said right before Jonna slipped in the thermometer.

"Well, Peder, how about you?" Jonna asked and he stood to his full height. "How have you been feeling?"

"I'm okay. Everybody's okay. Oh, except Edvin." He looked at the teenager on the table. "He coughs a lot."

Jonna checked the thermometer and showed the results to Teresa. "You were smart to follow doctor's directions. I'd say you're good as new."

"Toldja," Peder said. "You wanna go see Edvin now?"

"One minute." Jonna made notes on the paperwork, then spent an extra moment appreciating the painting. "Teresa, I hope this is hung for everyone to see. You should be proud of it. That's a lovely house."

Teresa appeared to be lost in her creation. "Papa let me paint these window boxes—the real ones," she said, not looking away, "and then Mama and me planted these flowers."

If she starts crying, I will, too.

Subtly, Jonna took a breath. Chances were virtually zero that this sister and brother would ever see their parents or this home again. She could only hope that new memories someday would make the old ones easier to handle.

"And that's why your beautiful painting is so important, Teresa. Be sure to finish it."

She couldn't wait to turn away and exhale. As Peder led her to Edvin, she wondered if she had enough strength for this job.

Edvin didn't look up when Peder introduced her. He turned the page in his book and read on.

"What are you reading?" Jonna asked.

He shrugged, his head still bowed. "Sheepherding."

"He got it yesterday," Peder said. "The English flier gave it to him so he wouldn't cry."

Edvin's head snapped up and he glared. "Not true! I wasn't going to cry! Go away." He spun away from them and coughed deeply as he returned to his book.

"About that cough," Jonna said. "Let me listen, won't you?" She stepped to his front and held up a stethoscope.

"Don't bother. It doesn't matter now."

"The doctor won't be happy if I don't do my job. Help me out, won't you?" She extended the diaphragm between the buttons of his shirt, surprised when he didn't brush her off. "How old are you?"

"Fourteen."

She considered his future, the odds of adoption, the chances he would leave here anytime soon, and forced those concerns aside. She had to focus on her work.

The heavy congestion she heard added to her worries. "Thank you. Now, how about temperature?"

Edvin exhaled, annoyed. He glowered at Peder as they awaited the thermometer's results.

"An English flier gave you this book?" Jonna glanced at the cover, and he nodded. "A pilot?"

"They come sometimes," Peder said. "They stay around here if they're hurt or escaping."

"I see." The thermometer indicated Edvin could be in trouble and Jonna took her time adding his information to her paperwork. "You mean a downed Allied pilot or a wounded soldier?"

"He was from another village," Peder added. "He came a few times, said he planned to take Edvin home with him, but not if he was sick."

"And I'm *not*," Edvin said. "He…He just chickened out." He flipped pages in his book and mumbled. "Who cares about going to England anyway."

Jonna appreciated Peder's information but thought it best not to dwell on what sounded like a failed attempt at adoption. As it was, Edvin seemed painfully defeated.

"Well, one thing is certain, Edvin: that cough of yours isn't doing you any good. And your temp is a little high, which I don't like. So, before things get worse, I'm recommending a visit with the doctor." He nodded as he turned pages.

Jonna closed her satchel and set a hand on his arm. "We can't lose hope, you know. You all probably hear that every day, I'm sure, because I hear it, too, but we can't. Good times will come."

Edvin finally looked up. His young, smooth cheeks were void of color, his dark eyes drained and haunted.

CHAPTER SEVENTEEN

Sam put her forehead down on the table in frustration. When she picked it back up, one of the many papers strewn across the table stuck. It was just as well, there was only so many more times she could see the look of disappointment in Nancy's eyes. This was one of many reasons she didn't mix business with feelings. Except she'd let that ship sail, the horse was out of the barn, the train was out of the station, the business-and-feelings potion was already brewing.

She pulled the paper off her forehead and rubbed her eyes. "Okay, one more time. I'm sorry I'm having trouble seeing the vision. Try me again. It's like this place, but not like here. And like the castle, but not a castle?"

Nancy sighed. "When you put it like that, I'm not sure why you're having trouble visualizing. Seems perfectly clear to me."

"Hey." Sam covered Nancy's hand with hers and squeezed. "You said you had it figured out. I believe you. All I need is help getting what's in there"—she tapped Nancy's temple—"into here." She tapped her own.

"Okay. In your book, there was an old lighthouse that was decommissioned and run down. The two women used it as shelter, right?" Nancy searched Sam's face.

Sam nodded, not sure where Nancy was going.

"They knew the history of the lighthouse, its maritime value, all of it. But that history wasn't preserved, and they were left with ruins. You and I are currently in a beautiful lighthouse with every modern amenity." Nancy indicated around them.

"But you hate that we don't know anything about the history of this lighthouse." Sam rolled her shoulders. "I'm still not seeing the big picture."

"That's because I'm not done." Nancy's smile took any sting out of her words. "You wanted a resort, I wanted a museum, why can't we have both?"

Sam felt her eyebrows reach for the sky. "You want a resort museum? Like the Louvre with cots and continental breakfast?"

Nancy laughed. "I said resort, not a youth hostel. Anyway, we can work on the branding. Why can't we have the place your Tove and Jonna stayed except no war and not crumbling around them? Or this place but with historical acknowledgement?"

Excitement bloomed in Sam's chest. "You are going to let me build the castle at my lighthouse."

"There will still be no castles at my lighthouse, but the castle is a good model. I think you knew that when you brought me there." Nancy hooked her pinky around Sam's little finger and gave their joined fingers a little wiggle.

"You're giving me too much credit." Sam snared Nancy's ring finger with her own. "I wanted to show you that the kind of resort I had in mind wasn't as awful as you might have been imagining. I chose somewhere I thought you'd like because of the history, but I didn't have a grand plan."

Nancy winked and entwined another of their fingers. "But we can. You want luxury, fine, I'll give you that, as long as there is also part of the island that is open to the public during the day."

"I can live with that. Let me get our paper." Sam searched through the scattered papers until she found the one with *bathrooms* and their signatures. She added *Overnight guests/luxury* and *open to the public during the day*. She signed next to each. "Your turn." She pushed the paper to Nancy and regretted it immediately when Nancy disentangled their hands to add her signature.

"Do you think your fancy-schmancy friends will be okay with a museum and the public at their private resort?" Nancy pushed their official document to the center of the table and took Sam's hand again.

Sam tapped her pen against her chin. "It wouldn't be for everyone, but it doesn't have to be. Not everyone likes a cruise either, but ships set sail every day. We'll find our crowd."

"*Our* crowd. I like that. I guess that means it's our lighthouse too?"

"Afraid so. At least if we plan on moving forward with this." Sam nodded solemnly and pointed at their agreement.

"You're a pain in the ass, Sam McMann. You made me like you. I have to give you joint custody of my lighthouse. What's next? I feel like the lighthouse is three steps beyond marriage and kids so that would be a step backward." Nancy looked playfully exasperated.

Sam choked on the sip of water she'd inconveniently taken as Nancy was talking. Marriage and kids? What the fuck? She knew Nancy was kidding. They both understood Sam's birthright, those responsibilities to her father's company. Nancy was only thinking of the most outlandish thing she could and tossing it out to make a joke, except it didn't land for Sam as she was sure Nancy intended. The idea of settling down with Nancy should feel like the wackiest idea in the world and yet, a wild, free, unruly part of her heart spoke loudly and clearly that it needn't. What was she supposed to do with that?

After clearing the water from her airway, Sam finally managed to respond. "I'm sure I'll come up with something." *How lame.*

She couldn't decipher the look on Nancy's face, but it passed quickly.

"Do you need another sip of water, or will that make things worse?"

"Stop proposing to me, we have work to do." Sam pointed to their signed agreement page.

Nancy looked nonplussed. "What are you talking about? I did no such thing."

Sam tapped the paper again faking stern, disciplined work habits. "Shall we?" She laughed when Nancy scowled. "Are you thinking new construction for our overnight guests?"

"No actually." Nancy's eyes lit up. "I was thinking they'd stay in the lighthouse, the building by the water, and the bunker building."

"Bunker building has to be the restaurant and bar. It's made for it. No one wants to sleep in a bunker. We can build more space for sleeping if we want to have more guests." Sam wrote *bunker bar* on the paper and signed.

"Awfully confident in my consent." Nancy took the pen from Sam and wrote *guests in lighthouse, building by water, additional space*. Then she added *dedicated museum space in every building*. She signed next to her last addition, and slid the paper back to Sam.

It was not lost on Sam that Nancy hadn't agreed to her bunker bar. "Where did you learn your negotiating skills?" Sam edged her chair closer to Nancy.

Nancy scooted her seat farther around the table from Sam. "From being one of five, and you keep all your sexiness over there while we're working. You're not going to ooze hotness all over me to get what you want. I have my weaknesses, but I'm not easy, not even jet-lagged and exhausted."

"I would never use a ploy like that." In truth Sam hadn't been trying to pull a fast one. She'd only wanted to get closer to Nancy because she craved the proximity. She'd gone out on a limb suggesting this lighthouse adventure as a date and now they were negotiating museum space and building usage.

Somehow, that really was okay with Sam, too. She was content spending time with Nancy, working on this project she'd started solo, but was now a joint venture. Maybe they could draw it out a few more months, or years, so she didn't have to return to reality and could continue whisking Nancy off on adventures, working closely together, and seeing if they could sneak in a real date. Sam sighed and melancholy hit hard.

"Hey, what's wrong?" Nancy now moved her chair around until she was right next to Sam. She frowned. "You didn't do that on purpose to get me closer, did you?"

"Added benefit I didn't anticipate. I was thinking that I want you to keep outmaneuvering me about lighthouse logistics, want us to keep flying off wherever we feel like instead of ever returning to my real world." Sam pulled their agreement over and began to sign next to *dedicated museum space*.

Nancy stilled Sam's hand. "Flying me around the world whenever and wherever I feel like? See, I knew you could come up with something surprising I'd like to think I'd say no to, but probably wouldn't. But no pity signing or the whole deal's off."

"Why are you agreeing to any of my ideas? I'm still suggesting rich people come to the island and have a unique experience most people won't be able to afford. Wasn't that what insulted you so much initially?" Sam leaned her elbow on the table and rested her head on her hand.

"Have you ever read any Jane Austen?" Nancy pulled Sam to her feet, grabbed a pen and the signature page, and pulled her out the door onto the deck overlooking the water.

"Of course. I'm not a barbarian." Sam sat in the chair Nancy pointed her toward.

Nancy pulled her own chair closer and sat. "Then you know it wasn't uncommon during that time for large estates to be open to the public for tours. The fees helped offset the substantial upkeep costs. Instead of the uber wealthy letting in the public to help pay for their mansions, we'll be the public letting in the uber wealthy to help pay for historical preservation."

"Smug. Is that the look on your face right now?" Sam ran her thumb over Nancy's lips and cupped her cheek. "Somehow it looks good on you."

"I prefer triumphant." Nancy leaned into Sam's touch, her voice barely above a whisper. "You don't have to go back you know."

That was the cold shower Sam needed to douse the moment. She pulled away and sat back heavily in her chair. "Would you be able to walk away from duty to your family?"

"I don't know. Mine has never asked of me what yours is asking of you." Nancy reached out again tentatively and laid her hand on Sam's. "But you deserve a fulfilling life, too. Happiness."

"Someday I'll take you to meet my father and then you can decide whether that still seems like a possibility."

Nancy put her hand on her forehead and dramatically faux-fainted back into her chair.

"OMG, you're going to take me to meet your parents? That's even better than being the only museum with two-ply toilet paper or finding out how many weapon-drink name puns you can come up with. We haven't even had a real date yet."

Sam tried not to pout. "You laugh but he's intense. I don't have a choice." She sat up as Nancy's words hit home. "Does this mean you're agreeing to the bar? Is it a pity concession?"

"Yes." Nancy looked at Sam seriously. "Every time you have a drink there, that slightly bitter aftertaste is a tiny hint of pity. If you don't stand up for yourself, that taste will get stronger and will morph into regret. I'm not talking about me here, although…" Grinning, she flipped her hair with a flourish. "All I mean is, what you want is important too."

Sam licked her lips. "Is it now?" She took her time surveying Nancy's soft curves and beautiful face.

Nancy moved from her chair onto Sam's lap. She put both hands behind Sam's neck and looked at her intensely. "I'm very hungry. It's time for you to take me," she leaned close and whispered in Sam's ear, "to dinner."

It was impossible, but Sam felt like all the bones in her body melted. How was Nancy able to play her so completely? "You are cruel. Maybe I will take you to meet my father as punishment."

"He doesn't scare me." Nancy stood and pulled Sam to her feet. "Let's go explore before we're both too tired to enjoy this amazing place you picked for us."

Sam tried to hide her disappointment. In the recent past, she'd have been overjoyed at the idea of a woman as stunning as Nancy on her arm. She'd have courted anyone with a camera to take pictures and post them anywhere and everywhere. Now though, she didn't want to share.

She couldn't say what they had, where it was going, or how long it might last, but she wanted all of it. She'd never allowed herself to want something just for herself. Surely a friendship would still be possible after this project ended, but what if that wasn't enough? Was Nancy right? Could she have more than what she'd been told and how high would the price be to get it?

CHAPTER EIGHTEEN

Sam gave Nancy a small nod of encouragement. Nancy rang the bell next to the formidable mahogany front door and they both stepped back and waited. Sam gulped down a few nerves when Mrs. Jones, a woman as forbidding as her door, welcomed them in.

"You're late." Mrs. Jones ushered them into the sitting room, each step punctuated by the thud of her cane. Sam and Nancy chose seats next to each other on a small loveseat.

Despite her very strong desire, Sam refrained from pointing out they were two minutes late and finding the old woman's house was nearly impossible.

Nancy didn't have such reservations. "The directions you gave us were crap, so I doubt you're surprised."

Mrs. Jones turned around faster than Sam thought possible for a woman of her age. Her eyebrows were sky high. "Do you not have GPS?"

"I assumed if you'd wanted us to use it you would have given us the address instead of a scavenger hunt. Either way, the adventure was fun." Nancy shrugged with a grin.

To Sam's shock, Mrs. Jones returned the smile. "And what about you?" She turned to Sam. "Have you made a final decision on whether you're only in this for personal peacocking?"

Sam's hand stilled with her glass of water halfway to her mouth. She'd never been insulted so fowl-ly. It was difficult to take offense.

Nancy made no attempt to suppress her giggles. "I would never have come up with that description, but that's exactly what your initial proposal was, peacocking. Your tail feathers were on full display and you were strutting around the island so we could all see. No wonder I didn't like you."

"Have we landed on one side of the like/don't like fence? I sensed some waffling earlier." Sam winked at Nancy.

"If you two are quite finished," Mrs. Jones interjected, reminding them they were in her sitting room on business. Despite her stern tone, Sam saw a warmth in her eyes. "Have you brought me a new proposal for the lighthouse?"

"We have." Nancy handed over their new proposal and she and Sam sat nervously while Mrs. Jones slowly read through each page.

Finally, she put the packet down and fixed each of them with a penetrating, unreadable, stare. "Ms. Calhoun, you were insistent on a museum in its purest form on the island. You hated everything about Ms. McMann's proposal for overnight guests and high-end clientele. What's changed?"

Sam turned to Nancy and waited for her to collect her thoughts. She hadn't noticed before that Nancy pursed her lips slightly and scrunched her nose when she was thinking. It was damn cute. Sam decided to say something thought-provoking the next time they were alone to elicit that look. She also wanted Nancy to think of her as interesting, intelligent. She was beginning to want a lot of things from Nancy and wanting was terrifying.

"What's changed," Nancy repeated, and smiled at Sam before turning back to Mrs. Jones. "I guess I've changed. I wanted history and my museum and I only knew one way for that to look. Spending time with Sam has shown me there might be other options."

Mrs. Jones frowned. "You changed for her?"

Sam laughed but quieted when both Nancy and Mrs. Jones glared at her. "I'm sorry, Mrs. Jones, it's just that you don't know Nancy all that well if you think she'd do that for me."

"I didn't change for her." Nancy looked slightly horrified. "But once I was open to the possibility of something different from what I'd proposed, it was easier to find the elements that were most important to me. It turned out overnight guests don't bother me as long as the historical piece is honored and available to everyone."

"And that's how you ended up with a bar in the bunker?" It looked like the words tasted sour coming out of Mrs. Jones's mouth.

"You'll have to join us for a drink at the grand opening." Nancy smiled proudly, either unaware or undeterred by Mrs. Jones's clear distaste for that aspect of the proposal.

"And you, Ms. McMann, how did you go from destination for the rich and famous to maritime museum?"

Sam shifted on the loveseat, buying herself time she didn't need. She knew why her feelings on the subject had changed. "I'm worried I'm going to sound a little too sentimental or like too much of a sap when I tell you." Sam brushed a nonexistent hair from her forehead. "Nancy's love of history is infectious. She took me to see a boat that rescued Denmark's Jewish population during World War II. We went on board and it blew my mind."

Mrs. Jones straightened in her seat. She looked a million miles away, as if mesmerized by a newsreel of the past. "I know that boat," she said softly. "Yes. I've visited the *Gerda III* many times."

"Then you understand. But Nancy took me there because of a book I've been reading. It's about two Danish women and one of them lived the same life as the *Gerda* crew. I can barely put the book down, and knowing that it's real, that those women were real...I don't have words to describe how that changed my perspective. Then, to be able to stand on the *Gerda*, on the deck of history? It was magical."

"And what of these two women? Do you mean to tell their story at your lighthouse?" Her gaze was back to steady and piercing.

Sam took a moment to consider. "The war forces them apart, but their lighthouse keeps them connected, keeps their hopes alive. Surely, there are similar untold stories about our lighthouse waiting for us to uncover and share with the world. How could I be opposed to that?"

Mrs. Jones smiled. It transformed her face and made her eyes twinkle. "I'm very proud of both of you. This is exactly the kind of creativity we were hoping you'd exhibit when we sent you on your way with a new mandate. I have to show this to the rest of the board and get their approval, but it's likely only a formality. I don't think it's premature to congratulate you on the acceptance of your proposal and transfer of ownership of the lighthouse."

Nancy squealed and threw her arms around Sam's neck. Sam returned the hug and then they both stood and politely shook Mrs. Jones's hand.

"No more playing hooky and whisking me all over the world," Nancy said, looping her arm through Sam's as they returned to their car. "We have so much work to do." She sounded a little overwhelmed.

"One day at a time. This is the fun part. Before we get to that, though, let's celebrate."

She was in a jovial mood. Finalizing their lighthouse proposal and having it be so enthusiastically accepted had her riding an adrenaline wave. But it was Nancy on her arm that had her heart really racing.

Dropping Nancy back at home and then heading to her own sterile hotel room was too lonely to consider. Even with the companionship of Tove and Jonna from her book, she knew she'd feel Nancy's absence too acutely. She was starting to notice the time they didn't spend together and how time seemed to drag endlessly onward. How did Tove and Jonna do it with no end in sight?

Sam caught her breath as she buckled into the seat next to Nancy and gave the driver directions. Tove and Jonna were lovers, soulmates. She and Nancy were business partners who enjoyed harmless flirtation. She and Nancy really were nothing like Tove and Jonna, right?

Nancy stared into the bottom of her cappuccino mug, disappointed to find it empty. She and Sam had stretched every course of their dinner to its breaking point, but with the end of her after-dinner coffee, the evening seemed to be at an end.

The shock of disappointment was more intense than she'd expected. The more time she spent with Sam the more she craved.

Where she'd initially assumed her to be snobby, aloof, and conceited, Sam was instead considerate, warm, and kind.

Nancy stared across at Sam, illuminated by two candles flickering lazily at their table. She was gorgeous. Lightning bolts shot through Nancy's stomach.

"It doesn't seem real that we own a lighthouse." The work ahead was a much safer topic than imagining how dark Sam's eyes might get when she came.

"I don't want to be done celebrating. Do you have to go home?" Sam looked surprised to have asked such a question.

"I stopped having a curfew in high school. I'm not in a rush to get away from you." Nancy reached across the table and took Sam's hand. "What did you have in mind?"

Sam looked at her hungrily but answered much more tamely than her expression suggested she might. "Do you like to dance?"

Nancy wasn't sure how Sam expected her to answer, looking at her like being in public was the only thing keeping their clothes on, so she settled for nodding. In fact, she wasn't sure how the table and anyone within Sam's line of sight wasn't on fire. She certainly was. Thankfully, mind reading wasn't a skill people possessed or she'd need an explicit content warning label. God, Sam was hot.

"Will you take me? Dancing, that is?" Sam amended quickly. "I don't know anywhere except places for tourists, and I don't want tourists. They'll have cameras and I don't want pictures." She lifted Nancy's hand to her mouth and kissed her knuckles.

"I thought you liked getting your picture in the tabloids." Nancy clutched both hands in her lap while Sam paid the bill.

Sam shook her head. "Not with you. You mean too much to me and that world means too little."

Nancy tamped down the little bit of hope that sprung up unbidden. Sam had made it clear where her life was headed, and her long-term plans didn't include a life in Rhode Island. "What does that mean?"

Sam looked lost. "I don't know."

"Okay. For now. Tonight, let's celebrate. And dance." Nancy took Sam's hand, led her out of the restaurant, and pulled her down the street. "You're in for more than you know, Sam McMann. I hope those shoes are more comfortable than they look."

"These shoes were made for my feet and my feet alone. I can go all night." Sam did a little tap dance spin move on the sidewalk ostensibly to prove her point. She looked ridiculous but also rather charming.

Nancy grabbed her and pulled her close. They crashed together, their faces and bodies only inches apart. It felt so good, Nancy considered vetoing dancing and bringing Sam home to put an end to their sexual tension and answer all her questions about Sam's orgasm eyes, but she wanted to go dancing. Sam might not want to show her off, but Nancy sure as hell wanted to strut her stuff with Sam. She wanted to spend the night dancing in Sam's arms, and she wanted to celebrate. There were always good reasons to have sex. Tonight, she wanted to get lost in the music and the embrace of a beautiful woman. And maybe some sex after. She was a "yes/and" kind of woman.

"You said you could go all night? Time to prove it." Nancy kissed Sam's cheek and pulled her down the sidewalk again.

Nancy led them from street level down a flight of steps to a nondescript door manned by a large wall with arms, legs, and a head, dressed all in black.

"Are you on the list?" The wall looked suspicious.

"Nancy Calhoun." Sam looked unsure beside her.

The wall checked his list, nodded, and opened the door for them. "Have a nice night, Ms. Calhoun."

"How'd you get on that giant meatball's list? I'm impressed and a little jealous. I can do that at fancy clubs, but I'm not cool enough to get into the weird warehouse door, sub-level clubs." Sam looked around.

"You'll continue to earn yourself points by pointing out the obvious. You have private jets and whole companies, but the cool points rain down like confetti over here." Nancy pointed at her head with both index fingers.

"I thought we were here to dance, not brag." Sam wrapped Nancy in a tight embrace from behind and lifted her off the ground.

Nancy squealed and kicked her feet. She didn't fight all that hard to free herself. She'd happily stay wrapped up tight in Sam's arms all night.

"Pierre told me you were here, Nance. I came out to see if you needed anything, but it looks like you brought everything you desire. I'm Della." Della extended her hand to Sam, forcing Nancy and Sam apart enough so Sam could shake. "Welcome to the multi-club. If Nancy no longer has use for you, my office is right around that corner. Show yourself in anytime." Della kissed Nancy's cheek, looked Sam over slowly, then turned back to Nancy with a knowing smile and fanned herself dramatically. As quickly as she'd appeared, Della was gone again.

"What just happened?" Sam glanced in the direction of Della's office, a perplexed look on her face.

Nancy led Sam to a desk manned by another mass of muscle. He had a clipboard and a wad of branded bracelets. Nancy gave her name again and she and Sam each got a bracelet and entry through the second level door.

"What happened is you now have to behave yourself or I'm turning you over to Della." Nancy winked at Sam. She had to shout to be heard over what was now a cacophony of music coming from multiple rooms.

Sam's eyebrows shot up. "And what does behaving myself look like? So I know how to stay in your good graces."

"Nice try, stud. You're going to have to feel your way through this one." Nancy evaluated her options: each room was a mini nightclub with a different musical style and feel. "I hope you like line dancing."

"I love it. I can boot scoot with anyone."

Before Nancy had a chance to worry about what she'd gotten herself into, they were in the door and fully immersed in a country music mega club. Sam found them a table and fought her way to the bar for drinks while Nancy scoped out the dancing. Beginners were intermingled with more experienced dancers, and everyone looked to be having a great time.

Even though it was Nancy's idea to try line dancing, the reality of actually taking to the dance floor stirred a serious case of performance anxiety. She concentrated on the rows of stomping, kicking, spinning, and shuffling boots without much luck decoding the secrets of the dance.

"I see your beautiful brain working overtime." Sam set the drinks on the table and took her hand. "Don't think. Just dance."

A new song started and Sam coaxed Nancy onto the floor. They lined up next to each other along with close to fifty others in a few uneven lines. The rows moved in unison to the right, sweeping Nancy along with it. She missed a boot slap and a hip shimmy, but she wasn't wearing boots and, without worrying about her hips, she could watch what Sam was doing with hers. Halfway through the song she wasn't thinking at all. She was content to be swept along with the crowd, joining the appropriate movement when she was able but otherwise happy to improvise as the music moved her.

They danced until they were both sweaty and breathing heavily. Nancy was about to call a timeout so she could catch her breath when a slow dance love song blanketed the room.

Sam extended her hand and gave Nancy a questioning look. Why she thought Nancy might say no was beyond her. She took Sam's hand and squeaked with surprise when Sam spun her into her arms.

Other couples moved around them following more traditional step patterns, but Sam didn't seem to care, and held Nancy close as they swayed to the music. Nancy rested her hand on Sam's chest instead of her shoulder and made no attempt to put any distance between them. Her heart raced simply looking into Sam's eyes. She could get lost in this woman.

But Sam managed to put feelings into words first.

"You get more beautiful every time I look at you." With a fingertip, she moved a lock of hair from Nancy's cheek. "I'm not sure how that's possible because you bowled me over the first time I saw you."

"Liar." Nancy leaned into Sam's touch. "The only thing bowling you over the day we met was the motion of the ocean."

Sam held her finger to her lips before pulling Nancy close once again. "It's my sappy declaration, I can fudge the unimportant details if I want."

Nancy traced along Sam's eyebrows, down the side of her face, and along her strong, well-defined jawbone. She tapped a finger on Sam's lips and was rewarded with a kiss against her hand that made her shiver. "I believe you were telling me how beautiful I am."

Sam's face softened and she smiled a lazy, knowing smile. "You're right. I was." Before Sam could continue, she was interrupted by a fellow club patron to their right.

"Are you Samantha McMann?" A man was standing at the edge of the dance floor, cell phone held in front of him, clearly recording their dance.

Nancy recoiled from the phone and pulled out of Sam's arms. Sam stepped between her and the camera wielding man, shielding her from view. "Turn around, don't look back, and go to the table. Keep your back to him and don't look at anyone else with a camera out."

As soon as she was out of touching distance, Nancy missed Sam. Not literally. Sam was only across the room talking to the rude camera guy. She missed her Sam, the woman who was open-minded about history, willing to fly to Ireland on a moment's notice to make Nancy happy, and was kind, curious, and loving. "Samantha McMann" had appeared the moment the camera came out and Nancy hated it. She didn't know that woman.

It had been easy to get carried away by the idea that Sam was a whole person and not the version of herself she allowed when she was temporarily away from her day-to-day reality. This encounter was a cold shower of reality. Nancy hated cold water. She wanted her Sam to stay. *When did she become my Sam?* She wanted Sam to choose to stay. Sam made her want a lot of things and that felt like a very vulnerable place to be.

CHAPTER NINETEEN

Kattinge, Denmark

Denmark's many varied islands had always been fascinating, exciting, but from this highpoint looking across to the glow of Copenhagen on Zealund, Tove saw them as foreboding. She and five others soon would cross the inland waters, stowed away on some vessel like the many countrymen she had shuttled across the Oresund. How she ached to see that water again and the light she shared with Jonna.

This mission would take her to Kattinge village on Zealund, not far enough east to reach the city of Copenhagen, and she mourned being so close yet so far. As their truck motored through darkness to the shore, she calculated the time she would need to reach the city, the docks, to spot Drogden's beacon. On foot, probably a day. By transport, an hour or two.

She leaned back against the truck wall and closed her eyes, contemplating her situation. Four others napped around her. Maybe one or more of them had roots in Copenhagen and a similar yearning to return, however briefly. Together, could they convince the driver to detour? When would she be so close again?

Everyone woke to a gruff voice ordering them out and on their way. Like the others, Tove readjusted the pack on her back and checked that the safety was set on her rifle, then jumped to the ground and ran for the tree line. From there, they would await an incoming trawler, then dash aboard as it departed.

Precision timing had become the top priority for everything, from camp meals and drills, to transport, rendezvous, and explosives, and Tove knew better than to imagine stealing a couple of hours for a side venture to the Copenhagen docks. This was a sabotage mission, although she and her comrades saw it as a rescue, and for every element of the plan, time was precious.

Now, she was among reinforcements rushing to the Zealund interior to succeed where the local Resistance cell had failed last night. Failing to destroy the Nazi post, that group had lost two members to arrest and two to gunfire. The rest of the cell had fled underground, and Tove expected some eventually would surface at her camp in the Jutland hills.

Finally ashore at an abandoned dock, they soon connected with a farmer who drove them to within a few miles of their objective. Her team's targets were the two key elements of the post left in operation: its headquarters and light tower. Of course, freeing their two comrades had to be the first order of business.

Skirting the wooded perimeter, the team divided its resources. The tower would be the first to go and provide enough distraction for the others to storm the headquarters and its depleted Nazi squad. Tove crossed her fingers that intelligence had been correct, and no Gestapo unit had arrived yet to retrieve the two Resistance prisoners.

The compound within the wire fencing was relatively small, all of it easily assessed, and most of it still smoldered from last night's destruction. But lamps burned brightly in the little headquarters building and those search lights still prowled the area.

Until the massive explosion lit up the night.

The search lights went black and, as Tove and three associates raced to the building, she heard men scream as they and their tower crashed to the ground.

Ahead, two sentries at the door swung their weapons into firing position, but an associate at Tove's side stopped, aimed, and shot them in place. Up the two steps, another associate kicked in the door and sprayed the room with bullets.

Tove shouldered through a side door and found both Resistance comrades chained to the floor, badly beaten. She grabbed an axe by the wood stove and hacked them free just as another associate produced keys to the shackles.

"Headlights!"

Grabbing their beaten comrades by the arms, they raced out and around the building. An associate tossed grenades through the window, and everyone bolted for the woods as a trio of vehicles roared into the area.

The small structure exploded into splinters as Tove ran, a million thoughts blurring her mind. She knew the Gestapo were overdue and regretted not having insisted on a change in plans. Behind her, officers shouted orders and guns began firing. She listened to her feet pound the turf, her breathing huff like a steam locomotive. *It's not going to end this way.*

With automatic weapons kicking up dirt to the rear, team members separated. Their eight different trails divided the gunfire, and the officers' commands grew frustrated and furious. Motors revved and grew louder, and headlights lit up selected spots in the woods.

"We're almost there!" a comrade yelled. "They can't drive in the damn woods!"

Guided by the glow of headlights, Tove and her comrades charged into the dense forest, crashing through the brush, aiming for areas not as brightly lit. The cars had to stop but gunfire followed them in.

Not far to her right, Tove heard a woman yelp in pain.

An associate she couldn't see issued a breathy call. "Are you all right?"

"M-my leg!" the woman yelled back, "but I-I think I can—" She cried out again and abruptly went silent.

In the dim light between the trees, Tove caught sight of her falling. She raced toward the spot, so difficult to pinpoint in the near darkness, but found her at last.

"Hurry!" she said on a breath and drew the associate's arm around her neck and hauled her to her feet. "We *have* to keep moving."

Erratic gunfire pinged off trees.

She was breathing so hard she couldn't hear if soldiers pursued them on foot. She just assumed they did. She was never more thankful than to *not* hear dogs on their scent.

The chase seemed to last all night.

Tove hurt everywhere but at least bullets hadn't been the cause. She'd slammed off of trees, tripped over branches and stumps, fallen into holes, and pulled muscles she didn't know she had, supporting her wounded comrade.

But now, mercifully, everything had gone quiet, and the pair collapsed beneath a thick pine to rest.

"I have no idea where we are," Tove admitted, wiping the slashes on her arms with her shirt. She could feel the stickiness of blood beneath her trousers, across her back, and through her hair. "And God knows where everyone else is."

"Or if they made it."

The woman was hard to see in the darkness. The vision of her chained to the floor had been a blur, so all Tove really knew was that she had long hair and that they were about the same size.

"How's your leg?"

"Wet." The woman's hand hovered over the thigh wound, obviously reluctant to touch it.

Tove leaned closer. "I think the blood's starting to dry around it." She sat back with another groan. "That's probably good, you know, that it's not…gushing or anything."

"Oh, God. Please." She ran her arm across her face. "I'm sorry you went through all that for me. Thank you for what you did."

"What name do you go by?"

"Dorit. My grandmother's. And you?"

"Well…They never said I had to use a different name."

"Their mistake. Use one. The Gestapo enjoys hunting down our families."

"At least the Gestapo didn't get a chance with you."

"Thanks to all of you. The soldiers took turns slapping us around through the night. They punched my friend until he passed out. I don't want to think about what the Gestapo planned to do."

"You don't have to, now." Tove stood with considerable effort. "I'm going to find you a walking stick so we can keep moving. I don't really know which way to go, but if we can avoid walking in circles, we might get lucky."

"We mustn't use the road you took," Dorit said when they started off, fumbling through the woods. "I imagine your group came from the western shore. We came from the inland direction two nights ago, and that would be better—if we can find it."

"Looks clear up ahead, but we should keep hidden."

Dorit stopped to rest again. "Yes, I think…If that's the way we came, there is a farm several miles from here, a *friendly* one."

Tove urged her to keep moving. "We must go. Daylight's coming." Despite their aches and pains, she knew finding refuge soon was critical and that Dorit's wound was working against them. No longer limping, Dorit leaned heavily on her staff, dragged her leg along, and Tove worried about her stamina. Leaving her behind was not an option.

She prayed Dorit's recollection of the forest road was correct, and as they kept to the trees along the route, she clung to the hope that the friendly farmhouse would soon appear.

They are Resistance sympathizers, according to Dorit, so will they take us in? The Gestapo certainly will arrive and search the place. Should I be going in the direction I arrived? My Jutland camp is a boat ride away, at the very least.

Copenhagen would be closer.

"Mila says I can rent the space above her shop." Jonna finished drying the supper dishes and turned to Hedda and Elin at the table. "I should have enough money by next month, after Christmas, that is."

She couldn't tell if they were happy or sad about her news, but figured they would appreciate having their home to themselves again. As a houseguest for nearly three months, she'd imposed enough. Personally, Jonna saw independence as the lone achievable goal in her new, foreign life, no matter how temporary, and she looked forward to it earnestly. Looking forward to *anything* helped her cope.

"You've done so well," Hedda said, "learning from Mila and assisting our doctor."

"But you'll miss us," Elin added, "and Mama's cooking."

Jonna conceded with a smile. "No doubt about it."

Hedda set down her teacup and shook a finger at her. "Be careful not to overdo yourself, Jonna. You are a hardworking young woman, so thoughtful, and I can imagine you 'helping' Mila by doing extra work. Your living upstairs like that will be convenient for her."

"Well, thank you for that, but I must keep busy."

"You are always busy," Elin said. She gestured to the front door. "Look, now, you will visit the dock? As you do every night?"

Hedda reached for Jonna's hand and tugged her to a chair. "Sit. You hold such a torch for your Tove, a torch as bright as Drogden itself, we know."

"A boat is bound to arrive with—"

"Yes," Hedda interrupted, "and a messenger will come if you are not there. We are only a little walk from the boats. It is winter, Jonna, and tonight it rains hard, not good for standing at the water, waiting and wishing."

Jonna really couldn't argue, but not going to the docks felt like admitting defeat, like she'd given up hoping. At least the sight of Drogden each night kept her flickering spirit alive. Tove had to be out there thinking the same way.

They passed the evening hours planning Jonna's apartment, which household items and pieces of furniture would be needed and where to acquire them, and how to decorate for the upcoming Christmas holiday.

Elin scoured through boxes of decorations, and Jonna struggled to pay attention to the items both mother and daughter detailed for her. The concept of Christmas without Tove, without Papa, simply left her feeling cold and alone. She forced smiles as various handmade trinkets were displayed on the table and absorbed as much as she could of the duo's genuine delight.

Elin's enthusiasm carried all the way through to bedtime, and, as she and Jonna settled in for the night, she propped herself on an elbow to watch Jonna scribble in her journal.

"Are you writing things about tonight? You should, you know, just so you don't forget."

"A few things, yes."

"I'm glad you're not moving until after Christmas, Jonna. I'm excited that you'll be with us."

"And I'm thankful for that. It means a lot, especially this Christmas."

"And I'm sorry you can't tell Tove about everything, like your apartment."

Jonna looked up, having just written that exact sentiment. "She'd be happy for me, but…"

"But what?"

"Well, a tiny Swedish flat is far from what we once dreamed."

Now, Elin sat up, cross-legged and eager to hear more. "Which was?"

"A cottage by the sea."

"Ahhh. I thought you might say Drogden, considering how much you miss living and working there."

"Oh, we would love that, if it were possible, but *women*?" She shook her head. "The Lighthouse Service would never agree, even though Tove insists I should succeed my father." The memory of Tove's fervent expression, that resolve on her noble face almost made Jonna sigh.

"Well, I'm with Tove." Elin flopped onto her back, then peeked at Jonna. "I think she loves you very much."

CHAPTER TWENTY

Copenhagen, Denmark

From a fourth-floor rooftop in Copenhagen, Tove defied the biting December wind and inhaled the salty air off the Oresund Strait. The Drogden Lighthouse was hardly visible from this distance, but flashes of its beacon filled Tove's heart with the warmth of a summer day.

Finally.

At this very late hour, she knew Jonna wouldn't be out there, looking back from the far shore, but connecting with Drogden felt like meeting her halfway. It had taken nearly three months of longing, life-threatening adventures, and hours of walking to get here, and had been worth the effort.

"Hans! Hey!" A comrade yanked Tove's sleeve. "Hans, stop daydreaming. Let's go."

She turned and followed her new associates into the stairwell and down to the street. She didn't object last week when they named her Hans, but the tag was hard to get used to. These newfound allies were from a different Resistance cell in the city, and she'd been surprised to sense that her reputation had preceded her. She had only needed to say "Drogden" to the leader to be absorbed into the ranks and immediately assigned one of the Resistance's most critical missions of the entire war.

Hers was one of two teams charged with destroying Copenhagen's main train depot. If all went as planned, the synchronized effort from east and west would leave massive craters along the tracks and a mountain of rubble on the building's foundation. Tove had carried explosives before, but this quantity demanded extra caution.

She tried to picture the sight of them from above, loaded with more necessities than weapons, darting from shadow to shadow through the alleys. She was no less an alley rat, silent and nimble, dark and vague. Her hair had grown darker and longer since her days aboard the *Engel*, and she wore it tied back, along with a black knit cap stretched down over her whole head. Like her comrades, she'd been supplied a thick canvas jacket, a military castoff as black as her trousers.

Huddled across the street from the depot, they eyed the wire fencing they would have to breach once the signal came. Thankfully, idle boxcars still sat exactly where they had been mapped and would provide cover once inside the rail yard. Soldiers would fire at anything that moved.

A muffled "boom" echoed within the depot and the team shot forward, snipped holes in the fencing, and scrambled through. They scattered to assigned positions, hid behind and between the box cars, then moved out to predetermined spots.

On open terrain, Tove flopped onto the tracks, reached over her shoulder, and pulled gear from her backpack. Trying not to fumble, she stretched fuse cords from bundles of dynamite sticks and set successive bundles along the track, taking their cords with her as she dragged herself along the rail. There was no time to check on the status of her mates.

No more than two minutes passed, she thought, and now the air filled with angry commands and gunfire.

Bullets pinged off the steel rails, plunged into the ground and the wooden ties. A distant storm of boots crunching in gravel began.

Tove shrugged out of her pack just as it was nicked by rifle fire and she rolled off the track, the long fuse cords twisted together in her fist. She tried not to hear, not to care about the comrades yelping in pain. Only igniting the fuses mattered. She hurried to flick a cigarette lighter to life, dropped it, then blinked when a bullet kicked dirt into her face.

Finally lit, the bundle of fuse cords sizzled away from her, and she rolled again, several times. A comrade lay just yards away, but Tove recognized the vacant death stare and knew she could not help her. The sounds of running boots, cursing, gunfire increased.

She darted for the nearest box car, dove beneath it as a series of explosions at the depot shook the ground.

"Come on!" she said to her work sizzling along the rails. "Now!"

Bullets hammered her box car and wood splintered everywhere.

She crawled to the opposite side and emerged face-to-face with the tall wire fence. With no cutters to make a hole through it, she climbed the box car wall, praying she could jump far enough.

Two familiar voices sounded from the street, shouting desperately for her to hurry.

Stooping on the car roof, Tove took a heavy breath, backed up several steps for some propulsion, and leaped for the fence.

Just seconds apart, her bundles of dynamite exploded in violent, ear-shattering eruptions. Caught in midair, Tove felt the slam of percussion waves—and then bullets. Knife-like fire sliced through her ribs, bored into her thigh, and then shattered her shoulder. Battered into a tumbling heap, she heard her own screams as she landed atop her comrades beyond the fence.

Jonna carried a basket of Hedda's confections into the orphanage on Christmas morning and was nearly overrun by excited children. These Jewish orphans might not celebrate this holiday, she mused, but that was no reason to deny them such treats. And bringing smiles to their faces brought a smile to hers.

Having exchanged gifts with Hedda and Elin earlier, and spoiled herself at Hedda's fabulous breakfast, Jonna couldn't sit by the tree with them for very long, fondly reminiscing about happy holidays. Hedda and Elin had lost a husband and father and certainly empathized with Jonna's loss, but their life adjustments just brought the instability of her life to the fore. Papa was gone but the love of her life was not.

Not really, right?

Despite the lack of communication with Tove, she refused to think otherwise…despite the news of the Resistance's heightened unrest at home, despite the not knowing. This holiday time of togetherness and goodwill made it difficult to hope.

Here, surrounded by delighted young spirits, Jonna let the happiness of the moment soothe her soul. There was no escaping the joy she'd brought to the orphanage today.

"Ah, Jonna! A blessed day for you today, dear girl."

She looked up from sorting treats on the table to find Rabbi Speiser approaching. A crinkly smile brightened his usually somber demeanor.

"So good to see you," she said and gestured to the delicious display. "Please, help yourself to Hedda's magic—before these imps make it all disappear."

Bent over the table, Speiser took his time inspecting and choosing. "This one." He munched into a cookie, eyes closed as he savored the taste.

"I haven't seen you around lately, Rabbi. I bet you're working too hard."

"Very busy in the villages to our north. We'll be receiving a few additions to our little family here soon."

"*More* children?"

He nodded as he took another cookie. "I'm afraid so. I'm dismayed to report that our neighbors are overflowing with little ones and need to make room, relocate some of the others. I offered what space we have left."

Jonna couldn't imagine this facility accommodating many more. They would have to be the last of the transfers to Strandhem. "Do you know how many? And when?"

"Don't know when," he said, "but I think there will be a girl and boy who are ten years old and another boy who is thirteen."

Automatically, Jonna considered Edvin and whether a new friend of thirteen would help his spirit.

"Oh," Speiser said, waving a hand. "Almost forgot I have a little something here that just might be for you." He drew a small, folded card from inside his jacket. "This was passed to me late yesterday as I left that village."

Firmly creased multiple times and coated with white paraffin, it fit easily in Jonna's palm. "Someone gave this to you?"

"Didn't know the man but he looked to be a farmer."

She turned the folded card over, saw no markings anywhere. "How could he tell it was for me?"

"He told me a fisherman put it in his hand. Apparently, the fisherman was simply instructed to get it to Sweden, and to just say the word 'Drogden.' Of course, hearing that, I immediately thought of you. I guess the farmer did, too, because everyone knows you're in Strandhem now. Rather intriguing, wouldn't you say? Of course, it *could* only mean something special to fishermen, but still…"

Or to me.

Jonna's heart jumped at the thought of a message from Tove. Her hands trembled and she wondered if she looked as breathless and dazed as she felt. Privacy. She needed privacy right now. She scanned the frolicking atmosphere around her, seeking a way out.

"Rabbi, could I ask a favor, please? Would you mind keeping an eye on all this for just a moment?"

"Oh, not at all."

"Thank you!" Clutching the card to her chest, Jonna grabbed the shawl Hedda had gifted her that morning and rushed outside.

Rounding the building, she swung the shawl over her shoulders and backhanded welling tears from her eyes. Finally, braced against the wall, she exhaled to steady herself and stared into her palm. The card couldn't measure more than two inches square, she thought, folded so often, so deliberately.

Please.

She cracked the wax and carefully unfolded each flap until the card reached its full size, similar to a post card. Hardly breathing, she eyed the gray lettering of a blunt pencil, and realized it was upside down. She blurted a sigh, impatient as she righted it, and bit her lip as she read:

Thoughts of you remain constant, bright, and comforting. Praying you are well, as am I. Remember that, together, we stand safe and strong. Never lose sight. Christmas is only a few weeks away, so let's welcome it with a shared hope and light for our future. You will always be the beautiful keeper of my heart. I love you.

Jonna spun to the wall and cried.

CHAPTER TWENTY-ONE

Strandhem, Sweden

Jonna stood back with hands on her hips, surveying the orphans' rearranged sleeping quarters. Bunk beds smelled of freshly milled pine and were sure to be claimed by everyone at once, regardless of age. The newcomers were due tomorrow, and the orphanage was abuzz.

"Jonna, I can't thank you enough for spending your free day here, *all* day and into the night."

Birta's satisfied smile somehow still beamed brightly, despite her bedraggled condition. It had been a strenuous day of tending the children while cleaning the place, not to mention assisting the volunteer carpenters.

"As long as Felix shows up on time," Jonna said, "I suppose we could wrap this up."

"This would be the perfect time, too, while everyone is occupied and content, all fed and scrubbed for bed." Birta shook her head as she collected her purse and coat. "That Felix. I wish my grandfather had been as much fun at his age. Imagine coping with six children at sixty-five years old?"

"Soon to be nine children, bless him. I know working here is good for him, being alone in the world, but... He's a special man to come here every night." Jonna marveled at his stamina.

"Attention! Attention, everyone! I'm here!" With a fluffy beard blanketing his chest like a bib, Felix filled the opened doorway with his huge bulk and the room with effervescent energy. Serenity of the past half hour vanished like air from a balloon.

Jonna shared a grin with Birta as children gathered around him, hopping, shouting, and clamoring for his attention.

"Hello, my young ones!" he bellowed down to them, "How are we tonight?"

"We are all well!" Birta had to yell over the din. "We *were* all quiet, not long for bed."

"Bah! Bedtime in a bit." Felix strode in, the two littlest children attached to his legs.

"That's our cue," Birta said, elbowing Jonna. "Good night, everyone! See you in the morning. Be good for Felix, now, and remember, new friends are coming tomorrow!"

The children cheered at the reminder as Jonna and Birta escaped out into the winter night.

They parted ways in the center of town and Jonna entered the back door of the seamstress shop, glad to be out of the cold. Her rooms upstairs held residual heat from the shop's coal stove, but the warmth didn't last long.

By the light of her little table lamp, she turned on the hot plate to heat water for tea and assessed last night's cheese and bread still suitable for a repeat supper.

All this was a far cry from Hedda's toasty kitchen, homemade meals, and entertaining conversation. But it was hers, and nobly earned. The hand-me-down furnishings from friends touched her deeply, and, topping it all was the view from her one meager window: Drogden's beacon flickered through the pines across the street.

Look where I am after three long months. How in the world...?

With a glance at the folded note on the table, Jonna fixed herself a mug of tea and picked at her plate of food. She would read Tove's words again, just as she had each morning, each evening since it arrived. Christmas Day. How appropriate for such a miraculous gift.

She toed off her shoes and placed her stockinged feet over the heating grate beneath the table as she ate. The warmth tingled up her legs and she slipped into the sweater she kept on the back of the chair. The quiet felt at once cavernous and confining, and she still wasn't sure what to do with or about it. *Wouldn't a radio be fine? Will I be here long enough to afford one?*

She knew that depended on the war, maybe on the success of the Resistance, which reportedly had been wreaking havoc of late. And that, like so many things these days, brought her concern back to Tove. *Are you involved? Please remember you promised not to do dangerous things.*

She unfolded the card again to see the words, to picture Tove's strong, weathered hand drawing the letters. How careful Tove had been, not to write their names or mention locations or happenings. The message was pointed and sparse but so heartfelt. If only a reply were possible.

She took her journal from the table drawer and began an entry.

Enjoying orphanage work. We're ready for the three additions tomorrow. Amazing, these villagers. Another visitor today, an American this time, asking about the adoption process. We all hope the older children won't be passed over, and tomorrow we will have three more to worry about.

Their plight steers my focus from this horrible separation from Tove. Missing her could drive me mad. Maybe I should look for new work that will give me more time at the orphanage. I should contribute as much as I can to the cause. Plus, helping them helps me.

Jonna tucked Tove's note inside the journal and put the book back in the drawer. Wandering into the chilly bedroom, she wrapped her arms around herself to spare a moment at the window. The reliable light flashed from the sea.

"I still see you."

Half the town must have turned out to welcome the newcomers because Jonna could hear the ruckus as she approached the door.

She entered to a wall of music blaring from the radio, excited children playing games, and decorations now sagging off the walls and ceiling. Apparently, it was still a busy day.

"Here she is!" Little Peder raced across the room and hugged Jonna's legs. "Come on!" he said, pulling her after him. "Come say hi."

Jonna waded into the crowd and Elin appeared, offering a cup of punch. They jumped aside as Felix lumbered by with the tiniest orphan under his arm and a youngster on his shoulders.

"He's been giving rides all evening," Elin said.

"That boy is Simon," Peder told Jonna, pointing to the child eating cake. "Teresa says he hasn't talked much."

"Maybe because he's busy eating," Elin said. "He already looks well fed. That shirt hardly fits him."

"Did the clothes we made arrive?" Jonna asked, hoping the extra work she and Mila put toward donations had been brought from the shop.

Birta appeared beside Jonna. "Indeed. We sorted them and put a pile on each child's bed."

Jonna nodded toward Simon, who now had cookies in each hand. "We can make alterations if they don't fit."

"And those two are talking now," Elin injected, directing their attention to Edvin and the oldest newcomer. "His name is Adam. It's taken them a couple of hours, but they're warming up to each other."

"Excellent, isn't it?" Birta asked Jonna. "The last newcomer is over there. Well, she's behind Hedda and those women from the church."

When one of the women turned aside, the girl and Jonna spotted each other simultaneously.

"Jonna!" Eyes wide, mouth agape, the youngster bolted across the room.

"Naysa!" Jonna blinked back tears, equally stunned to see the little girl she remembered from Drogden racing toward her. "I can't believe it's you!"

"You're here! You're here!" Naysa exclaimed, looking up from their hug. "I'm so happy!"

Jonna crouched to her level. "I am, too. You look well. Maybe a bit thin in these cheeks, but..." She poked her cheek playfully.

"I-I never thought I'd see—" Naysa dropped her head and sniffed. She wiped her eyes with her sleeve. "Thank you for remembering me."

Jonna took her by the shoulders. "My God, Naysa. You're a treasure! How could I not? No tears, okay?"

Naysa rubbed her eyes. "Tove's here too, isn't she?" She scanned the crowd. "I don't see her. Where is she?"

"No, I'm afraid she isn't."

"Why not?"

Jonna cleared her throat. "Well...That's a story for another time."

"But why?" Naysa's insistence stopped abruptly. "Oh no! Did she die?" Tears began immediately. "Please say she didn't die! Please!"

Jonna cupped the wet cheeks. "No, no, honey. She didn't die." She steered Naysa to a quieter spot in the room and wiped the tears with a napkin. "Calm yourself now. Please don't worry. Tove is needed back home, that's all."

"But, Jonna, she belongs with you where it's safe."

"All Danish men and woman have rallied to fight for our country. Fishermen, teachers, grocers, priests, entire families... everyone. Tove has valuable skills to lend, to do her part."

"So...so why did you come here without her?"

Jonna tenderly stroked back some of Naysa's mussed hair. "The Gestapo...Well, they believe my papa and I were spying on the Nazis at Drogden, so—"

"Did they kill your papa?"

"Yes, they did, and were coming for me, next."

"Coming for you like they were coming for me?"

"Exactly. And we are so grateful for those who brought us here, saved us, and for those who fight such evil. We wish them well with all our hearts—especially Tove." She wiped Naysa's last tear and tipped her chin up. "Now, *you* are right here, safe and sound, and have all these new friends by your side."

Naysa threw herself back into Jonna's arms. "Every day I wished to go back, just to see you and Tove, everyone I knew. I wished so hard not to be an orphan."

"Look at me." Jonna held her out at arm's length again. "I am an orphan, too. I understand. See these children here? They are just like us. We all share something special, like a family does. A new family and an important one. You mustn't let loneliness take charge of you."

Naysa nodded toward her feet. "I know, but…"

"Oh, it's hard. Believe me, I feel it, too, and so do they." Naysa glanced around at the other children. "So, who better to help build new memories? All of us together, we can do this. We're not alone. *You* aren't alone."

"Everything okay here?" Elin offered Naysa a cookie.

"Just a private moment between old friends," Jonna said and winked at Naysa.

"Good to hear. Naysa, why don't you show Jonna which bunk bed you chose and your new clothes? Did you know that Jonna helped make them?"

"You did?" Naysa stared at Jonna, floored.

"I did," Jonna stated, tilting her nose up, "and helped build your bed as well. After this busy day, I bet you can't wait to use it."

"I already tested it, the top bunk."

Jonna chuckled at that. Still the same fearless little girl at heart. "And what did you think?"

"I like it. It's soft, comfortable. And it's warm up there."

"My bed's nice, too, Naysa," Simon said from her shoulder.

"This is Simon," Naysa told Jonna. "And, Simon, this is my friend Jonna. She worked at Drogden and I used to visit her there."

"At the lighthouse?" The concept obviously excited him. "Jonna, will you and Naysa tell us Drogden stories?"

"We can do that, can't we?" She looked to Naysa and back to Simon. "I think we have some really good ones to share. You'll see."

❖

"I need to get back to Copenhagen, dammit." Tove groused at the pillow stuffed at her back, tired of being bedridden and propped onto her good side. "There's no chance of getting word to Jonna from this god-forsaken place."

The short, stocky woman turned from the tray of medical supplies and slouched onto a hip. "Will you stop complaining? Mountains were moved to get you back here, Hans. In fact," she stepped closer and shook her finger at Tove, "you're lucky just to be above ground, shot to pieces like you were. And all we hear from you is bitching?"

Tove frowned toward the farmhouse window. She didn't like seeing the truth—or the irritation—in the woman's face. Kirsten was the gruff-and-tough sort, better suited to active missions than doctoring, but she was Tove's favorite nurse of those recruited by the Resistance because she never sugar-coated anything. Patience, however, had never been Tove's strong suit. Jonna would have agreed.

"But what good am I here?" she asked, daring to look back.

"Right now, you're not good for anything anywhere."

"But it's been almost a month, right?"

"Five *glorious* weeks."

"God. I could have sent something to her by now if I was in—"

"How many times are you going to whine about this? If you were still in Copenhagen, they'd have to bounce you from one hiding place to the next and wouldn't you heal fast that way?" Shaking her head, she busied herself preparing a fresh wrap for Tove's shoulder. "Besides, there just happens to be *three* of us nurses in this camp right now. Be grateful you arrived at such a moment because two were scheduled to leave yesterday. Someday, we *all* hope you'll count your blessings."

"Aw, I really do," Tove said on a sigh. "I appreciate all of you, Kirsten. I do, honestly. It's just…"

She returned to the view outside. Another snowy day, somehow back again in remote Jutland. During her "therapy walk" this morning, she'd seen the heavy accumulation from yesterday, the pair of faithful old trucks sidelined behind the barn. The sight made her miss the adventure of sailing through the white stuff, miss how Jonna delighted in throwing it.

"How long since you've seen her?"

The compassionate tone caught Tove by surprise. "October."

"I suppose there's been no communication."

"I sent a note, as cryptic as I could write it, sometime in the middle of December but who knows if it even made it to Sweden."

"But if it did?" Armed with fresh bandages, Kirsten came to the bedside. "Imagine her frustration, not being able to answer you."

"It's hell, not knowing how she's doing over there."

"All reports say everyone is doing well. Hard not to, compared to what life is like for Jews here now…if there are any left."

"She's not Jewish. Just wanted."

"Ah. She has something the Gestapo values."

"She worked Drogden Light."

Kirsten paused. "I remember that tragedy. Everyone heard of it. The Gestapo ran wild, hunting for those associated with the place."

"She made it out."

"I'm sure she's just as desperate to learn about you."

"How much longer before I get out of here?"

Kirsten chortled as she unwrapped Tove's sling. "No time soon, and you're crazy if you think you can make it to Sweden. You were in fine shape before all this, strong and muscular from whatever work you did, but your body has suffered badly."

"But these weeks here must have done *some* good."

"Look. Yes, it's good you are taking steps now, but your leg is very weak. Growing back tissue and muscle takes time. Also, these four broken ribs will steal your breath with every move you make. And ribs heal slowly. But most of all, this shoulder may never be a work of art. To have all the pieces back together, good as new, requires serious care. The doctor told you to expect lots of rehabilitation, lots of hard work."

Tove couldn't argue with that assessment. Restricted breathing and just one good arm and leg amounted to serious loss. They sapped the fire from a Resistance fighter and salt from a sailor's blood. Hard to accept, spelled out like that, and Tove regretted having forced the issue. She had to be patient, but that was a tall order. Getting another note to Jonna, once she researched the means, would have to see her through this mess.

"Do you know of any transport leaving for a city connection?"

Now, Kirsten laughed outright. "I know your eyesight is clear, but I do wonder about your brain." She finished tying the new sling and stepped back. "The sleigh is bound to go into the village eventually, and that's as close to a city as we'll get. Did you forget where you are? Copenhagen is not just over the next hill, Hans."

"I need to pass along another note. That farmer who supplies us, he passed my note along in December. Maybe he'll take another. When is he coming again?"

"I don't have that information, but I can tell you that the doctor sent a messenger off on foot with an urgent request for medical supplies. With five patients here now, we're stretching what little we have, but because of all the snow and with more on the way…"

"Well, then, he might have some idea of when a delivery could come. Will I see him tonight?"

"After the supper meal, yes." She nodded with satisfaction as she assessed the wrap around Tove's chest and the bullet wound beneath it. "Listen, Hans. Stop deluding yourself. I doubt the doctor expects a quick response, even for his medical request. For now, the snow's put a halt to everything. So…A week? Maybe more? Who knows?"

Weeks, Tove thought, before she'd have a chance to send something. *Time to focus on what to write.*

"Could you hand me the pencil and paper, please?"

Pressing onto the mattress with her good hand, she struggled to inch back cautiously into a more upright position. The task was exhausting, but she eventually settled against a pillow and tried to catch her breath. A sharp cough caught her by surprise, and pain lanced through her midsection. She clamped her good arm around her chest and blinked up at Kirsten through watery eyes.

"Please let there be magic in those pills you've got."

"All that we can offer," Kirsten said, medication in her palm, water glass at the ready. "You're due for them, anyway."

"They don't help much." Tove swallowed the two tablets.

"You'd notice the difference without them. Trust me." She set paper and pencil on Tove's lap and patted her head. "Now behave. No plotting your escape."

CHAPTER TWENTY-TWO

Strandhem, Sweden

"I like coming up here, even if it is cold."

Jonna studied Naysa's dreamy gaze at the Oresund and wondered what else rambled through the girl's mind, if these little excursions to the promontory helped or hindered that longing for home. Jonna had needed months of this view before hope and comfort eased the heartache. She smiled, thinking Naysa might follow the same course.

"Days like this," Jonna said, scanning the sunny sky, "you can almost feel spring trying to push winter aside." She sat on the blanket beside Naysa and watched her take a huge bite of her bread-and-jam snack. "Can you imagine places in the world where it's never cold?"

"I'd swim every day."

"Every day and night."

"Did you ever swim at night at the lighthouse?"

"Never. That would have been scary. Hardly during the day, either. Those waves crashing against us were usually too rough."

"Well, I remember sitting on the steps with Tove, letting the waves splash our feet."

Jonna chuckled at the memory. "You keep that a secret between you two. She wasn't supposed to take any of you children down those steps."

"Did she get in trouble?"

Jonna bumped her shoulder. "Nothing she couldn't talk her way out of."

"Nothing's too dangerous for Tove. She's brave." Naysa chomped into her bread and turned to Jonna as she chewed. "I know you miss her. I wish we knew how she was doing, too."

"We have to believe, don't we?" Jonna tried to focus on her own bread, but a myriad of unwelcome images threatened her self-control. "Just keep sending her happy thoughts, wishes for courage and safety."

Naysa gestured toward the sea. "I heard that big gun again last night, out there at Drogden."

"The Nazis are always trying to stop Allied planes from flying over."

"Every day I pray things will get better, Jonna. I mean, I know bad people are out there doing bad things, but people like Tove are out there, too, making them stop. I *do* believe."

Jonna touched Naysa's chin fondly. "You are a smart girl, you know, and very brave. Thank you for making me smile."

Naysa blushed and took another bite. "At first, I wasn't brave, you know. I cried all the time, until I used up all my tears. Didn't you?"

"I did."

"But now, I only cry when I think about Mother and Father, what the Germans probably did to them."

"Do you cry about being alone?"

"Once in a while, but I believe a new family will want me someday if I'm good. We were told that right away at the orphanage and Rabbi Speiser said it here. I know Mother and Father are watching from Heaven, too, so I always try to be good."

Such a pragmatic outlook from a remarkable ten-year-old. Assurances about their future were standard practice, but these older orphans faced difficult odds. Speiser had said that, too. Only last week, two of their youngest charges were adopted while inquiries about twelve-year-old Tilde were abandoned.

Even though it meant risking crushing disappointment, Jonna saw no choice but to reinforce Naysa's indomitable spirit.

"If *I* could pick a new place to live," she pondered aloud, "I think…maybe…Spain."

"Spain? Why Spain?"

"It's warm there and I could swim every day."

Naysa perked up at the topic. "I'd pick…Ireland. It's so pretty in our schoolbooks and they have lots of sheep."

"Oh, you like sheep, do you?"

"I do. And the ocean. Ireland has plenty of that."

"Because it's an island."

"And warmer than here. But not as warm as Florida, so maybe I'll go there."

"Florida? Where did that come from? You would like to live in America?"

"I think so. Is that too far?"

"Well, it's not on this continent."

"Hm. I might still like it."

Jonna leaned against her side. "And leave Drogden behind?"

"Oh, you're right." Her gaze locked onto Jonna with purpose. "We need to choose closer places."

Jonna sent her a frown, agreeing half-heartedly. "You know." She pointed toward Drogden. "I see Papa every time I see that beacon."

"And Tove, too?"

"Without fail. Just as I dream she sees me from her shore."

"It's good that the light can be seen from both sides of the strait, isn't it? Day or night, it's always there for us." Naysa stared toward the lighthouse until it blinked. "It's like we're all still holding hands."

Beautiful July afternoons were meant for beautiful thoughts and pleasantries, not for dwelling on war. Granted, Tove took satisfaction in the news of the Allied advance toward Paris, but always wound up dreaming of being with Jonna somewhere very far away. It was comforting to imagine Jonna and her new friends had safe, easy access to a radio and the latest war news, maybe even the Resistance's successes in Copenhagen.

Around her in the low-slung cool of the tavern, townspeople voiced excited opinions and itched for the British to bear down on the Nazi fatherland. They marveled at the rumblings of a Polish uprising and prayed the Russians would help that effort. And oh, how they raved about the heightened sabotage in Copenhagen that was driving the Nazis insane.

Tove finished her tankard of ale, relishing the break before tomorrow's lineup of meetings. Although she preferred being a hands-on mission participant, her cane and compromised shoulder had long since reassigned her to behind-the-scenes work. Administering counterfeit papers kept her plenty busy, and leading pistol drills and seamanship lessons provided some spice to daily life, but she looked forward to the return of her physical abilities, working aboard the *Engel*, and the freedom to enjoy both.

For now, however, the upcoming mission was her priority, regardless of who was sent into action. During the past month, she and a sizeable team had filtered into this obscure fishing hamlet of cottages and cobbled streets because of its proximity to Copenhagen. Only a solitary Nazi patrol rolled through every other day simply to be a nuisance, a reminder of who was in charge. The soldiers routinely stomped along the docks, helped themselves to shop merchandise, and barked at townspeople before driving off. Life was good, all things considered.

Tove tried to relax, watching villagers shuffle past on their errands. Horse-drawn carts clattered by the tavern's opened door, and perfumed summer air occasionally wafted in from flowery window boxes. The setting teased her to recollect perfect days and dream of more, days she'd hoped to be spending with Jonna by now.

There would be no appreciating the view from the Copenhagen docks during this mission, no chance to see Drogden. Other saboteurs with life-and-death things to worry about would take her place. The danger of initiating a daylight uprising in the heart of the city was equaled only by that of destroying the huge telephone building after sunset.

Gaiety among several comrades abruptly distracted her. Chattering brightly, they maneuvered to her table and seated themselves around her. Tankards thumped onto the rough wood surface, and one was pushed toward her.

"Here," said Liva, a fresh-faced young blonde, a newcomer to Tove's shooting class. "Too hot a day for you to run dry."

"Everyone's enjoying this free afternoon, I see." She had to grin at the carefree expressions, their enthusiasm, but knew they barely had the skills necessary for what was to come. All three were younger than twenty-one and would be among the two dozen comrades sent into action in just a few days.

"So, what was our instructor dreaming about?" Liva asked.

"An end to our nightmare, I suppose."

Rakkel, an outspoken redhead and one of Tove's best students, raised her drink. "Can't blame you for that." She winked before taking a sip.

"You all should try the kottfarslimpa before we leave here," Tove said. "Highly recommended." The loaf of ground beef and sausage would provide hearty, much needed sustenance. "Supplies are dwindling here, so eat while you can. Be mindful of keeping your strength up."

"If I eat much more in this village, I'll have to add holes to my belt." Dag ran a palm over his substantial stomach and Tove figured he'd already sampled more than his share. "Last night," he went on, sighing, "the kroppkakor, those balls of pork, onion and potato? In cream? Ohhh."

"Rationing is catching up to these isolated villages," she reminded them, "so we're lucky to get such meals."

"Dag's been lucky, all right," Liva said. "He tried to dance it off, last night back at the barn."

Tove raised an eyebrow at him. "I heard a reprimand was issued."

Dag averted his eyes. "The radio was too loud."

"There were only a few minutes of it," Rakkel said, "but we should have known better."

Liva nudged Tove's arm. "There is dancing here tonight. They say some musicians usually stop by and people dance along. Do you dance?"

Rakkel leaned toward Liva across the table. "If you haven't noticed her cane by now, you should disqualify yourself."

Now, Liva looked as crestfallen as Dag.

Tove had to laugh. "I try to rely on it less each day, but… Maybe in a few months."

"Hey," Dag pointed to a comrade hurrying into the tavern. "Jesper's out of breath."

Rakkel left them and spoke briefly with the young man in the doorway before sending him on his way. She strode back to their table and leaned on her palms.

"The damn patrol is on the next street," she reported in a hush.

"But Nazis aren't due till tomorrow." Dag looked to Tove as if she had more accurate information.

"Apparently not," she told him. "Let's move. I'd rather we split up or mingle."

They stood in unison and Tove wound her way between tables toward the back door, cursing the cane that slowed her progress. She saw Liva claim a space along the bar and Dag exit the front just before a Nazi lieutenant entered. Rakkel turned with a tankard in each hand, as if to offer him an ale.

Hearing the tavern fall silent, Tove eased the back door open. A soldier blocked her path, hefted his rifle to his hip.

"Back up." His crisp command was loud enough for everyone behind her to hear.

"No need to leave on our account, fräulein," the lieutenant called from the middle of the room. He noticed the cane as Tove turned. "You wouldn't make us chase you, now, would you?" he asked with a laugh. "Most inhospitable." He nodded to the soldier.

Tove felt the rifle press across her back. She was urged forward to within spitting distance of the lieutenant.

"It's clear that old age hasn't befallen you," he said, making a point to survey her entire frame. "So why the cane? To me you appear able-bodied."

"An accident, but the leg is almost healed."

"What kind of 'accident'?"

"Tractor. I was run over."

"You are a farmer?"

"I am." Anxiety and resentment bubbled in Tove's veins, made her heart pound as she labored to appear honest and duly respectful. But, with her patience pressing from the inside, it was a difficult role to play. This Nazi expected subservience from her, not fearless confidence. He reveled in his authority, and she despised everything about him.

"A *stupid* farmer," he proclaimed. "A typical, stupid Danish farmer." He snickered as he shook his head. "I'm always amazed that Danes manage to grow anything edible."

"German gluttony in our country has proved otherwise, Lieutenant." The words just came out.

He seized her hand and wrenched it over to examine her palm. The bruising twist almost drove Tove to her knees. Pain rocketed up to her bad shoulder and the fragile wound flared. She swallowed hard and gritted her teeth.

She leaned heavily on her cane as he searched her palm for hard-earned callouses or dirt or some proof. She knew her callouses had faded since her days on the *Engel*, but the scars of rough work still remained.

He thrust her hand down. "How brazen of you, fräulein." He snatched away her cane, broke it over his knee, and threw the pieces across the room. "Like so many others, you will learn your place." He slammed his boot heel into Tove's thigh, and she collapsed, writhing in pain. "Stupid Dane."

He strode out with the lone soldier in tow, and patrons and comrades hurried to Tove's aid.

❖

"Visitation days bring life to the orphanage," Birta said as she and Jonna watched the orphans mingle with adults in the churchyard.

"I love seeing the children happy like this. It gives me hope for them."

"All these adults are looking to adopt?"

"Oh, no, but the woman with her arm in a sling? That's Rita, an American pilot. This is her third visit, the second this week. She's especially interested."

"A pilot?" Jonna had never heard of women serving as pilots.

"They have their own unit, she told me, and they shuttle planes for the flyboys. Her husband is one of them, although they haven't seen each other in a while. Some two weeks ago, the Royal Navy plucked her from the sea. She suffered only that broken arm."

"You don't say!"

"I do! Isn't that exciting?"

"Absolutely. I see Peder has taken a liking to her."

"Denmark's most adorable ambassador. But Rita spends most of her time with Tilde and Naysa, the oldest girls, which has me holding my breath. I *do* hope her attention doesn't lead them on."

Jonna observed the interactions curiously as visitor time came to a close. Tilde accepted the book Rita offered, shook her hand, and went to a distant bench to read alone. Naysa accepted her book, glanced inside, and hugged her immediately. Rita even kissed Naysa's cheek before they waved good-bye.

"Well, that was telling," Jonna mused aloud. "Has our American pilot said when she's leaving Sweden?"

"Not exactly, and she may not be allowed to say, but she hinted that both her and her husband's tours of duty will expire soon. I know she can't wait for an upcoming rendezvous."

"Well, I'm sure I'm going to hear all the news any minute now."

Within seconds, Naysa was hurrying toward her at the gate, book held high.

"Jonna! Look what I got!" She opened the book atop the fencepost and pulled out a folded map. "Rita gave this to me." She hurried to unfold a large, atlas-type map. "It's America!"

"Wow. This should keep you busy."

"I know! Now I'll know where everything is. See? Here's Florida. And this is Texas. And—"

"You like Rita a lot."

"I do," Naysa said, eyes glued to the map. "And she likes me. Look! I found Washington, DC. It's so little."

Jonna and Birta exchanged hapless grins.

"There's an hour or so before the supper bell, Naysa," Birta said. "Why don't you and Jonna go for a walk or something on this warm afternoon, enjoy the change of scenery?"

Naysa sighed, laboring to fold the map.

"I want to hear about your day," Jonna said, leading Naysa toward their favorite promontory spot. "Rita visits a lot, doesn't she?"

"This was her third time. She crashed in the ocean, you know. That's how she broke her arm."

"She sounds very adventurous—and very lucky."

"She is. Today, she brought presents for Tilde and me. Tilde doesn't talk much, though. I'm not sure she likes her."

"Why not?"

Naysa shrugged. "Maybe because Rita likes me better."

"Ah. I'm sure Rita tries to be fair, but Tilde is a bit shy. Perhaps she's uncomfortable talking to adults or isn't used to it. Heaven knows, *you've* never had a problem with that."

"Not me. I like talking to people most of the time."

They sat on their usual patch of grass overlooking the Oresund and Jonna inspected Naysa's new book. "This looks full of fun things. *The Many Waters of Florida.*"

"Rita knows I love the ocean and animals. She said they have plenty where she and her husband live. Did I tell you they live in Florida? That's where Miami is." She smoothed the map across her thighs and began tracing the state's long oceanfront. "Here it is."

"So, what's she like?"

"Rita? Oh, she's fun. She's been lots of places. She's even seen real American cowboys."

"What do you like most about her?"

"I don't know. She's pretty." Naysa shrugged and stared out to the sea. "She has a soft voice, and she looks at me when we talk, like we do, like Tove does. And sometimes I think she's a better listener than Mother was."

"Do she and her husband have any children?"

Naysa shook her head. "But she loves being around them. She was a teacher before the war. Her husband likes children too, she said. He sounds rich, but she's really nice so he must be, too."

"I see."

"I hope she still gets to fly when the war's over because she likes it so much." Naysa returned to gazing at the map.

"You don't think she will?"

"Well, she said if they started a family, she would stay home."

"I hope that would make her happy."

"Oh, they're excited to start a family soon."

"Is that all she said about it?"

"Uh-huh. I can write to her anytime I want, you know, and she will write back. She said a little voice told her it was important that we stay in touch." She looked to Jonna. "Do you think an angel told her?"

Jonna's heart skipped. A piece of her felt responsible, somehow, with a curious obligation to guide, even protect. As one orphan to another, she *was* Naysa's sole remaining connection to her heritage and previous life.

She slid an arm around the thin shoulders and squeezed. "An angel? Maybe so, honey."

CHAPTER TWENTY-THREE

Sam hardly noticed the low-level nausea that the medicine wasn't able to drive away on the boat ride out to the lighthouse. She craned her neck hoping to catch a glimpse of Nancy even though they were still much too far away to make out that kind of detail.

She hadn't seen Nancy since the disaster at the multi-club except when they signed the contract and other paperwork with Mrs. Jones. Sam had finally given in to her brother's increasingly urgent and annoying requests for her to fly home and show her face. She'd spent two weeks calming him down and visiting her father.

The water taxi finally pulled up to the dock and Sam wobbled her way out of the boat and onto dry land. Now that she owned a lighthouse, she needed to work on her disembarking skills. How long before she stopped looking like an idiot around boats?

At the top of the stairs, she was greeted by a much more bustling scene than she'd expected. Nancy was there along with the board members, but there were also a fair number of media members and other self-important looking people in suits she didn't recognize. Nancy spotted her and waved her over.

Sam had come straight from the airport and her flight had been delayed so she was late. She'd hoped to talk to Nancy for a few minutes before the hoopla began, but it wasn't meant to be. Things had felt different between them when they'd talked since the incident at the club, and she needed to right that ship. She missed whatever it was that she and Nancy had.

Before she could do more than smile and offer a "hello," someone handed her a hard hat and a shovel. The handle was only half the height she was used to. No sooner did everyone have a hat and shovel, than they were being directed toward a fresh pile of dirt, lined up, and posed.

"This feels like prom, getting posed for pictures with silly props," Nancy whispered to Sam.

"I wouldn't know. I was at a business conference with my father and brother." Sam rolled her eyes.

Nancy leaned on her shovel with one hand and put her other hand on her hip. "Are you serious?"

"Ms. Calhoun, you're out of position." The flustered photography assistant clearly didn't care about Sam's high school days.

"I would come up with a more believable lie if I had a secret to cover up. Now tell me, who was your prom date?" Sam was careful not to draw the ire of the photo assistant although she did turn to get a better view of Nancy.

"Eugene Kazloski. But I spent the evening dancing with his ex-girlfriend, Bianca. Poor guy had a reputation for turning girls gay. Wasn't true, but there were a lot of us who came out after dating him." Nancy pointed Sam back in the proper direction as they faced another round of inspections.

Done with groundbreaking pictures, of which there were many, Sam tried to find a moment alone with Nancy. When she finally spotted her, she was on the far side of the lighthouse, away from the group, looking out over miles of Narragansett Bay.

"You found my hiding spot." Nancy didn't look at her.

Sam stopped and didn't move closer. "Are you hiding from me?"

Nancy turned around, her expression soft. "No, never. I could do without all the politicians crowding our photo ops and tramping around our island, though."

"Is that who all those people are?" Sam looked back over her shoulder. "Rhode Island has a population of about one hundred, right? Why does it need so much government?"

"Smartass. How was your trip? Is your father feeling any better?" She looked genuinely concerned.

"He's still in the hospital. I can't tell if that's something I should worry about or if it's a rich man taking advantage of having an entire hospital wing's staff at his beck and call." Sam felt her jaw tighten. It had been doing that a lot since she left for the West Coast.

"Look, if you pull any of that rich girl crap with me, I'm not sure I can even be friends with you. You've been warned. I come from a family of fishermen. If you've got a hook through your thumb but the only way to get the fish off the hook is rip your thumb in half, that's what you do." Nancy mimed the hook extraction.

"Is this something I have to do to show my devotion? Is it a test or some kind of hazing ritual?" Sam risked taking a step closer.

"It's the final act in all of our family's wedding ceremonies."

Sam froze. What the hell?

"I'm teasing you. It's going to be a long project working together if all this awkward jumpiness continues between us. Can we agree what happened at the club was unfortunate but was only a reminder of what we already knew?" Nancy looked at the ground, not at Sam.

"I'm dying to know what we already knew."

Nancy did look at her this time and raised her eyebrows. "Did you not know that you are you and I am me?"

"Do you have a cipher key or some interpretive device I could borrow?" Sam was floundering. "I wanted to kiss you before the shit wagon with the camera interrupted us. Is that something that 'I' would want? Can still want?"

Suddenly Nancy looked unsure. With an odd sense of relief, Sam thought she might not be the only one on unsteady ground.

"Are you hungry?"

"I am, thank you for asking." Both Nancy and Sam spun around, caught off guard by Mrs. Jones's voice behind them. "Which is why I came over to find you and bid you farewell. Thank you for posing for all those interminable photos. The moment they heard about your project, the politicians circled like vultures. Galskab!"

"I brought a picnic. Would you like to join us?" Nancy pointed to a basket Sam hadn't noticed.

Mrs. Jones's eyes twinkled happily. "Oh no, dear. Time spent overlooking the water is meant for deep conversations on love and life. Two women destined for love don't need an old woman getting in the way."

Sam started to protest the characterization of their relationship but Nancy's sharp elbow to her ribs ended any rebuttal she had planned.

"Thank you, Mrs. Jones. The bay is especially beautiful today." Nancy had been looking out over the water, but her eyes traveled to Sam when she said "beautiful."

Sam felt exposed under Nancy's glance, especially with Mrs. Jones there as witness. What was Nancy playing at? Wasn't the event at the club enough to prove what a liability she was to Nancy? But damn, if her stomach didn't flutter uncontrollably as Nancy's eyes searched her face and scanned her body.

Mrs. Jones clapped once, looking delighted, and headed back the way she'd come.

"Why did you let her think we were falling in love?" Sam helped Nancy spread the blanket and kneeled to unpack the food. Apparently, a picnic was next on her agenda.

"You mean you aren't falling in love with me?" Nancy stopped scooting across the blanket, a pint of pasta salad in one hand.

"I, um." Sam rubbed the back of her neck. What was she supposed to say? "Yes" felt like pandering. "No" was too harsh and maybe not entirely truthful. Yikes, where did that come from?

Nancy didn't let Sam off the hook right away, but finally her serious expression broke and she laughed. "Sam, please don't answer. I'm kidding. Mrs. Jones wanted to think we're falling in love, so let her think that. It doesn't harm anyone. Besides, maybe she knows something we don't. But mostly, I'm hungry and I wanted to have lunch with you. I didn't think she'd argue if I agreed with her."

Sam nodded. The logic was sound even if Mrs. Jones's comment still made her uncomfortable. She didn't have an answer as to why.

"You weren't on social media with all the hot women of the West Coast while you were away. What happened? Were you feeling okay?" Nancy's tone was teasing, but the lightness didn't reach her eyes.

"You happened. I'm sure you aren't interested in hearing any of this after what happened when we were dancing, but you're the most extraordinary woman I've ever met. Why would I want to spend meaningless time with someone else?" Sam busied herself pulling out cutlery and napkins. She felt the need to fill the silence that seemed to stretch between them like a bowstring. "But why are you stalking me on social media? Should I be worried?"

"Damn it, Sam."

Sam looked up, afraid Nancy was upset with her. Nancy did look upset, but not furious. "What can I do—"

"Shut up." Nancy surged forward like a crashing wave, put hands to both sides of Sam's face, and pulled Sam close. "I'll stop if you want me to stop."

Sam was throbbing with anticipation and excitement. *Finally, we're kissing?* "Don't stop."

Their lips came together gently but Sam's insides sizzled with the voltage of an hours-long thunderstorm. She wanted more. She drew Nancy closer. They lost their balance and tumbled together to the blanket. Sam ended up on her back, looking up at Nancy framed by flaming red curls and a cloudless blue sky.

There was no tentativeness to this kiss. Sam was intoxicated by the sweet softness of Nancy's lips. She flicked out her tongue to drink in more and was rewarded when Nancy mirrored her advance.

Nancy leaned down further and deepened the kiss. Sam's stomach clenched and flipped. *God, this woman can kiss.*

Much too quickly for Sam's liking, Nancy slowed their frantic pace and kissed her once, twice, chastely. "I really wish you'd been bad at that." She backed away and sat down, well out of kissing distance.

"Thanks. I think?" Sam sat up, leaning on her elbows. "You are very good, too, but that's not a disappointment to me."

"I didn't say I was disappointed." Nancy looked affronted.

"It was implied. And if my kissing is offensively good, I won't subject you to its awesomeness again. Fear not, I will keep my skills to myself." Sam mocked sealing her lips and tossing the key.

Nancy walked on her knees across the blanket, directly into Sam's personal space. "I think that's an empty threat, McMann."

"It's 'McMann,' now, is it?" Sam knew her voice was trembling. Why did Nancy calling her by her last name make her clit throb?

Nancy moved back a few inches. "Do you mind?" Her smile said she knew full well that Sam didn't mind one bit.

Sam didn't answer. Instead, she pulled Nancy to her and kissed her again. So much for keeping her lips to herself. When they broke the kiss this time, they were both breathing heavily.

"Before we get too carried away, we should talk." Nancy moved away again.

"Uh-oh. Are we about to have the 'it's not you, it's me' talk?" Sam searched Nancy's face for a clue.

Nancy laughed. "Oh no, it's definitely you."

Sam was so caught off guard she didn't react immediately. When she did, she joined in on Nancy's laughter. "Rude."

"No one is ambushing us in clubs to get video of me. I'm not the one stubbornly insisting on inheriting the family business and making myself miserable. Look, Sam, I really like you, a lot, but I don't want to be yet another in a string of women on your arm in the tabloids. And what happens when we finish this project together?" Nancy wrung her hands, looking sad.

The collar on Sam's shirt felt too restrictive suddenly. What was she supposed to say? Nancy would never be just another woman in a lineup of them, but short of making some kind of announcement, how would the paparazzi know that? They would fill in their own blanks without a story provided by Sam or the McManns.

"I have to go home when this is done. I don't have a choice. My brother's already mad enough about time I've taken off."

"This is only a partially self-serving question." Nancy looked pensive. "Why is your brother telling you what to do? I thought it was going to be your company."

Sam nodded. "That's true, but right now it's our father's. Phillip is better with the day-to-day management than I am. I've always been a little jealous about his skills and knowledge in that area." She scooted closer and took Nancy's hand. "I like you a lot, too. I like being with you. I like whisking you off around the world. I really like kissing you. But I can't offer you anything more than what I already have. And after the incident at the club, it's probably even less now. I don't know where that leaves us."

Nancy leaned her head on Sam's shoulder. "It leaves us right where we are. On a beautiful island, overlooking the water, having a picnic. I don't know about the rest. This probably won't shock you, but I like the chance to build a little history in my relationships, too. I've never dated anyone with a timer. I'm not sure I'm built for that."

Sam felt her brow knit. "It doesn't sound very romantic when you put it that way."

"Romantic or not, I like you enough to consider it." Nancy handed Sam a plate and nudged a pint of potato salad her way. "But that can wait for another day. I'm hungry."

Sam piled her plate high and settled next to Nancy. It was good to be back on solid footing with her after the awkwardness of the past few weeks. She tried hard to ignore the feeling that the tectonic plates of her life were rubbing together more aggressively and preparing for a massive quake of change. It had her on edge. If only she knew which direction the change might be coming from.

CHAPTER TWENTY-FOUR

Strandhem, Sweden

Within a couple of weeks, Jonna found herself facing yet another of life's inevitabilities. Rita's husband now accompanied her on visits to the orphanage, much to Naysa's unbridled delight, and it was just a matter of time and red tape before life changed for all of them.

The couple's military discharges were due soon and they often spoke excitedly of finally going home to America.

"I'm convinced they'll submit papers for Naysa any day now."

She watched Hedda glance at Elin at the kitchen table, knowing they expected her to be happy about this development. But Jonna couldn't get past the twinge of emptiness that Naysa's departure would bring.

Of course, I want the best for her. An eleven-year-old orphan being adopted by a caring, well-established couple in America would be a miracle, a blessing. But...

"Naysa must know what's going on," Elin said.

"She grows more hopeful by the day. I've tried to caution her, in case the Lewins are denied, although I can't see why they would be. But I think Naysa is just as convinced as I am that it's going to happen."

Hedda placed her hand over Jonna's. "And she's aware of what she will leave behind?"

"We've talked about it, to a degree. For an eleven-year-old, she has many fond memories but more than her share of bad ones, so I've tried to be careful what I say. She's a smart little girl, though, and seems to be handling things well. She should remember her past, just not dwell on her losses."

"But *you* do."

Jonna met Hedda's knowing, steady gaze. Elin offered a sympathetic smile.

"I suppose I do. It's hard not to, losing someone from home again."

"That's so understandable, dear," Hedda said, "but you have given Naysa so much since she's come here, a brightness in her step, a faith in people's goodness that she might not have found again. She will have a home, a loving family, and heaven knows how much more in America. You've saved that little girl and you should be proud."

Elin tipped forward and whispered, "Tove would be so happy, wouldn't she?"

Jonna's eyes filled. It was true, Tove would be ecstatic. Her benevolence, her big heart had brought Naysa and the other children to Drogden, and the affection Jonna and Tove offered had kept goodwill alive in those innocent souls. "Yes, Tove definitely would be happy."

"So, there." Hedda sat back, smiling. "You are stronger than you think, Jonna. You've shown that to everyone here, to yourself. Now, I imagine the adoption process could be finalized as soon as October, and that may seem sudden, but you'll get through these next few weeks. This is a triumph you should treasure."

"I suppose you're right."

She scooted her chair back from the table and stood with a sigh.

"Are you heading home now to listen to your radio?" Elin's eyes danced at the idea and made Jonna chuckle.

"Eventually. I think I need a little stroll first to help clear my head."

"Big day tomorrow." Elin walked her to the door. "Are you all still going out on the water?"

"We are if Leo's still available. Why don't you join us if you're free?"

"I'd love that! Sure, thank you."

Jonna had to smile as she meandered toward the shops in town. She would probably need the supervisory help for the joyride aboard Leo's boat. She took a deep, cleansing breath against the memories of Tove and herself chasing rambunctious youngsters around Drogden's perimeter.

Those fond memories lingered long after she had settled into bed, and they woke with her the next morning. The sun hadn't been up an hour before she found herself smiling at the waterfront, even earlier than Leo, whose boat still dozed at the dock. *Guess my spirit knows I need this fun day as much as the children do.*

Her timing could not have been better.

At the very end of the pier, Jonna squinted into the growing sunshine just above water. It made spotting Drogden's flicker impossible but that was simply due to Mother Nature's clock. The sound of lapping waves was comforting, as was the rapping of lines on Leo's boat—and the distant sound of an approaching boat.

She shaded her eyes with her hand and found the dark spot advancing on her location along the coast. No local fishermen were due in, all were accounted for, so a delivery of refugees could be at hand.

Two men from the village arrived behind her, and then Rabbi Speiser. *Yes, welcoming more refugees.* She had played this scene before, some eleven months ago, and remembered every detail of every second.

The boat advanced and Jonna's heart caught in her throat. She could recognize the *Engel* in her sleep, but here she was wide awake. *Will I ever run out of tears?*

Breathless at the arrival of a long-lost friend, Jonna watched as the intrepid lighthouse tender cut its engine and drew along the vacant side of the pier. Crewmen Frans and Vidar leapt onto the dock to secure the boat while Rolf addressed people gathered on its deck. One by one, nine weary men and women were helped onto Swedish soil.

Seemingly out of nowhere, Captain Holsten wrapped Jonna in a bear hug. She threw her arms around him and spoke through tears. No one reminded her of Papa and "family" more than this man.

"I don't believe this!" She kissed his bristly cheek several times. "It's been so very long. Thank God I was here at this moment!"

"Dear Jonna. We are all just as thankful." He held her at arm's length. "Frans spotted you from way out, through the glasses, and the boys all cheered." He pulled her in for another hug. "I almost sounded the horn."

"You are well? You're a sight for my sore eyes, Captain. And the crew? How have you been?"

"We're surviving, Jonna. Thank the *Engel*, not me."

Rolf then interrupted for a hug, and then Frans and Vidar. She caught the signal Rolf sent Holsten and her heart sank, knowing they had to leave. Drogden—and its Nazis—awaited them.

"I know we rarely make it to this village, and I wish I could say when or even *if* we will return," Holsten told her, a palm heavy on her back, "but I've no way to know. You just take care and hang on, Jonna. It's what your papa would have wanted." She hugged him hard. He kissed her forehead and climbed aboard.

Vidar and Frans hugged her again and followed him, but Rolf hung back and took her hands.

"I'm sorry this has to be so rushed," he said, his dark eyebrows narrowing, "because I'm so excited to see you looking so good, but…but just listen: A fisherman some miles west of Copenhagen recognized Tove only last week. He heard she's an instructor with the Resistance, someone with rank, I guess."

"She might be in Copenhagen?"

Rolf shook his head. "The man didn't know. Honestly, no one knows where any of them are based and that's for their own safety. He said no one's seen her anywhere near the water for ages, probably because they're still safeguarding her, so he was surprised. He…he saw her using a cane."

Jonna inhaled hard.

Rolf squeezed her hands. "It could be just a disguise, Jonna, but it is likely she was wounded."

"Wounded?" Jonna's voice cracked.

"Sh. The fisherman's sister is a nurse who's 'helping' the cause and she apparently had Tove as a patient. Well, she suspected it was Tove. I guess they call her Hansel or Hans now for her own protection. Anyway, she said Hans drove them crazy, harping about Drogden, wanting to contact you. Sounds like she's missing you madly, Jonna, and I'm sure she's spent all this time trying to tell you."

"Oh, Rolf." She swiped away tears. "You have no idea what it means to hear this. No idea."

He tugged her to his chest. "I do. So, never lose hope. We are winning the war, Jonna, and all this is bound to settle itself soon." He gripped her by the shoulders and a smile broke through his thick mustache. "I have to go, but I will pass word of you as soon as I can."

The very thought of connecting with Tove, however indirectly, had Jonna's mind whirling. Finally, after so very long, a chance to reach her? There was so much to say, so much she wanted her to know.

She couldn't speak. She watched Rolf gallantly kiss her hands then turn and vault aboard the *Engel*. Everyone shouted good-byes to her, but all she could do was wave.

❖

I must admit, under different circumstances, we could be fast friends, Rita and I, and I think her husband, Derek, is a likeable sort, kind and caring. I'm happy they will be helping at least one little soul shine brightly after all this madness.

Jonna returned her journal to the drawer. Writing for nearly an hour had been cathartic, but, damn, if there wasn't always more to say. But not right now. Today, she had one last morning to share with Naysa before Rita and Derek arrived to take their newly adopted daughter home to America.

Bundled from head to toe in clothes provided by the Lewins, Naysa ran through the ankle-deep snow and into Jonna's outstretched arms. The excitement in her face said it all and they hugged hard and long.

"Let's go to the confectioner's," Jonna said, taking the mittened hand. Naysa quickly looked up, her smile widening. "Well," Jonna explained, "we need to celebrate your special day."

Snow had covered their scarves and shoulders by the time they entered the sweets shop, and Jonna barely had time to brush it from Naysa's head before she was off to make her selections. After prolonged deliberation, a varied assortment of sweets was bagged and paid for, and Jonna guided a very preoccupied Naysa back out into the wintry day.

"Don't eat all of them now, silly girl. Save some for later and tomorrow, maybe longer." She doubted the advice registered.

"I'm going on an airplane, Jonna," Naysa said into the bag.

"And a long boat ride."

Naysa popped a candy into her mouth and offered the bag to Jonna. "Try a red one."

Jonna selected the designated treat. "Did you have a good breakfast? It's going to be a long day, you know."

Naysa nodded vigorously. With the candy stuffed into her cheek, she said, "Birta gave me a little extra and then we packed my valise. I decided to wear this new blue dress because it matches my boots."

"The Lewins thought of everything, didn't they?"

"Rita said I probably won't need boots in Florida. It doesn't snow there. It just rains."

"Will you live close to the water?"

"Uh-huh and they have a boat." She stopped them in the middle of the street and took Jonna's arm. "Know what? There's a lighthouse not far from where I'm going to live, and we can go there!"

Jonna made a point to show just as much joy in that revelation. Knowing that a lighthouse remained dear to Naysa warmed her heart. "Well, aren't you the lucky girl? That's wonderful." She tapped Naysa's nose affectionately. "I think it means happiness awaits you. Everyone should have a lighthouse looking out for them."

Naysa practically hopped in place. "I thought so, too!" She looked sharply toward the end of the street, toward the docks and the worn path to the promontory. "Can we go to our spot and watch Drogden?"

Jonna squinted at the path through the falling snow. "Hm. Well…" She shrugged and claimed Naysa's hand. "Why not try, huh?"

Naysa nodded. "I know it's snowing but we can do it." She held Jonna's hand firmly as they strolled along, letting go only to wave at a farmer passing on his horse-drawn wagon. "That's Gris."

"Is it? You know him? I'm surprised he didn't call your name."

Naysa laughed. "Gris is the *horse*, Jonna. I've met him before. Elin introduced us."

"Oh, I see. But…isn't gris the Swedish word for pig?"

"He eats like a pig."

Now, Jonna laughed, and realized how good it felt, reminiscent of times past, the two of them so lighthearted. Here they were now, forced so far from their homes, eating candy, and hiking to the promontory through the snow. A cherished moment.

At the outlook, they stopped and stared in Drogden's direction. The curtain of snow cut visibility to far less than a mile, but Jonna knew they both hoped to detect a flicker of light. *Just a wink, please.*

With a deflated sigh, Naysa stuffed her candy bag into her coat pocket. "I just wanted one more look."

Jonna draped an arm around her shoulders and drew Naysa to her side. "We know it's out there, honey, just a few miles farther than we'd like."

"Do you think you'll ever go back?"

"To Drogden?" Naysa nodded but didn't look away from the sea. "Yes, definitely. I won't be in charge, but—"

"But you should be, like Tove says."

Jonna had to smile. "And I thank you both, but it's not likely. It won't stop me from visiting, though. I intend to do that."

"Tove will visit, too, won't she?"

"I'm sure."

"I miss her, Jonna. She's okay over there, isn't she? Back home? I mean…I don't want to make you sad, but…Well, I guess I'm sad, too. You'll have to say good-bye to her for me."

Jonna squeezed her closer. "We send her our deepest, strongest wishes, Naysa, and have to believe she is well. I miss her terribly, yes, and it makes me sad, but good times are coming. You," Jonna gave her a little shake, "you are the first of many victories to come. Happy times are beginning."

"You know what I wish?" Naysa swiped snow from her eyelashes and looked up at her. "I wish for you and Tove to make Drogden your home and welcome families and children like me and guide ships and take care of each other and live there happily ever after." She added a perfunctory nod before turning back to the sea.

"Well. If I could grant you that wish, I would this very second." Jonna leaned down and kissed Naysa's cheek. "In return, and I know Tove would agree with me, we wish *you* all the happiness in the world."

"Drogden always made us happy, didn't it? It kept us together, no matter where we were, but now I'm going so far away. You and Tove mustn't let it get lonely. If only I could see it one last time. I need to say good-bye."

Jonna bent to Naysa's ear. "How about this: If you think of your Florida lighthouse as Drogden's sister spirit, you're not really saying good-bye. After all, they speak the same language and serve the same noble purpose, don't they? When you're out on your family's boat, take your new lighthouse into your heart the way you welcomed Drogden."

Naysa's rapt gaze grew distant with the concept. Her jaw slackened in wonder, and then she spun back to Drogden. Suddenly, she gasped and pointed. "Look, Jonna! Just then! I saw it!" She spared Jonna a glance. "Did you see it, too?"

Jonna narrowed her eyes in the lighthouse's direction and, as if between the millions of snowflakes, a blink of light appeared. "Oh my God, I did! Yes! I saw it!"

Naysa bounced for joy and hugged Jonna hard. "Drogden made it through the snow!"

Drogden has bid you farewell.

CHAPTER TWENTY-FIVE

Copenhagen

Tove found it difficult to remain focused. A city block from the Copenhagen docks, she dodged from one shadowy place into the next, struggling with a weighty sack of coal for the hospital. Still, as much as she needed to concentrate on the icy walkways, she fought the desire to search for the *Engel*.

At last, she deposited her precious cargo behind trash bins in the hospital alley, knowing one of the many supportive medical personnel would retrieve it soon. Winter had descended with a vengeance, a month ahead of schedule, but Nazis didn't care who froze to death.

She rubbed her arms vigorously as she plotted her exit from the area. She chose another deserted, mostly dark route that skirted the docks and, this time, couldn't resist the temptation.

The warehouse by the water was all too familiar and, abandoned many months ago, it no longer served as the Resistance's holding place for desperate refugees. She ducked inside when sentries came into view along the docks. That hadn't changed.

With the door open an inch, she spotted the *Engel* in the row of boats. For a moment, she imagined slipping into its cargo hold and being secreted to Sweden, to Jonna. Had it been thirteen months since she'd been aboard? Since she'd felt warmth and desire in Jonna's arms, the fit of them together?

A faint but familiar whistle caught her ear, and she closed the door almost completely. The sound grew louder as the whistler passed and Tove finally recognized the tune. *Could it be?* She peered after the man, tall, bearded, with a sea bag over his shoulder. *Rolf!*

Tove hissed at him through the crack in the door and his stride slowed. She hissed again. He stopped and inspected his left shoe. He swung his bag to the ground and appeared to rummage through it. With a glance around, he surveyed the area casually then resumed rummaging, whistling.

Rolf pulled a pair of shoes from his bag and looked for a place to sit. Grinning at his antics, Tove watched him limp closer and prop himself against the warehouse.

"Something in your shoe, sailor?" Tove whispered firmly.

Never looking her way, Rolf pulled off his gloves and proceeded to change his shoes. "Only one person I know stupid enough to come this close."

"Good to see you, too."

"Same here. You've been missed."

"Been busy."

"Getting shot up, I heard."

"Some. Any run to Strandhem?"

"Month ago. Jonna's doing well. She cried, seeing us and missing you."

Tove felt her throat tighten. *Not a time to lose control.* Rolf was stalling, tying his shoes so slowly he was bound to be spotted soon. Tove madly raced through everything she wanted to say and know and chose the most important.

"Name a place," she whispered, her voice breaking.

"Vidar's cottage, before dawn."

"I'll be there."

"Bring coal."

He pushed off from the warehouse wall and puffed warm breath into his palms before tugging on his gloves. With the seabag over his shoulder, he ambled off to the *Engel* without another word. She heard him exchange his standard greeting with the sentries and breathed a sigh of relief that all was well.

Now, all she had to do was get back to safety tonight, coordinate a massive conflagration mission tomorrow, and then travel miles across the city before dawn. *And the bluster off the water says the weather's changing for the worse.*

❖

Tove confronted the relentless storm head-on—from the seat of a stolen bicycle. The hat pulled low over her eyes and the scarf across her face provided some protection, but the cold and dampness quickly ate through her jacket, trousers, and gloves.

She peddled hard, slid around curves, and took several spills in her haste to cross the city. Twice she drove behind trees to hide from Nazi patrols. By the time she reached Vidar's cottage, she was a ghostly vision of snow. At the back door, she greeted his wife with a frosted backpack filled with coal and was immediately urged out of her jacket and into one of Vidar's heavy sweaters.

Maneuvering her frozen limbs was difficult but the farthest thing from her mind, once she spotted Vidar, Rolf, and Frans seated around the kitchen table. They greeted her with great flourish, then teased her about taking so long to arrive. When she removed her hat, they teased more.

"You don't own scissors?" Frans asked, referencing the hair that extended halfway down her back.

"A rat's nest waiting to happen, if you ask me." Rolf shook his head. "When the open sea gets a hold of all that?" He snorted.

"Stop," she said, enjoying the familiar banter. "You three look like what the sea threw ashore."

"Hard work," Vidar injected, handing her a cup of coffee. "After all, we're one mate down and have to do your work, too."

"Hey, I've been busy." She held the cup in both hands, glad to be without gloves. "I've thought about all of you, the *Engel* so much. Not a day has gone by…"

"Drogden is crazy, Tove," Rolf said. "Those damn Nazis don't have a clue what they're doing out there."

Frans leaned toward her. "Last month, the beacon was dark for almost a week."

"No! A week?" Tove was shocked.

"They love shooting at Allied planes coming down the strait, but those Nazi boys can't hit a thing. They try, though. One idiot lost control of that cannon, swung it too far around and shot out the lens."

"Oh, my God!" Tove's first thought was of Jonna's horrified reaction.

"So, then," Frans went on, excited to finish, "two nights later, one of their supply ships ran up the rocks beside Drogden and split wide open."

Still stunned, she looked at each of them, saw their grins, and broke into laughter. "Their own damn fault."

"Stupid soldiers *and* stupid sailors," Vidar said.

"Wow. They must keep you busy, looking after the place." An image of Jonna in that compact kitchen floated to mind. "Rolf, you've seen Jonna?"

He finished sipping and nodded. "We have and she looks wonderful, Tove. I told her that you had been spotted a while ago—with a cane. I had to be honest. I told her you'd probably been wounded."

"Damn, Rolf. Who knows what she thinks now?"

"But I said we'd heard you were doing well and being a pain to everyone about missing her."

Tove felt her heart lighten. "You said that, too?"

"I did."

"Fisherman from the *Sohest*, his sister was your nurse, we heard." Frans grinned, waiting for her reaction.

"My nurse?" Tove had to think back. Those weeks of recuperation last winter were an agonizing, frustrating blur. "Um... Kirsten was the name she went by. And, yeah, I guess I...well, I may have nagged a little."

"More than a little, apparently," Frans said.

"So, Jonna's getting by? Where did she settle? Is she still in Strandhem? Do you know what she's doing? How about friends—"

Rolf held up a palm. "Slow down. When we saw her, there wasn't time for small talk, so we really didn't learn much. Any information comes through two or three people, sometimes more."

"I heard she was repairing fishing nets," Vidar said, "but that was a long time ago."

"It was hard for us," Frans nodded to his mates, "not knowing about *you*. All we knew was that the Resistance was keeping you away from the Gestapo, and, really, that was the most important thing."

"And we figured the Underground would take you in," Rolf finished. "Once that happened, we knew you'd disappear."

"Oh, disappear is the perfect word. Things happened so fast, my head spun. I never knew anything about guns or dynamite or things like that, but they train you hard and fast."

"And you *were* wounded, weren't you?"

She nodded at Rolf, knowing her mates wouldn't ask when or where. "Sometimes, it's like a bad dream." She snickered. "But it was real." She pointed from one body part to the next. "Shoulder, chest, and thigh, all at once. I guess I snapped about like a fish out of water."

They all grimaced. Frans pressed forward on his elbows. "You manage okay now, no cane?"

"Is riding the bicycle a problem?" Vidar asked.

"The cane, on occasion. Pedaling is good for me, but the shoulder…"

"Well, carrying coal can't help. But thanks for bringing some, by the way. Sorry if it was a burden."

She patted Vidar's hand. "I'm glad I could bring it. The shoulder I'm just going to have to live with, I think."

"I'm sure that not communicating with Jonna took getting used to," Rolf said.

She was touched by his understanding. "I must have sent dozens of messages, even risked sending a few notes, but there was no way to know if anything reached her, let alone receive something from her. It's been…difficult, yes."

"Well, at least it looks like the tide is turning against Hitler," Vidar said. "So many regions have been liberated."

"Are you still making runs to Sweden?"

"Not quite so often," Rolf answered. "That run to Strandhem in October was the only one of the year. The Nazis grow desperate these days, though, so we still run to the bigger villages, mostly for political fugitives and military evacuations."

Frans added, "Just a few weeks ago, Holsten had us pick up a dozen Danes and *bring them back.*"

"Back? Seriously? Fugitives?"

"Mostly our soldiers who escaped, but refugees, too. There's a Danish military camp up the Swedish coast. They reorganize, train others to return to the fight."

"That's amazing," Tove said. "They've managed, by the grace of God, to escape this Hell over here, and then risk everything by coming back?"

"To defend their homeland. Without it, what have you got?" Rolf asked. "Some things are worth the risk…just like sending a secret note to another country." He tilted his head slightly and challenged her with a look.

His message rumbled loudly in Tove's head. Maybe it was the companionable setting, the hint of "normalcy" with old friends in this kitchen that gave her pause and made room for free thinking.

What if *she* went to Sweden? Would Jonna return with her to continue the fight? Both she and Jonna had endured prolonged separation for her own safety, so, maybe they should stay and not return at all. But every Dane was a patriot, after all, and every Dane was in the fight. Dare she and Jonna enjoy sanctuary together, take advantage of patriots' sacrifice defending their homeland?

Regardless, the temptation to heal her aching heart with Jonna intensified with each passing second. She'd considered it many times during the past year, but never had it felt so compelling. Now, her palms grew damp. Even her heart rate increased.

There's really only one way to know.

"Hey." Vidar waved his hand in front of her face. "Where'd you go?"

Tove blinked and scrubbed her face with both hands. The men chuckled while Vidar put their empty cups in the sink, signaling that this comforting session was about to end. Her mates needed to begin their workday, and Tove wished she could head to the *Engel* with them.

Rolf waited as Tove rose and removed Vidar's borrowed sweater. Both acts took effort and she knew her stiff motions were telling.

"Come back if you can," he said gently. "We do this every Tuesday." He set a palm on her shoulder at the back door. "You're wise to keep a distance from the docks. There's always a chance some soldier or officer will remember you." He grinned as she fitted her cap onto her head. "The long hair isn't much of a disguise."

Tove reached up and stuffed it inside her coat. "It gets in the way, and I've been meaning to cut it."

"Holsten wouldn't want you to."

Recalling their captain's fatherly approach made Tove smile. "Please give him my best. And you—all of you—take care, okay?"

"Will you be able to come here again?" Vidar asked.

"I seldom know anything in advance, but I'll try. Thanks for welcoming me, Vidar. I know you risked a great deal having me here, but just seeing the three of you felt like coming home." She met Rolf's eyes with serious intent. "You've given me a lot to think about."

Chapter Twenty-six

Strandhem, Sweden

Jonna fitted the load of cumbersome netting into the till on Leo's fishing boat, latched the heavy lid closed, and straightened wearily. As her frosty breath blew back at her in the lantern's dim light, she tried to catch bits of conversation happening below deck. The crew disagreed about something, a night trip, she heard, and Leo was asserting his command.

"Well, then, the rest of you stay. I'm fine with just the two of us. We'll make do."

"It's not our fight," argued a crewman.

"Actually, it is."

"Well, it's definitely not our place."

"We could bring the devil upon us," said another crewman.

"We won't be alone," Leo countered. "Another Swedish boat has agreed to this, and two Danes, remember."

"But, with just you and Bjorn aboard, what can you do? One steers while the other shoots?"

"While the Nazis machine-gun holes in our precious livelihood? Leo, it's a doomed plan."

"No, it's not," Leo insisted. "With enough boats as distraction, at least a couple will get close enough to fire or use the dynamite."

"Close enough?" The crewman's voice rose with incredulity. "How close to Drogden's rocks do you think you'll get before you capsize or sink?"

Shocked at the mention of Drogden, Jonna moved closer to the cabin door to eavesdrop.

"I told you earlier, we're not the main vessel," Leo stated. "We're going to be one of the distractions. The main element will come from the west and have the means to take out that gun."

Jonna returned to the dock in a daze, trying to fathom what she'd heard. Apparently, the neutral Swedes planned to assist the Resistance in destroying Drogden's anti-aircraft battery. However, such success was bound to include losing the lighthouse as well. By the sound of things, numerous vessels contributing to the effort virtually assured maximum damage.

How can they even consider this? They are fishermen, and Drogden plays a vital role in their daily lives. As Swedes, they cannot violate the neutrality agreement with Germany.

Arms wrapped around herself in the gnawing wind, she stood stoically, numbed by it all. Maybe this plot came from the Allies, believing the Resistance better suited for the delicate operation. An attack by an Allied plane, she had to admit, definitely would not be delicate.

But...dynamite? How delicate will that be?

All five of Leo's crewmen emerged from the meeting and filed past her, barely offering a greeting. Their demeanor spoke volumes about their success at changing Leo's mind.

"Jonna, come!" From his cabin door, Leo waved her forward. "Get out of the damn cold, woman! Do you want tea?" He went inside as Jonna returned to the deck.

"Tea sounds wonderful," she said, eager to shed her coat. "Thanks, Leo." She watched him brew her a cup. "Your nets are good as new."

His eyebrows rose, as if he'd forgotten about her work. "Ah. Thanks. You...You folded them into the till? Meticulously as always, I'm sure." Handing her the cup, he forced a little smile but looked worried. He obviously knew she had been aboard during that crew meeting and probably had overheard a great deal.

Officially, it isn't any of my business...but it is.

Jonna decided to take the casual approach. "Your nets are stowed away properly as requested," she said with a grin. "You all put in a long day today, I see. Wives won't be happy."

He sat back and pinched the bridge of his nose. "Wives aren't happy with me right now, no. Mine hasn't been for some time." Suddenly, he leaned forward. "I have to ask for your confidence, Jonna. I'm sure you got an earful here earlier. It got a little loud—"

"Loud?" Jonna repeated with a laugh. "A little."

"Damn. I should have…" He shook his head. "But what you heard? It can't go any further."

"Leo." She set her cup down firmly and flattened her palms on the table. "It's been over a year, I know, but did you forget what brought me to Strandhem?"

His shoulders relaxed and he laughed lightly. "I guess I did. I'm sorry. No one here has worked with the Resistance longer than you, and no one has lost more."

Jonna clinked her teacup to his and drank.

"Just promise me Drogden won't be destroyed."

"If only I could make such a promise. I know we're supposed to stay out of it, but they need our help. You know what Drogden means to us all. If we can't disable that battery, the Allies will do it themselves—and they won't fuss about the damage." He exhaled heavily toward the ceiling. "I just wish my crew agreed."

"It's a lot to ask, the least of which is Swedish involvement."

"I know. You're right, but aren't we mariners the ones who know Drogden best? We know just how to approach it, when and where." He raised his cup. "Hell, you, of all people, know that."

The notion stopped Jonna in mid-sip. Suddenly unsteady, she put her cup down and they held each other's gaze for several seconds. Leo's penetrating eyes said he could be reading her mind— and there was a jumble of conflicting thoughts to read.

"I don't imagine a Dane would be breaking any neutrality rules," she said, not looking away. "So…maybe I should join you."

❖

Tove spent the rest of the crystalline December afternoon absorbing the sunshine, ignoring the emptiness in her belly, and cursing bone-chilling cold that renewed the need for her cane. Thoughts of Jonna in her arms along the Drogden rail, soothed by breezes and a sapphire sea, were no match for her latest profound concern.

Just last night, she had decided to cross the Oresund and reunite with Jonna. The *Engel* would take her, she was sure of it. But first, she was obligated to see the upcoming Resistance mission through to fruition.

Far from an act of sabotage, this one would likely lead to serious combat, and although the logistics meeting she'd just conducted had gone well, she opposed the mission with every ounce of her being. The plan to "eliminate" the Nazi stronghold at Drogden had her heart, stomach, and common sense in a nauseating twist.

As much as she yearned to see, let alone visit the lighthouse again, and certainly wanted to oust those Germans, she couldn't get past the likelihood of Drogden being destroyed. Appointed technical advisor because of her expertise with the Oresund and the lighthouse, she nevertheless was helpless to stop the effort.

It would break your heart to know what's in store, my sweet Jonna. I can hardly stand it myself. Hopefully, you won't learn of it until our lives have turned for the better. I miss our special place almost as much as I miss you.

As she approached the village's main road, a young boy raced to her side from out of nowhere.

"The cobbler says your shoes are ready."

Baffled, Tove looked down into the excited eyes. "The cobbler?"

"That's what I said." He frowned, impatient. "I see you got a cane, right?"

"What of it?"

The boy tipped forward, confidentially. "They call you Hans?" Tove straightened and the boy noticed. "Yeah, so, the cobbler closes soon." He ran off down an alley.

Leary of messages from strangers, Tove briefly stared after him before ambling along to the cobbler's shop. With her next team meeting scheduled for tomorrow night, *this* was unexpected.

The bell above the door chimed as she entered, and the elderly cobbler simply jutted a thumb toward a curtained doorway in the rear. With the tip of her cane, she parted the curtain just enough to recognize her team leader and two comrades at the table.

"Hans. Good. Sit." The leader looked far more harried than he had earlier at their logistics meeting. "Change of plans," he said as she took a seat. "We've lost three days."

The news stunned her, made her heart pound. She was ready but she wasn't.

"What happened to Friday night?"

"Waiting that long risks discovery. The Allies have moved up the timetable for their sweep down the Oresund, and that damn gun at Drogden cannot be sitting out there."

Tove could only nod. "We still must avoid taking out the beacon."

"We'll do our best. The anti-aircraft battery is the real target, but things could get messy. Now, do you foresee any problems with this change?"

Concentrating was hard but necessary. In the scratches of the old tabletop, she saw a myriad of navigational courses drawing her to Drogden, not to Jonna.

"There's no significant tidal change to worry about and this fair weather should hold until Sunday," she thought aloud. "The boat is roomy, broad, and fast. Its engine is stronger than most. It will be ready. I don't foresee any problems, as long as supplies arrive in time." Her stomach turned at the image of explosives by the crateload.

"Supplies are due tomorrow," a comrade said. "Already on their way."

His associate added, "I've sent word to the other boats. Each will approach differently, so, based on what you've said about their defenses, the Nazis will be spread too thin to cope with all the boats at once."

But these are just fishing boats. They are bound to suffer significant damage from riflery.

"Our boat here will carry the heaviest weapons and the landing party," the leader said. "Docking alongside—"

"But we've been over this," Tove said. "Close enough for a landing…Just one grenade dropped from the platform—"

"Not with sentries trying to rebuff fire from all directions. We're storming that place, as long as the captain can tie up."

Once suspicious of inbound craft, the Nazis surely will sound the alarm, and then patrol boats will arrive and the unthinkable will happen.

"So, Hans, you know our captain?"

The leader didn't seem fazed by the magnitude of risk. Or maybe he simply couldn't afford to show it. Tove felt twitchy, just sitting in the chair.

"I know *of* him," she said. "Reliable and skilled on the water for decades."

"He's familiar with the lighthouse?"

"As much as any fisherman, I suppose."

He slapped the table. "Dammit. We're counting on him being better than most." He covered his face and growled into his palms. "We can't gamble with just 'any fisherman' leading the way."

Tove didn't know what else to tell him. She knew the captain could maneuver through a hurricane, but a hail of gunfire? And, like most fishermen, his daily routine probably had brought him to Drogden only occasionally. Yet, he was a tough old salt, cut from the same cloth as Captain Holsten.

The leader's stern look bored into her. "Listen, Hans. I want you on that boat with him. That's our best solution. No one knows it better."

A million factors careened through her head, all centered around a mission she would cancel if she could. Could she direct action away from the tower? Would any of them survive heavy machine guns on the Oresund? Was she fit enough to participate? Would Jonna advise against it?

Fate seems determined to test me, dearest Jonna. I'll have to try.

"Very well."

Everyone stood and her comrades left her with the leader.

"We could lose every boat," she said evenly.

"We took only volunteers. Everyone is aware."

"We must target only that gun battery. Drogden is so much more than a landmark for the Allies. It's everything to mariners, too, of both shores." *And to me. To us.*

"I'm confident all of you will do your best. Your help with this plan has been invaluable." He offered a handshake and a knowing smile. "*Hans.* Your lifelong devotion to Drogden says it all."

CHAPTER TWENTY-SEVEN

Nancy pulled into the driveway at her sister's house and gathered her handbag and beach towel. She hadn't been taking advantage of Eloise's Friday afternoon open pool policy often enough lately. She made time today, although she also wanted the company of her siblings, pool or no pool.

She and Sam hadn't talked any more over the past few weeks about what they were or could be to each other. Nancy felt like the ball was in her court, but she didn't know how to return serve and that had her unsettled.

Every time Nancy visited Eloise's home, she was jealous of the impeccable interior decorating, the immaculate lawn, and picture-perfect backyard. Today, she didn't care about any of that. The most glorious sight was all four of her siblings in their bathing suits splashing in the pool or lounging nearby.

"Oh, well, well, well, look who it is. You vaguely resemble my long lost sister, but I think she's still on her world tour." Sean splashed her from the shallow end.

"I heard it's now a galactic tour. She's on the planet Pluto." Kevin saluted with a guacamole-laden chip.

Nancy stole Kevin's chip before he could eat it and flopped in the lounge chair between Eloise and him. "I've been building a dream. That's not easy."

"Especially when you have something dreamy to look at and distract you, right?" Eloise looked at Nancy with one raised eyebrow. "And, Kevin, Pluto's not a planet anymore."

"Not a planet? What happened to it? Did it blow up or something?" Kevin sat up and helped himself to more chips.

"It's been reclassified as a dwarf planet, but I'm not interested in space science right now. I want to hear about Nancy's lady troubles." Eloise turned so she was fully facing Nancy.

Since they were kids, Eloise had always known when Nancy was upset or something was bugging her. She could usually diagnose the problem as well, sometimes more effectively than Nancy could herself.

"I'd ask how you knew, but what's the point." Nancy sighed as Sean and Casey hauled themselves out of the pool and joined them on the loungers. "But, first of all," she continued, "it's not really lady troubles exactly." Why was she feeling so defensive? "More like a lady conundrum."

Kevin, Sean, and Casey didn't have any sympathy for Nancy. They all agreed they didn't have any lady troubles or conundrums and she was extremely lucky to have either. They pretended to stop paying attention while she and Eloise talked, but Nancy knew better.

"What's the problem, Nan? If you've got any feelings for her, I can attest that she looks at you like you hung the moon." Eloise moved to Nancy's lounger and despite the heat, they cuddled next to each other like they'd been doing since they were kids.

"I've got lots of feelings for her. Too many feelings." Nancy knew she was frowning.

Unbidden images sprang to mind, their trip to Ireland, sitting on the back deck of the Connecticut lighthouse, strolling Mystic Seaport. The grumpy fog clouding up her gut dissipated with the gentle swirl of the memories.

"Whoa, what was that? That smile was…was…?" Eloise made an exploding motion with her hands. "Your whole face lit up. I've never seen you look so happy."

"I was thinking about Sam."

Sean looked at Nancy and Eloise with a perfectly ridiculous expression. "I'm thinking about Sam, too. Is my face as adorably moony?"

"You said you weren't listening." Eloise threw a chip at him and he went back to feigned indifference.

"If she can make your face do what it just did, then what's the problem?" Eloise snuggled closer.

This was how every major life decision between the two of them had been made. Nancy couldn't imagine having this conversation any other way. She considered Eloise's question. When put so simply, especially in the face of wonderful memories, it was hard to remember what exactly her lady problems were. But all she had to do was start to picture the future and it all came back.

"She has an expiration date, that's the problem." Nancy put her head on her sister's shoulder and closed her eyes.

"Nan, she's not canned goods. What are you talking about?" Eloise gave Nancy a gentle poke in the ribs, right where she knew she was most ticklish.

"Hey, that's not cool. I'm having a vulnerable moment here." Nancy squirmed away from her sister's prodding but not far enough to break their connection. "After the lighthouse project is done, Sam's going back to the West Coast and resuming her duties as heir to the family business. She doesn't have time for anything else."

"I'm in the supermarket a lot for supplies for our tours, and, if the tabloids are to be believed, Sam is not all-work-and-no-play back at home." Casey stopped pretending he wasn't listening and turned around so he could more naturally join the conversation. "Why can't you be the one in all the pictures instead of a parade of different women?"

Nancy felt her muscles tense and wondered if she was white as a sheet. She certainly felt it. "I don't want to be in any tabloid pictures. Ever."

"Not even if it's the price of being with her?" Kevin turned back to the conversation, too.

In Sam's most recent update on the adventures of Tove and Jonna from her book, those two were a country—a world away from each other—but still held out hope of being reunited. They survived the long separation with sporadic, cryptic communication, Nancy mused, so who was she to complain about a few pictures in a trashy magazine, even if they suggested Sam was in a relationship with a beautiful woman?

"It's not really a price." Nancy sighed. "But it doesn't change the fact that she's leaving as soon as the project's done."

"Hmm." Kevin tapped his chin. "If only she knew someone who owns a private plane and can be ready to go in thirty minutes." He frowned more deeply and rested his chin in his hand in an exaggerated thinking pose. "Oh wait, she's the one with the private plane and a willingness to travel."

"He's right. If you're going to be bicoastal or try long distance, the one to do it with is an ultra-wealthy hottie who takes you around the world because she got bored on a Tuesday." Eloise looked quite proud of herself.

"I hadn't considered the private jet." Nancy shivered when she thought of the last time she was on that plane. How she'd ever been able to maintain she didn't like Sam was beyond her. "But I still have trouble signing on for something I know will be part-time at best. Maybe it's my love of history coming through, but I want something that can grow roots if I'm going to really let my heart out to play." Nancy returned her head to Eloise's shoulder.

"Nan, no history can be made without living in the present." Kevin patted Nancy's leg in what looked like his attempt at being reassuring.

"Whoa, big brother, that's very profound." Nancy took his hand and gave it a squeeze. "Thank you, guys. I needed a little time with you. I do have to wonder though, why are you pushing me so enthusiastically into getting my heart broken?"

Eloise sat up, nearly dumping Nancy from the longer. "Oh, for cripe's sake. You have no way of knowing that's what's going to happen. Tell your brain to stop spinning every disaster scenario you can come up with and stop for a minute to imagine how that woman looks at you." Eloise gave Nancy a long stare. "Can you picture it?"

Nancy nodded. She felt the smile tugging at the corners of her mouth. She loved the way Sam looked at her. It made her feel like Sam was gazing at a priceless relic thought lost to history. It made her feel like she was beautiful, exciting, and cherished.

She was snapped out of her mushy moment by Sean making a retching sound and Casey making obnoxiously loud kissing sounds.

"Look at our little sister, so in love with a woman who loves her back. So sad for her." Kevin fake cried dramatically. "You know we will have to go and threaten to break her kneecaps if she hurts you, right?" He turned serious quickly.

Nancy rolled her eyes. "You've been making that threat since I started dating. Wait." She paused and rewound what Kevin said in her head. "I'm not in love with Sam."

All four of her siblings howled with laughter.

"I am in love with Sam?" She looked to Eloise. Her sister shrugged. "Holy shit, I am in love with Sam."

Nancy's brothers and sister cheered. "Now you've joined the party." Sean scooped her up and slung her over his shoulder.

"And this is a pool party." Casey pulled off her shoes.

"Don't you dare." Nancy slapped Sean's back but he didn't seem to care.

Eloise retrieved her cell phone from her pocket and her sunglasses from her face. "Sorry, sis. Nothing I can do to stop this from happening."

"You're right about that." Kevin grabbed Eloise.

Before Nancy could protest further, all five Calhoun siblings were in the pool. She came up sputtering and shoved Sean back under as soon as he appeared next to her. He had a big, goofy grin on his face when he popped back up a few feet away.

"You're lucky I have my suit on." Nancy tried to hold a straight face as she attempted to glare at her brother.

Sean looked unconcerned. "I've changed your diapers. You think I care about seeing your bra?"

"You haven't changed any of my diapers recently, and given how much older you are, it won't be long until I'm changing yours." She laughed at Sean's horrified look.

They swam and splashed around in the pool and Nancy felt at peace, like she always did around her family. Except, for the first time in her life, it felt like something was missing. Not something, someone. She missed Sam.

Now, though, she'd admitted something to herself that she couldn't take back. She was in love with Sam and didn't know what to do about it. What if Sam didn't feel the same way? What if she did?

"I thought I told you to keep your brain from running through the disaster scenarios and freaking yourself out." Eloise joined Nancy on the edge of the pool.

"I'm not picturing any disasters. I'm trying to figure out what to do now that I know that I'm in love with Sam."

"Well, what were you planning on doing with her before you said those words out loud?" Eloise bumped Nancy's shoulder with her own.

Nancy felt her cheeks heat, but she raised an eyebrow defiantly and held her sister's eye contact.

Eloise's ears pinked. "Okay. That's not what I meant, but I guess it answers my question." Eloise took Nancy's hand. "Just call her and stop acting weird."

"I'm going to do that." Nancy pulled herself from the pool and trotted to grab her towel. She circled back to give her sister a kiss on the head. "I love you, sis."

"Yeah, yeah. Tell Sam she's welcome to join the pool party." Eloise shooed her away.

Nancy slipped into her sandals, grabbed her phone, and moved to the deck for a little privacy. After talking to her siblings and making some surprising discoveries, the idea of not exploring things with Sam felt ludicrous. And given that, Sam needed to get poolside in a sexy, preferably revealing, bathing suit.

Sam didn't answer until Nancy was convinced the call was going to go to voice mail.

"Hey, hot stuff. Did you pack a bathing suit when you came out east?"

"Hi. It's nice to hear your voice." Sam's voice was flat and devoid of the verve and sparkle that made her her.

"Sam, what's wrong?" Nancy gripped the phone tightly.

"My father's dead." There was no emotion in her voice. She sounded in shock.

Nancy's stomach churned and her jaw tensed. It felt like the world she imagined was being blown apart by the winds of change, which was selfish. How must Sam be feeling?

"Can I come over? What do you need?" Nancy put her head in her hand. Was there a more helpless feeling than what she was experiencing right now?

"I'm about to board a plane back home. There's an emergency board meeting as soon as I land. Nancy, I don't want any of this. I wasn't ready to give up everything we've started." Finally, some emotion came through in Sam's voice.

Nancy took a breath so she wouldn't start sobbing. "You don't have to lose me. I love you, Sam."

"I don't deserve that. Now more than ever, I can't give you what you need. Reality caught up with me. I have to go." It was obvious Sam was crying.

"You listen to me, Samantha McMann." Nancy jabbed at the air as if Sam could see her. "You don't get to decide what I deserve. It took me a while to figure it out, but I want you. You don't get to tell me not to love you and, whatever you tell yourself, I know you care about me, too. As long as we have that, we can figure out the rest. Think about your Tove and Jonna. All that they went through. If they can do *that*, we can do this. Let me be there for you."

"I don't know how to do that. All I know right now is what I have to do for the company." Sam sounded like her heart was breaking. "I do care about you, you're right, but my personal needs aren't important anymore. I'm the CEO of the company, that's the only thing that matters."

"Damn it, Sam, that's not true. You matter. We matter." It felt strange to be fighting so hard for something she'd had to be convinced she wanted only a few hours prior. But now she knew that Sam was where she belonged.

"Let me get through the board meeting and I'll call you. We can talk more then."

"Of course. If you need me to come with you or meet you there, say the word. You don't have to do this alone." Nancy wanted to run to her but knew this would only work if Sam wanted to meet her halfway.

Sam thanked her and hung up, her voice back to its flat monotone.

Nancy set her phone down and put her head in her hands and cried. She was sad for Sam losing her father and as she'd explained it, her freedom and what might have been between Sam and her. A few months ago, she would have done anything to get Sam off the island and away from the lighthouse and now the thought of going back to finish the project without her was unbearable.

She wiped at her tears and took a few deep breaths. She needed to pull herself together. Enough with the doom and gloom. Nothing was official one way or the other between the two of them and she would finish the lighthouse project on her own because the finished product was going to be incredible.

While Nancy warred with hope and despair, Eloise joined her and slipped an arm around her shoulders. They didn't speak, but Eloise's comfort was exactly what Nancy needed. Why did she have to come to the realization she was in love only to have Sam fly off without her?

She wanted to believe there was space in Sam's life for her, but given the way Sam had described the demands on her time even before her father died, she wasn't optimistic. Something dramatic would have to change and she wasn't sure Sam was willing or capable of making change happen. If that was the case, Nancy couldn't see a scenario where she wasn't on the outside of Sam's life looking in, and that was the last place she wanted to be.

CHAPTER TWENTY-EIGHT

Sam walked out of the board meeting in a daze. Since Phillip had called and told her their father was dead, it felt like she was running through quicksand. The board vote had gone exactly as expected and she was now chairperson and CEO of the company, as her father had always wished. Hopefully, wherever he was, he was happy because Sam was not.

She'd been replaying the phone call with Nancy in her head since the moment they hung up. Nancy loved her. Despite her grief, shock, and disbelief, that had still resonated. Why couldn't she have had a few more months with Nancy and their lighthouse? Why did he have to die now?

Sam slammed the door to her father's—*her*—office. She wasn't ready to sit behind the desk, so she slumped onto the sofa along one wall. Nancy deserved a phone call, but what would she say? Sam had seen what being the wife of a CEO had been like for her mother. She was essentially a single parent with an additional full-time job of being a perfect wife and hostess at a moment's notice. Sam would never ask Nancy to climb into that cage. She wished she'd asked her mother more about her life when she was still alive. All anyone cared about was what her father or Sam and her brother were doing. It must have been lonely.

Phillip flung open the office door without knocking and poured two drinks from the bar next to the desk before saying anything. He downed the first in a single shot and returned the glass. The second he brought to the couch with him and slumped down next to Sam.

"No, thank you. Nothing for me." Sam rolled her eyes at her brother.

"Oh fuck off, it's your bar now, you can serve yourself." Phillip's words were harsh, but his tone and delivery were anything but. He looked distraught. "Can you believe this is all yours now?"

Sam looked around at the office and all it represented. "Do you remember playing in here as a kid?"

"You remember playing? I remember business lessons that seemed like fun because when you're a kid everything can be a game if you try hard enough." Phillip made a sour face.

"I always thought you loved those lessons and everything he taught us."

"Not at first, but when you're the spare to the heir you can't afford to not be invested in every piece of advice he spewed out." Phillip took a big swig of his drink.

Sam evaluated her brother as if for the first time. "I might have figured you all wrong. I resented what a know-it-all you were and how much you seemed just like him. You're good in all the ways I'm not. I wish I'd known you were so bitter about it."

"You resented me?" Phillip nearly choked on his drink. "The old loon ignored everything except the unremarkable order of our birth to determine what was best for this company. You don't care about it like I do. I used to hate you for that."

"But not now?" Sam had never had anything resembling a heart-to-heart with her brother. Now they were having a lifetime of clearly needed family therapy condensed into a small session without the aid of a professional. To say her head was spinning was an understatement.

Phillip finished his drink and stood. He toured the room looking like movement was essential to maintaining his sanity in the moment. Eventually, he spoke. "Nah. It took me a while, but I finally saw you were as stuck as me. Must have sucked being you and forced into something you had no interest in."

Sam nodded her agreement. "Do you think he loved us?"

"Not enough to care what we wanted." Phillip returned to the couch. "Speaking of, tell me about this project you've been working on. Even when I was calling to yell at you, I could tell how happy you were."

Thoughts of Nancy flooded her mind. Her stomach churned and it didn't feel like there was enough oxygen in the room. Sam leaned forward and cradled her head in her hands. "I was so happy with her."

"Her?" Phillip gave a her shoulder a slap. "You told me you were building a lighthouse or an island or something. Now you're saying this whole time you were shacked up with some girl? What the hell?"

Sam could feel her face heat, her body seize with pent-up emotion. She shoved a finger into his face. "I was not shacked up. I was working on the lighthouse project like I said. My partner on the project was Nancy Calhoun and I…" Sam dropped her head to the back of the sofa. "Holy shit, I fell in love with her."

Phillip's smile lit up his face. He looked genuinely and enthusiastically happy for her. "Good for you. It's about time someone tamed you. When can I meet her?"

"You can't. Or you won't. How can I ask her to share my life when this is what it looks like now?" Sam motioned around the office. "She'd hate living here full-time and being expected to smile and support me but never have an opinion of her own."

Sam's heart ached. She imagined Nancy framed by the blue sky, stunningly beautiful, or animatedly describing an esoteric historical fact very few would find delightful. What was Nancy doing right now? Was she at the lighthouse? It was almost too much to think about.

Phillip pulled Sam from her forlorn musings. "What century are you living in? Expectations have changed since Mom was the trophy wife, and even if they haven't, you're the boss. You can do whatever you damn well please."

A strangled laugh escaped before Sam could squash it. "If only that were true. I feel more trapped than I ever have. I don't know how to run a company."

"No shit." Phillip rolled his eyes but was smiling. "I'll do for you what I always did for him. I'll make you look good and make sure this ship doesn't go down."

That comment relit the spark of a fantastical dream she'd harbored as a child. When the pressure from her father felt like more than she could stand, she'd always dreamt about handing the company to Phillip and walking away from her responsibilities. What if she could fulfill her duty and still find her own happiness?

"What do you mean, 'what you did for him'? How much of the day-to-day was he running the last few years?"

It was Phillip's turn to laugh. "He hadn't been involved in keeping this company going in years. I wasn't allowed to tell anyone, even you."

"What would make you happy, Lippy?"

"For you not to call me that, for one." Phillip didn't look that angry at the use of his childhood nickname. "Truthfully, I want the company, but I'd have to murder you to get it and I'm not a monster."

"Thank you for not plotting my demise. It seems like there might be a solution we can all live with. I have something you want. I don't want what I have. Match made in heaven." Sam looked keenly at her brother, allowing herself to feel hopeful for the first time in a very long time. She didn't think about Nancy, that was a step too far, but she did think about what life would be like without the weight of the company on her shoulders.

"You can't be serious." He looked incredulous. "They named you head of this company an hour ago and now you want me to take over?"

Sam got up to pour herself a drink now. It seemed like a good time. "Sure, consider it my first official act. Can it be done?"

"You're chair of the board, CEO, and majority owner. You can do just about anything you want." Realization of what they were actually talking about seemed to sink in as Phillip was talking. His eyes grew wider. "If you do this, there's no take-backsies. You can't hand me the company and then, in a month, decide you want to come back to play boss lady."

"Same to you. I don't want to hear any whining in a few weeks about how hard the job is and that you want to dump it all back in my lap." Sam had butterflies flittering through her stomach. "Do you want the company? I'll give you my titles and the responsibility as soon as we can get the board reconvened."

Phillip looked pensive. He tugged on his ear, a sign since he was a baby that he was working through something thorny. "Yes, I want the company but not your titles. At least not yet. If you hand them over now, it'll look like there's a leadership crisis, that neither of us knows what we're doing. Since that's only half true," he looked at her pointedly, "you stay as figurehead leader and we can transition you out in a year or two."

It felt like a trap door opened beneath her and dropped Sam into one of the circles of hell. She'd allowed herself to hope and now all she'd wished for was yanked away.

"I can't wait that long. I need to get back to Rhode Island." The giant office felt too small and confining, the tasteful decor looked jarring. She needed Nancy back in her life to set her world right. She had to get to her and tell her she loved her, too.

"Whoa, take a breath." Phillip put a hand on her shoulder. "The transition is only on paper. You do whatever you need to do. I've got you. Remember, this is what I was raised to do and for some weird reason, I love it."

Sam sprang to her feet, excitement bubbling through her. She kissed his forehead. "If you change your mind, don't call me. I won't answer." She grabbed the one item she'd brought with her into the office and headed for the door.

"Where are you going?" Phillip wandered after her.

"The airport. I need to get back to my girl, but don't think I'm not going to check up on you. My name's still at the top. You don't get to slack off and make me look bad. I might hate it, but I still know enough about the business to keep you in line."

Phillip pinched the bridge of his nose. "This is going to be a nightmare for me, isn't it?"

"At its worst. Don't forget you begged for it." Sam closed the office door, then re-opened it. "Thank you and I love you."

She didn't wait for his reply before heading to the elevator, phone in hand. She tried Nancy's cell first, but she didn't answer. Her office line was next on the list. She didn't pick up there, either. She started to leave a message but was interrupted by Casey answering the call.

"She's not here, Sam, and unless you give me a damn good reason, I'm not going to tell her you called. My sister's incredible and if you're too dumb to see it, I'm not going to assist you in hurting her further."

Sam hadn't expected a Casey-shaped roadblock.

"I exorcised my idiocy a few minutes ago. I want to talk to her. Please?" Sam was going back to Rhode Island whether Casey provided any information or not, but it would be helpful if she didn't have to do a door-to-door search when she got there.

"She's not here. She's out on the island finishing the project you abandoned. If you're coming back, make sure you know if it's for good. You're not going to get another chance if you screw up again. She deserves better." Casey was in full protective big brother mode.

Sam made every promise she could think of that she wouldn't hurt Nancy, but knew words only went so far, and Casey wasn't the one she needed to convince.

The plane was fueled and ready for her when she got to the airport. If the pilot and crew were ever annoyed by her last-minute requests and summons, they never showed it.

"Ms. McMann, welcome aboard. The captain is preparing for an immediate departure as you requested. She asked me to tell you the flight may be pretty bumpy as we approach New England. There is a storm brewing off the coast." The flight attendant helped Sam get settled and efficiently set about preparing the cabin.

Sam didn't care if she had to crawl through a hurricane or drive through a wall of fire, she was getting back to Nancy today. She leaned back in her seat and closed her eyes. Emotions swirled and bubbled in her gut, but the ones that rose to the top were love and hope.

She finally knew her own heart and had found a pathway for them to be together. Would Nancy believe they could after all that effort Sam spent insisting they couldn't? She clung to hope. Nancy loved her. Repeating that sent her insides into a shimmy. Soon, she'd see Nancy and be able to declare her own love. She fell asleep dreaming of Nancy's beaming smile, crashing waves, and a lighthouse's flashing beacon. The pull of Nancy and their lighthouse was finally guiding her home.

CHAPTER TWENTY-NINE

Oresund Strait
Denmark

Having spent two harried days at the Danish training enclave north of Strandhem, Jonna thought herself sufficiently prepared for this night. But knowing she could use a pistol or a mortar or machine gun did little to calm her nerves now.

She stood in the wheelhouse, transfixed by her first glimpse of Drogden rising above the horizon. As if magnetically drawn to the beacon, they motored across the inky water without lights, the engine set to an almost inaudible drone. Bjorn, Leo's first mate, explained that three other boats were similarly approaching the lighthouse from various directions, and no doubt were as on schedule as Leo.

"No sign of them yet," he said and handed his binoculars to Jonna.

Nostalgia tightened her throat as she viewed Drogden's full form. It stood some thirty feet tall, dark against the night sky, and topped with a tiny star of yellow light. Intermittently, the tower brightened as the beacon revolved. Too clearly, she saw her father polishing that lens, cranking the alert siren, laughing over a game of cards...and the *Engel* crew devouring her meals, the children running races around the perimeter, and Tove, embracing her for the first time.

Will you believe I'm doing this, Tove? The need is great, for Drogden, for our country. What it means to us, you and I, goes without saying. How I wish we were standing together! I have sat by idly for too long, and now I am afraid but not helpless. The calling to this place has brought me to my feet, my love. I'm sure you understand.

"It's been so long since I've seen Drogden," she said, taken by each timely rotation of light.

"I want it to look like that when we're done." Leo checked his watch and returned his hand to the helm. "We're lucky to have good seas tonight. Everyone should be on schedule."

"All seems quiet. No searchlights yet," Bjorn added.

"The main boat out of the Copenhagen area should be approaching directly from the west, the opposite side, so searchlights will probably focus on it first. Keep your eyes open."

"I think I see a boat." Jonna gave the glasses back to Bjorn. "To the north, see it?"

"You're right." Bjorn pivoted to look south. "And there's the other one. We're all in position."

"Except we can't see the other side," Jonna said, "the Copenhagen boat."

Leo checked his watch again. "We have to trust that it's already advancing. Time we all moved in closer."

"I'm going out to listen," Bjorn said and opened the door.

Leo stopped him as the bitter wind blew in. "Be ready. At the first sound of trouble…a siren or gunfire…" Bjorn gave a quick nod and left. As Jonna buttoned her coat to follow, Leo added, "I can't imagine all that this place means to you. Please be careful."

Before closing the door behind her, Jonna took another good look at Drogden. They were close enough now to see the cottages on either side of the tower. Newly-built sheds stood near the gun battery. No doubt soldiers had finally seen the need for such shelter or maybe the sheds were for ammunition. She wondered about the caliber of Nazis stationed there since her departure and hoped they were still as inept.

Ducking into the wind, she focused on following the plan they had devised in Strandhem. She brought a box of ammunition magazines to where the machine gun had been bolted to the deck.

Thankfully, Bjorn had military experience with it, and she knew how to assist. She pried open a crate of mortar rounds and slid a projectile out of its transport tube. Could she and Bjorn launch these from the boat and strike *only* the gun battery? The impact of the two-pound device made her blood race. *So much destruction from what looks like a baby torpedo.*

A low howling sounded over the rushing wind and Jonna spun to look at Bjorn. The wailing increased in pitch and volume. She knew the sound well. A Nazi lookout was cranking the Drogden alert siren.

They hurried to lean over the gunnel and see the lighthouse ahead. Less than a quarter mile away and closing fast, Leo pressed his engine. Searchlights on the far side stopped their random scanning to focus on something, no doubt the Copenhagen boat. Shouted commands now carried across the waves from the Drogden platform, and soldiers ran to designated posts. Jonna felt her heart rate increase.

It was time to give the Nazis more than they could handle and reclaim Drogden.

❖

That electrified sun near Drogden's beacon finally settled its beam on Tove's boat. Beside her at the helm, Captain Jensen simply locked his steadfast gaze into a squint and charged his *Rejse* toward the granite wall. None of his three hundred pounds even flinched. Tove turned away from the blinding light and chose to check the open deck behind her, glad to see it was empty but for random piles of canvas-covered cargo.

Jensen's six fishermen hid in their cabin while a dozen Resistance fighters waited in the cargo hold, all of them heavily armed. Nazi lookouts would only see an uninvited, idle fishing boat cruising their way, but that obviously concerned them enough to sound the alarm.

"That damn thing's as bad as those lights," Jensen grumbled. "Wish we could blow them all out."

"Shooting out the searchlights up there risks hitting the beacon," Tove said, "but we can take care of that alarm—hopefully before their patrol boats hear it." She shook her head at the annoying wail. "Send a friendly hello. Sound your horn."

Jensen tooted the horn twice and drew his *Rejse* closer to the steps along Drogden's side. Mercifully, the alarm stopped.

Peering up through the wheelhouse window, Tove watched sentries scurry in comical disarray as they sought their designated positions along the rail. She exchanged a nod with Jensen and took a breath to steady herself, then opened the door and yelled.

Men poured onto the deck like wharf rats. Three stood their ground and sprayed machine gunfire up at soldiers along the railing while Jensen steered into Drogden's protective fenders. A fisherman leaped onto the steps before the *Rejse* bounced away, and another tossed him lines to draw the boat in.

Jensen wrestled the waves, laboring to dock the boat in a hurry. His cursing nearly drowned out other distant blasts. "Finally!" he yelled. "We're set!"

"Hear that?" Tove shouted over the noise around them. "The other boats. Perfect timing!"

Gunshots and explosions could be heard from varying directions. Then the siren began again. Nazis were crying for help. The firing from on high diminished enough to know that the sentries had scrambled to counter multiple attacks.

Meanwhile, as fishermen with rifles kept Nazi fire to a minimum, two men readied a mortar on the deck. A Resistance fighter machine-gunned the horn off of the alarm siren.

Tove gestured toward the half-dozen fighters rushing up the steps.

"We have to unleash everything we've got now."

Bullets pierced the wheelhouse ceiling and Tove and Jensen dropped to their knees. The window shattered and Tove shook the glass off her sleeves, then scrambled outside.

She hustled directly to the mortar team. "The far end," she said, pointing to the distant reaches of Drogden's oval platform. "The battery's there."

"Gonna try but no promises!"

The three of them ducked as bullets pounded the deck around them.

"I don't care if you have to blow off the end of the island," she shouted, "just don't hit the damn tower!"

She ran to the gunnel, watching more fighters take the stairs. She jumped across to the granite landing and pain shot into her hip, dropping her to all fours. She had asked too much of her leg, but couldn't afford to care.

Pressed to Drogden's wall, she climbed with pistol in hand and eyes glued to the top. An explosion made the entire structure tremble. Some part of Drogden suffered dearly, but, although sizeable, the explosion wasn't big enough to have been the gun battery.

Rapid, frantic gunfire sounded ahead, and she hoped it meant the Resistance fighters who preceded her had survived that blast. Then another explosion came, staggering her on the steps. *Scars on this beloved place will last a lifetime.*

Near the top now, she lowered her head further, gun at the ready, and tried not to remember the last time she made this familiar climb. Jonna had been here, greeting her with open arms.

"Halt!"

Tove fired.

The sentry's corresponding shot singed her arm as he toppled to the waves below.

Dozens of shots rang out on the platform. Peeking over the top, she found a Resistance fighter dead several feet away and another—Dag—a few yards beyond her. She swallowed hard at the loss of her brave young friend.

Bullets seemed to rip along the railing from all sides as determined fishermen played their parts. Several fighters shot from behind the gun battery sheds, and she prayed her other comrades had not been lost. Nazi sentries, now firing from windows in the cottages and tower, appeared to be concentrating primarily on targets on the opposite side.

It was then Tove remembered the flimsy, emergency stairway on the other side of the island, and she assumed some brave fisherman had made that climb. Admittedly, she was thankful they had drawn the Nazis' attention.

She raced to the cottage, wincing at her aching leg, and hurled herself to the base of the wall, clear of any gunfire from above. But now, armed with only a pistol and facing the unmanageable distance to the gun battery, she swore at her predicament. Until she spotted the grenade clipped to Dag's jacket. *Can I get to it and then the battery? How far can I press my agility, my luck?*

A flurry of pistol fire then mixed with furious Danish voices, and Tove strained to discern the words. Suddenly, someone darted across the platform, blindly squeezing off wild shots back toward the tower and cottages. Tove flattened herself on the ground and held her breath.

The daring figure fell to the platform, screaming in a woman's voice. Guns erupted in her defense as she dragged herself behind the battery. Seizing the moment to retrieve Dag's grenade, Tove rushed into the open, yanked it off his jacket, and looked to the injured woman behind the battery.

"Use this then run!" she shouted, ready to send her the grenade.

The woman struggled onto a knee and, for a half-second, they faced each other across the platform.

CHAPTER THIRTY

Drogden Lighthouse, Denmark

A deafening explosion pounded the island's wall and knocked Jonna onto her side. The blazing fire in her calf howled for attention. *Why now?* She struggled back to her knees, taken by that Resistance fighter still holding his crouch out there in the open.

Please let me catch whatever is coming my way!

He readied something, probably a grenade, but was he hesitating or…in shock? His voice, that firm alto, replayed in her head.

Can't be.

The black knit cap and unruly blond hair hanging from it were little help, but Jonna had no time to think.

"Tove?"

"Jonna?"

"Oh, my God!"

"Hurry! Take this now!"

With all her senses reeling, Jonna caught the grenade. Breathless, she checked her surroundings and cringed at the realization that the remaining fighters sheltered behind what she now saw were ammunition sheds. Luckily, they were aware of what she was about to do.

Once she activated the grenade, everyone—including her, somehow—would have to run to safety. She had to trust they would provide covering fire, because, wounded or not, with Tove miraculously just yards away, she had to move or be blown to bits.

She held the grenade to the base of the battery, pulled the pin, and staggered to her feet.

The fighters unloaded at every Nazi position as they ran from the area. Jonna hobbled as fast as she could to where Tove huddled against the cottage wall and threw herself into her arms.

In the same motion, it seemed, Tove swung her onto her back and covered her with her body.

The deafening explosion erupted in two rounds and tossed their entwined forms toward the stairs. The loaded anti-aircraft gun blew apart and then the nearby supply of ammunition tore a chunk from the platform and the island's wall.

Steel, cement, and granite shrapnel rained everywhere, and Jonna heard Tove gasp, felt her flinch, and knew she had been stricken by debris.

"Tove! Are you—speak to me!"

"That was the good shoulder," Tove groaned, struggling to raise her head. "Jonna. Am I dreaming?"

Tove's eyes were dark with pain and exhaustion, but her attempt at a smile made Jonna's vision blur.

"If you are, then so am I." She cupped Tove's face in both hands and kissed her.

Two figures rushed to either side of them and went to their knees.

"Hans! Move!" a woman snapped. "Let's go, you two. Now!"

Jonna rose to a knee and gasped at the pain. "We're both hit."

"Something got my shoulder," Tove said as the woman helped her stand. Bent forward from her wound, she managed to guide Jonna up.

"So, you're Hans?" Jonna asked.

The woman's sharp eyes flashed to Tove. "My teacher."

"Jonna," Tove said through a wince, "this is Rakkel. Yes, I'm Hans."

"Come on!" the other fighter shouted. "The last two vermin have been taken away. The lighthouse has been cleared!"

Rakkel studied the dark sea beyond the platform. "We can't delay. Patrols will arrive any time now."

Jonna scanned her surroundings, the blight of damage, the bodies of comrades being hastily carried away. She hardly saw what used to be. Gazing up the whitewashed tower, she caught the beacon's flash.

"Nothing will erase our memories here. Not even this."

"And we'll make more," Tove said before sagging within Rakkel's grip.

Jonna limped closer and slid an arm around her waist. "We'll hold each other up." She drew Tove to her hip. "Rakkel, tell your leader Tove's gone with me. Until it's time to come home, we'll be in Sweden."

CHAPTER THIRTY-ONE

August 1947
Copenhagen, Denmark

"A few scattered weeks a year won't be enough." Jonna frowned at Drogden as they sailed away on the *Engel*. "Do you seriously think the Lighthouse Service will honor its promise?"

"Of course, it will," Tove stated. "After what you did? What your father did? Having you fill in for the keeper now and then will prove the job should be yours full-time."

"But we just spent five days there and I miss it already. My next chance won't come until October." She pouted. "Am I whining?"

"Like a child."

She sighed and closed her eyes to the summer sun. "I guess I *do* have other important work to do."

"And you've been slacking. How far along is the book?"

"Not very. Hey, writing isn't easy, especially without you. Recalling details of that period is uncomfortable, so many months feeling unsettled and lost, sad."

"And scared." Tove linked their arms as they gazed back at Drogden. "Never imagined we'd end up doing all we did." She shook her head slightly. "Hard to believe."

"I'm glad, excited, actually, that we decided to preserve our story, but it's so emotional. A trying exercise for us both." Jonna leaned against her along the gunnel. "You know, Tove Salling, if I had more help…"

"I promise to be a better collaborator, be more available. At least my hours on the *Engel* aren't as long as they used to be."

Jonna stroked Tove's warm cheek with the back of her fingers. Tove never seemed to worry about giving more hours to others than she had in her day. With their brief getaway to Drogden behind them now, Tove would return to work on the *Engel* and spend her free time with Jonna, preparing their new business enterprise on the docks.

"We could be open in a month or so," Tove reminded her. "Once we hire an assistant or two, our little sailing shop shouldn't demand much of our time at all."

"It would be wonderful to go to Drogden whenever we wanted—even if the Lighthouse Service gives my keeper's job to someone else."

"So, shopkeeper instead of lighthouse keeper would be okay?"

"I suppose so." She couldn't help but smile at Tove's hopeful expression. "And you will be okay with less of this?" She waved her hand to encompass the *Engel*, Drogden, and the Oresund. "Offering boating lessons to children will require some of those hours, you know."

"Captain Holsten knows we need to grow our new business. Besides, it's not as if either of us will be far from all this." She gestured to the strait. "I'll survive working here a little less to be with you a lot more." She nuzzled Jonna's ear.

Jonna hooked a finger inside a button of Tove's shirt and tugged her closer. "As long as we are together, cooking, writing, sailing, I don't care, and, honestly, it doesn't matter where, a little place we might find or if my family's flat is still available or…or even Drog—"

Tove's lips swept her away, resolute and divinely soft. Embracing at the *Engel*'s stern, Jonna could feel Tove's yearning against her hips, in the hands pressed to her back. The kiss lingered, grew, and Jonna wanted more. When they finally parted, she smiled at Tove's slow recovery. She could live forever on kisses like that.

"We should find us a cottage by the sea," Tove said gently.

Jonna warmed all over, just remembering that conversation from so long ago.

Awash in warm breezes off the Oresund and the feel of Tove's strength around her waist, Jonna's nerves simmered with memories. She hadn't thought any experience would surpass that special night on Salthoven, until their ultimate reunion in Sweden. The Drogden mission had left them both wounded and spent, but exultant to be together.

"Yes," she said, finally finding her voice. "I'd like searching for such a place to be our next mission."

"It has to be within view of Drogden." Tove kissed the tip of Jonna's nose. "Wherever we end up, whatever we do, love will guide us. And as for all of this," she added, her eyes twinkling, "the *Engel*, Drogden? They'll always be a part of us, my dearest Jonna, and we're inseparable."

Chapter Thirty-two

Nancy watched the water taxi pull away from the dock. The construction workers and everyone else on the island were aboard. She could have crammed on with them, but there were still a few last-minute items she wanted to check off her to-do list. Besides, since Sam left, there wasn't a lot enticing her back to the mainland.

She looked at the sky. The clouds looked darker and more menacing than they had when she'd turned down the ride off the island. The predicted storm wasn't supposed to roll in until the middle of the night. Hopefully, that was still true and she'd be snuggly tucked into her bed at home listening to the sounds of the rain and thunder overnight.

After one last look at the gathering storm, Nancy returned to the lighthouse. She'd spread old pictures, maps, and news clippings about the lighthouse across the floor in the main room. She picked her way through them, careful not to step on any, evaluating each as she passed.

Work on the lighthouse and adjacent buildings was nearing completion so she had begun focusing her energy on the look and feel of the interior spaces, with a special emphasis on the presentation of history. The items laid out on the floor were finalists to be framed and hung in places of prominence.

She picked up a black-and-white picture of the lighthouse. The original was taken at least one hundred years prior. She looked up toward the lantern above. *What must this wondrous building have seen in the past century?*

Her historical ruminations were interrupted by a loud crack of thunder. She nearly jumped out of her skin. She glanced out the window and it looked like the lights had been turned off on the world. A tingle of unease creep-crawled down her spine. If the storm blew in early, there was no way she'd get off the island.

Nancy used her phone to check the latest forecast and her fears were confirmed. The storm was upon her, hours earlier than predicted and more intense. Her phone lit up with text notifications from her family. They knew she'd been on the island today and wanted to know that she'd made it safely back to shore.

In responding to their concerns, hers melted away. This lighthouse had seen far worse in all its time. She would be safe here. She had food and water and shelter. Company would be nice, but she'd never minded solitude in small doses.

She climbed to the lantern room and evaluated the churning water below. She'd seen plenty of angry seas living with a family as closely connected to the water as hers, and this rivaled some of the most cantankerous.

Nancy did a double take as she scanned the Newport coastline. She rubbed her eyes, but they weren't deceiving her. Heading toward the island, nearly swallowed by the whitecaps and erratic waves, was a boat far too small to be out in such unfriendly weather. She watched, barely breathing, as the craft drew closer to the lighthouse. That the water taxi would make such a run now didn't make sense. The captain had been working these waters nearly as long as Nancy had been alive. He wouldn't risk his boat or his life to return for her. Not when she was safe and secure where she was.

The little boat continued its approach, getting tossed around violently as it did. Nancy was not eager to climb aboard and would instead insist they ride out the storm in the lighthouse. As the boat neared the dock, she knew it was in trouble and that whoever was captaining was not the skipper she knew. This person was in well over their head.

She clamored down the stairs, flung open the door, and raced across the island to the dock. She watched in horror as the boat was caught by a wave and thrown against the rocks. Remarkably, the boat was still afloat when the waves ebbed, but it was only seconds before the next crashing wave sent it back against the jagged shore, this time rending it in two.

Nancy rushed to the water's edge. Would anyone have survived such violence and need her assistance? She scanned the water, trying to pick out anyone needing rescue. Before she was able to discern whether anyone was alive in the rageful sea, a particularly sizable wave slammed ashore and deposited fiberglass shards, a cooler, and one wet, bedraggled human facedown in the sand.

There was no time for Nancy to do anything except drag the body farther ashore before waves sucked him back out to sea. Only once she was certain they were a safe distance onto the sand did she check for signs of life. Before she could flip the body, it stirred.

Startled, Nancy scrambled back, then she gasped to see Sam turn over. She sat up slowly, dazed, and began coughing up saltwater. Still stunned, Nancy collected herself and quickly stopped Sam from moving further.

"What the hell were you thinking? And don't move, I need to have a look at you. God, it's good to see you, you absolute idiot."

"Surprise," Sam croaked and smiled weakly. "By your reaction, I'm guessing my big romantic gesture fell a little short."

"The boat. Where's the captain? Oh, my God!" Nancy jumped up to head for the water, but Sam caught her arm.

"Only…me," she managed. "I was the captain. Should have asked for driving lessons before I bought the boat." She stood gingerly and rolled her neck, arms, and feet. "I'm going to be sore as hell, but I think I'm in one piece."

Nancy stood and crossed her arms, partly against the cold, driving rain, but mostly in anger. "You're lucky the sea chose to spit you out. What were you thinking, Sam?"

Sam looked at her feet. She was pale and suddenly shaky. Nancy's anger melted away. There was time for that later. She needed to get Sam inside, out of the rain, and make sure she really was okay.

"Come with me. Anything you brought belongs to the ocean now. Are you okay to walk up to the lighthouse?" Nancy took Sam's hand and tugged gently to get her moving.

"I'd crawl if it meant getting out of the rain."

They stumbled back toward shelter, taking considerably longer than Nancy had in her haste to reach the stricken vessel. By the time they made it through the lighthouse door, they were both drenched to the bone and shivering uncontrollably.

Once inside, Nancy continued guiding Sam who seemed in shock and only hesitated a moment when faced with the carefully arranged items on the floor. She set out on a path directly through the room but stopped short when Sam resisted.

"We'll get them wet." Sam pointed to the photos and other documents on the floor. "I'm not going to be the reason your precious history really is lost."

Nancy turned and truly looked at Sam for the first time since she'd crashed ashore. She searched her face and brushed a wet and sandy lock of hair off her cheek. "Fuck history, Sam. I care about you, right here, right now, in the present." She started again and this time Sam followed her. "I need to warm you up and look you over. Then, when I'm sure you're not going to die, I'm going to yell at you for a very long time."

"Always nice to know what's on the agenda." Sam's voice had none of its usual spark.

Nancy deposited Sam in a kitchen chair and set about dealing with their immediate needs. Having those tasks allowed her to ignore the emotions that were as restless and wild as the sea outside. She put a pot of water on to boil and searched the storage bins of food until she found tea. Since it was so expensive and time consuming to bring things out to the island, they'd stocked the small lighthouse kitchen with large quantities of a few essentials. The construction foreman was never without a hot cup of tea nearby.

In another stroke of luck, a first shipment of bedding had arrived earlier in the week. It was supposed to be used in marketing photos but now was destined for a more noble purpose. Most of the bedding she left in the main room of the lighthouse for later use, but she brought a blanket back to the kitchen and draped it over Sam's shoulders. Sam pulled it close.

Once the tea was ready, Nancy grabbed mugs, snacks, and Sam, and returned to the main room. She shoved her precious historical artifacts roughly to the side and spread the bedding and pillows on the floor.

"If we get in there now it will be wet and cold immediately. No choice but to remove some clothing and set it out to dry." Nancy tried to keep her voice level. It was a crisis, but she was still asking Sam to disrobe. Her heart rate kicked up.

"This is what it took for you to ask me to get naked?" Sam struggled with her shirt, but her hands were shaking too badly.

"Hey." Nancy raised an eyebrow in warning. She pulled Sam's shirt over her head. "The jokes aren't going to keep you out of trouble."

Once down to their underwear, they scooted between the sheets and two fluffy duvets. Nancy held her close.

"Your heart is pounding." Sam lifted her head from Nancy's chest and looked at her with concern. "I'm sorry."

"Jesus, Sam, you have a lot to explain to me, but start with what you're doing here and why you brought that boat out in this weather."

Sam sat up and took Nancy's hand. "I love you. That's the answer to both questions. It's the answer to so much in my life. I love you. That's why I'm here."

Nancy was at a loss. She'd wanted to hear Sam say those words since she'd realized the depth of her feelings, but what about everything else. Was love enough?

"Where did that come from? You haven't called or been in touch and now all of a sudden you had to see me in the middle of a storm? My phone still works, even now, you know." Nancy ignored the tears that were pooling in the corners of her eyes.

Sam rubbed both hands over her face and sighed. "I wasn't thinking. I haven't been thinking lately. I screwed up so much time we could have had together, I didn't want to waste anymore without you knowing how I felt. Rushing back to the lighthouse and declaring my love felt like a big romantic gesture you might appreciate."

"And now what? You go back home and I don't hear from you for weeks on end while you live your real life? I get to be the mistress to your company and you'll sneak off to be with me when you have a few free minutes?" Nancy moved away and wrapped her arms around her knees.

"God, I'm screwing this up." Sam looked distraught. "Let me start over." She sat up and held out her hand.

Nancy didn't accept the offered shake so Sam took Nancy's hand and joined them for a shake. She didn't let go when social niceties dictated one should, and instead entwined their fingers and held on.

"I'm Samantha McMann, CEO in name only of a big dumb company I have no interest in running. I didn't realize until I was back in the boardroom that I was stuck in a trap with an easy escape. I'm taking it. I'm in love with you. That's what I want as the first line of my obituary, that I loved Nancy Calhoun with all of my heart. They can mention the company as a footnote if there's room. I'm yours if you'll have me."

Nancy wiped away the tears that had begun falling in earnest. "The company isn't a footnote, Sam. You've made it clear it's who you are."

Sam shook her head swiftly enough to send water spraying across their blanket nest. "No. It's who my father wanted me to be, but it's not me. I didn't know there was a difference until I met you."

With a fullness, a dizzying warmth rushing into her chest, Nancy wanted to believe what Sam was saying, to get lost in her arms, but she held back. "What about your brother and the tabloids and all the hot actresses and models who would be heartbroken without you? I don't compare to any of them."

"God, you're right, you don't. You are so beautiful and brilliant and stunning and creative and gorgeous."

Nancy threw a pillow at Sam. "You're going to make me blush." She batted her eyelashes dramatically.

"My point is you have no comparator in my eyes. I only see you. As for my brother, he loves the business and the company. I gave full control of the company to him."

"So, you went from CEO to unemployed and now's when you choose to come woo me?" Nancy scooted closer to Sam and cupped her cheek. It was rough with the ocean's salt residue.

"I was hoping you and I could find ways to keep ourselves busy and spend some of my money together." Sam looked adorably hopeful. "If you would reconsider being in the spotlight on my arm, there's an entire charitable side to my company that could use far more care than it's currently getting. Maybe we could focus our attention there?"

Nancy considered. Could it possibly be as good as it sounded? She didn't need the wealth or influence, but she knew they were part of Sam. So, too, was increased scrutiny and some invasion of privacy. "This isn't all a joke, right? You're not going to disappear on me again if I say yes?"

"I bought a boat I had no idea what to do with so I could sail through a storm to get to you. I'm very serious." Sam's voice was as soft, as revealing as the look in her eyes.

There was no point drawing out the inquisition further. She was Sam's and had been for a long time. Like the lighthouse, they'd find a way to blend their lives together seamlessly, no matter how opposed they appeared.

"I tried so hard to not like you." Nancy pulled Sam close and kissed her. "But I accidentally fell in love with you instead."

They stayed like that, holding each other close and kissing, until Sam's ordeal caught up with her and she drifted to sleep. Nancy held her and listened to her even, steady breaths. She was certain the ferocity of the storm outside paled in comparison to the depths of her feelings for the woman asleep in her arms. Mrs. Jones had been right after all. They were two women destined for love. Nancy had never had a sweeter end to a journey.

Sam woke disoriented, hesitant to move. She smelled like the ocean and was stiff and sore. Her terrifying trip across the bay and violent marooning rushed back, and she struggled against something pinning her in place, not yet awake enough to distinguish memory from present.

"It's okay. Whatever it was, you were dreaming."

Sam fully opened her eyes and was greeted by Nancy's concern and her comforting arms. "I'm okay. I forgot where I was. I thought you were the ocean trying to kill me again." She sat up and stretched.

It wasn't until that moment that she remembered that she wasn't wearing anything other than a bra and boxer briefs. Even more importantly, Nancy was similarly attired. Sam played her finger along Nancy's hairline, down her cheek, and along her neck. She skirted her collarbone and swirled her touch around her pulse point.

"You know, Tove and Jonna were shipwrecked on an island together, too." Sam raised her eyebrows in what she hoped was a suggestive way.

"I'm not shipwrecked." Nancy kissed the pad of each of Sam's fingers. "That's a title only you can claim."

Sam pulled her hand back and gave an exaggerated sigh. "That's too bad. I was hoping we could spend our time shipwrecked similarly to how they spent theirs."

Nancy inched closer and reconnected their hands. "I'm sure we're allowed creative license. Tell me how they spent their time."

"It's much better if I show you." Sam closed the distance between them and kissed Nancy onto her back. "Tell me if you want me to stop."

"You better not." Nancy yanked Sam down to her breast. "I've waited too long for this."

Sam withheld the attention Nancy sought. Her fingers tingled in anticipation of finally getting to touch Nancy. Her mouth watered. She wasn't going to rush.

"You want me to touch you here?" Sam hovered her hands over Nancy's breasts, still covered by her lacy, hot pink bra. "I don't think so, not yet."

Nancy whimpered. Sam's heart skittered. She'd barely touched her and already Nancy was so responsive. It was heady and emboldened Sam.

"I think I'll start here." Sam flattened her palms across Nancy's stomach and traced a lazy path with her tongue. "I want to memorize your body."

Before Sam knew what had happened, she was on her back with Nancy on top of her. Nancy pinned her hands above her head and leaned down to whisper in Sam's ear. "I think I get the idea. You'll have time to memorize my body, I promise, a lifetime. But right now, I want you to tell me how you want to be fucked."

Sam's center clenched so abruptly it shot pleasure through her stomach and down her legs. She was worried she would come if Nancy continued speaking. She'd never been topped, but the idea she was about to be sent her blood pumping to exactly where she needed it.

"I want you." Sam kissed Nancy, hard.

"You're going to have me. Spread your legs for me, babe. I want you too." Nancy nudged Sam's legs apart and settled between them.

Nancy's weight on her and the added pressure to her center had Sam feeling wanton. She pumped her hips looking for something, anything, to provide some relief. She was throbbing and hard but Nancy stayed away, teasing her.

"You're beautiful." Nancy removed both their bras and shimmied out of her briefs while straddling Sam.

Sam watched the show and knew she was dripping wet. Nancy's body was too perfect, Sam couldn't help herself. She took a breast in each hand and teased Nancy's nipples. She was rewarded with a loud moan of pleasure and Nancy removing her boxers with expert efficiency. The cool air touched Sam's wet center and made her shiver. What was Nancy doing to her?

Nancy kissed her again, revving Sam up with the intensity of their frantic kissing and groping, only to dial it back down. Sam wasn't sure her clit could take the orgasmic roller coaster much longer.

"I want to watch you touch yourself while I get my fill of these." Nancy circled her tongue around one of Sam's nipples. "Then we're going to switch and I'm going to watch you play with your breasts while I make you come."

"If you keep talking to me like that, I'm going to embarrass myself and come in my own hand." Sam did as she was told and ran her fingers through her slick, wet folds.

Nancy's eyes flickered with unrestrained desire. Sam had never felt more beautiful or wanted. "You won't come until you're in my mouth."

The command sent another shockwave directly to Sam's clit. "You better get your mouth to work." She increased the speed of her ministrations.

Nancy wasted no time. She devoured first one, then the other breast, sucking Sam's nipples into her mouth and circling them with her tongue. She bit gently and then more roughly as Sam moaned with pleasure.

Sam was close to the edge and desperate for all Nancy had promised. She stopped the motion of her own hand and pushed Nancy down, urging her to move to her aching, dripping center.

Nancy circled the tip of her tongue over Sam's clit with enough pressure to keep Sam teetering on the edge, but not enough to drive her over. She seemed to sense when Sam was about to cross the point of no return because she pulled back and rested her head on Sam's thigh. "Do you know how long I've wanted you in my mouth? Are you ready to come for me?"

Sam made a noise she hoped conveyed everything she was feeling and brought her hands to her own breasts. She took a nipple between the thumb and index finger of each hand and squeezed. "Make me come."

Nancy licked along her clit then sucked it entirely in her mouth. She circled and sucked, finding every nerve capable of enhancing Sam's pleasure. When Sam didn't think it possible to feel more, Nancy plunged first one, then another finger inside and Sam careened over the edge, crying Nancy's name as she came.

When Sam opened her eyes, Nancy was on all fours, between her legs, leaning over her looking stunning and in love. "I'm glad you're not bad at that." Sam smiled as she watched Nancy sort out the compliment.

While she was occupied, Sam traced her finger down the center of Nancy's chest and abdomen and directly to her center. She swirled her fingers through the wet heat and sank two fingers deep inside.

Nancy dropped onto her elbows, resting her forehead on Sam's chest, and settled deeper on Sam's hand. "Yes, Sam. More."

Sam pulled her fingers out and thrust back in, thrilling at the feel of Nancy's walls contracting around her hand. She found a rhythm and matched the movement of Nancy's hips against her. Nancy moved her hips faster and moaned more loudly as Sam increased her own speed and depth.

"Fuck me. So close. Fuck me, Sam. Fuck me." Nancy worked her hips hard against Sam's hand, her pace more erratic.

Sam caught Nancy in a fiery kiss and pushed deep inside her. Nancy screamed out her pleasure and came in two giant waves.

Sam stayed in deep, letting Nancy ride out the aftershocks before pulling out slowly and collecting Nancy in her arms. "I don't know why there are so many books about the misery of being shipwrecked."

Nancy bit Sam's lower lip and then kissed the spot. "I shouldn't have rewarded you for your foolishness but I couldn't help it. I love you too damn much."

"This lighthouse knew what it was doing, bringing us together. In you, I found home and if I ever get lost, the lighthouse can lead me back." Sam traced a meandering circle along Nancy's back.

Nancy propped herself on her elbows and gazed at Sam. "Saying things like that guarantees neither of us will get any sleep tonight." She cupped Sam's center and squeezed.

Sam didn't want to get any sleep. She wanted to drink up every moment with Nancy. They'd fought each other and fate, but in the end the lighthouse had won. She knew it would always be a symbol of their love, strong, steady, and bright.

EPILOGUE

Six months later

Nancy woke to the sound of a symphony of sea birds and rolling waves lapping at every shore of their island. She stretched and ran her hand up Sam's naked torso. Before she reached her breasts, Sam caught Nancy's hand and kissed her palm.

"Are you sure you want to go through with this? It's not too late to keep the island all to ourselves. We could repeat last night in every room, and when we're done we can start again." Sam raised her eyebrows cheekily.

"You're a scoundrel, you know that? It is far too late to call off the grand opening of our lighthouse dream project. But I love waking up naked with you and the sound of the sea, so we'll need to find ways to do it as often as possible." Nancy kissed Sam deeply before hopping out of bed.

"Where are you going? I'm still naked and we still have the whole island to ourselves for a little while longer." Sam posed provocatively.

Nancy stayed as far away as she could manage in the bedroom of the luxury suite. "You're nearly impossible to resist, but I don't want to greet any early birds screaming your name. Besides, I have a surprise for you."

That got Sam's attention. "I love surprises. You should have led with that." She was up and hopping one-legged into pants and pulling a shirt over her head before Nancy could say more. "Come on, what are you waiting for?" Sam tossed a shirt Nancy's way.

"I'm a little offended you're so eager to cover these." Nancy cupped her breasts.

"I know where they live and half the fun is uncovering them. Now, what's the surprise?"

Nancy took her time pulling on clothes and freshening up in the bathroom. She didn't dare make Sam wait while she showered. The poor woman would likely explode. As it was, she found Sam on the couch practically vibrating out of her seat with anticipation.

"Okay, love, let me get my laptop." Nancy retrieved her computer and sat snuggled tightly in Sam's arm. "I know how much you loved that book about Tove and Jonna. I thought you might also like this."

Nancy pushed play on the video of Tove and Jonna being interviewed about their book in the nineties, marking the fiftieth anniversary of the end of the war.

As soon as the two women appeared on screen, Sam gasped and covered her mouth. "Where did you find this?"

"A lot of great history is gathering dust in archives somewhere. Or in this case, a back cabinet of the internet." She kissed Sam's cheek.

They watched in silence as Tove and Jonna answered the interviewer's questions. Most focused on Tove's time with the Resistance and the final mission to retake Drogden. Their love was never mentioned but it was easy to see how deeply it still ran between them.

"The way they look at each other is so beautiful." Sam paused the video. "Do you think that's what people see when we look at each other?"

"I can't speak for anyone else as to what they do or don't see, but that look is how I feel whenever I look at you." Nancy took Sam's hand and leaned her head on Sam's chest.

"You took the words right out of my mouth."

Sam restarted the video and they watched the last few minutes as wrapped up in each other as what was playing on the screen. It wasn't until the interviewer asked the final question that they both snapped back full attention.

"Did they say they moved to Florida?" Sam looked at Nancy hopefully. "Do you think there's any way they could still be alive?"

Nancy's heart leapt with the possibility before reality let the air out of the balloon of hope. "They'd be over one hundred if they were. But I think I might know someone who has the answer. Check out the second video." Nancy pointed Sam to the second half of her surprise.

The second video was one Nancy hadn't seen yet either. It was amateur movie quality and clearly taken in someone's home. Tove and Jonna were easy to recognize despite having aged at least twenty years from the prior video.

"It's Tove's ninetieth birthday. How did you get this video?" Sam looked at Nancy, stunned. "This couldn't have been hiding somewhere on the internet waiting for you to stumble upon it."

Nancy was at a loss for words. It was an incredible gift to see these two amazing women still so deeply in love after seventy years. She didn't know how to explain to Sam how she'd gotten the video or her suspicion about who had provided it, but it turned out she didn't need to.

Before she could answer Sam's query, Jonna gestured off camera. "Naysa, come join us. You should be in this picture too."

"Naysa?" Sam leaned forward as the young girl from her book, now a grown woman in her eighties entered the picture. For the second time, Sam gasped. "Mrs. Jones?" She looked at Nancy. "Did you know?"

"Happy Birthday to You" played from the laptop. Nancy's heart was full. "I suspected. She was the one who gave me this. She must have changed her name when she came to America as a child. It was a common thing back then."

Sam frowned. "How the hell did you figure it out?"

Nancy laughed. "The book, her love of lighthouses, and she swore in Danish the day she told us we were going to fall in love. It made me question whether she'd been there, back then. I didn't have any idea she was Naysa until I watched just now with you."

Sam pulled Nancy to her and kissed her. "Thank you. I don't know how you managed to make me a history nerd, but Tove and Jonna, the *Gerda III*, Drogden, it feels so alive to me. Do you think people will walk away from our lighthouse feeling like this?"

"I hope so. And if they don't, I hope they remember this being the best resort they've ever visited, with the most amazing bar, and views that can't be replicated anywhere else in the world." Nancy pulled Sam to her feet and wove her hands under her shirt and up her back.

"I guess we'd better go open it up to the world then." Sam pulled Nancy down the hall toward the shower.

Despite their best efforts to keep their hands to themselves, they weren't terribly successful and were very nearly late to their own party. Thankfully, they didn't have far to travel since the grand opening celebration was a stone's throw away from the suite where they'd stayed the night.

As they walked toward the fanfare and ceremony awaiting them, Nancy took Sam's hand. She'd never felt more at home than she did in that moment. "Will you take me to Drogden one day? I want you to tell me her story."

Sam grinned widely. "You tell me when you want to leave and we'll be on our way."

They took their seats next to the board members and other dignitaries. Even though they were the owners of the lighthouse and resort, today didn't seem to be about them. Plenty of others wanted to be seen which was gratifying for Nancy. The more people invested in their lighthouse, the more people would come to visit.

After too many had talked for far too long, Nancy stood. Her belly was full of butterflies. She saw her family in the small crowd and smiled. Sam gave her hand a squeeze before letting go. She took a breath. She could do this.

"Thank you all for being here today. When Sam and I started this project, we had very different ideas about what this day should look like. It took quite a bit of arguing and a bit of gentle coaxing, but we came to this place of joined vision. We are honoring the past and looking to the future. Before we start the party, I want to make one final unveiling." Nancy motioned to one of the construction crew at the main lighthouse building just to her right.

He pulled down a sheet covering a large bronze plaque.

"This lighthouse is one in a vast network of sister spirits. These sisters speak the same language and serve the same noble purpose, to stand sentry over our waterways and protect mariners as they pass dangerous shores. Whether you are visiting our lighthouse or one across the world, these beautiful sisters will always help guide you safely home." Nancy nodded slightly to the applauding crowd before returning to her seat.

Mrs. Jones leaned over and took her hand, tears in her eyes. "That was beautiful, my child. I knew this lighthouse was in good hands with the two of you. Sam, thank you for opening your heart to Drogden and Tove and Jonna. Their legacy should never be lost to history and not just because they saved me. And as for the two of you, love each other well."

Somehow, Nancy just knew they would. She saw the same devotion in Sam's eyes that she had seen in Tove's in the videos. She hadn't thought happiness of this magnitude was possible. It didn't feel like her chest could hold it all inside. She took Sam's hand and held it tightly.

Mrs. Jones surprised her with a tap on the knee with her cane.

"You two," she began confidentially. "Remember when each of you thought you had *the* answer?" As she shook her head, her craggily smile spoke volumes. "A lighthouse is so much bigger than a single dream. That's why, for years, there were chains of them, sisters arm-in-arm overseeing vast distances."

She leaned on her cane as she stood to leave, but turned with still more to say. "Ever since I was a little girl, I believed the beam was magical. So bright and proud, through thick and thin, it speaks, doesn't it? Touches you from afar. That's how a lighthouse shares love, you know." She winked, preparing to shuffle away. "I'm so very happy it guided you two home."

About the Authors

CF Frizzell

A life-long Massachusetts resident with backgrounds in journalism and telecom, CF Frizzell writes in various genres with a reporter's penchant for detail and depth. She is a Golden Crown Literary Society multiple-award winner for novels in both contemporary and historical romance. Her *Measure of Devotion*, set in the American Civil War, has been honored as a 2023 finalist by the American Fiction Awards in three categories: Historical Fiction, LGBTQ+ Fiction, and Historical Romance.

CF "Friz" Frizzell credits Bold Strokes Books powerhouse authors Lee Lynch, Radclyffe, and the generous BSB family for inspiration. Her introduction to BSB began as a rabid reader, advanced to volunteer BSB proofreader, and then to hopeful, aspiring writer, winning the 2015 GCLS Debut Author Award for her historical romance, *Stick McLaughlin: The Prohibition Years*. She is into history, sports, and Guild guitars—and her truly amazing wife, Kathy, and their chocolate Lab, Chessa.

Jesse J. Thoma

Although she works best under the pressure of a deadline, Jesse Thoma balks at being told what to do. Despite that, she's no fool and knows she'd be lost without her editor's brilliance. While writing, Jesse is usually under the close supervision of a snoring dog and judgmental cat or two. *Guide Us Home* is Jesse's tenth novel. *Seneca Falls* was a finalist for a Lambda Literary Award in romance. *Data Capture, Serenity*, and *Courage* were finalists for the Golden Crowne Literary Society "Goldie" Award.

Books Available from Bold Strokes Books

Blood Rage by Illeandra Young. A stolen artifact, a family in the dark, an entire city on edge. Can SPEAR agent Danika Karson juggle all three over a weekend with the "in-laws," while an unknown, malevolent entity lies in wait upon her very skin? (978-1-63679-539-3)

Ghost Town by R.E. Ward. Blair Wyndon and Leif Henderson are set to prove ghosts exist when the mystery suddenly turns deadly. Someone or something else is in Masonville, and if they don't find a way to escape, they might never leave. (978-1-63679-523-2)

Good Christian Girls by Elizabeth Bradshaw. In this heartfelt coming of age lesbian romance, Lacey and Jo help each other untangle who they are from who everyone says they're supposed to be. (978-1-63679-555-3)

Guide Us Home by CF Frizzell and Jesse J. Thoma. When acquisition of an abandoned lighthouse pits ambitious competitors Nancy and Sam against each other, it takes a WWII tale of two brave women to make them see the light. (978-1-63679-533-1)

Lost Harbor by Kimberly Cooper Griffin. For Alice and Bridget's love to survive, they must find a way to reconcile the most important passions in their lives—devotion to the church and each other. (978-1-63679-463-1)

Never a Bridesmaid by Spencer Greene. As her sister's wedding gets closer, Jessica finds that her hatred for the maid of honor is a bit more complicated than she thought. Could it be something more than hatred? (978-1-63679-559-1)

The Rewind by Nicole Stiling. For police detective Cami Lyons and crime reporter Alicia Flynn, some choices break hearts. Others leave a body count. (978-1-63679-572-0)

Turning Point by Cathy Dunnell. When Asha and her former high school bully Jody struggle to deny their growing attraction, can they move forward without going back? (978-1-63679-549-2)

When Tomorrow Comes by D. Jackson Leigh. Teague Maxwell, convinced she will die before she turns 41, hires animal rescue owner Baye Cobb to rehome her extensive menagerie. (978-1-63679-557-7)

You Had Me at Merlot by Melissa Brayden. Leighton and Jamie have all the ingredients to turn their attraction into love, but it's a recipe for disaster. (978-1-63679-543-0)

All Things Beautiful by Alaina Erdell. Casey Norford only planned to learn to paint like her mentor, Leighton Vaughn, not sleep with her. (978-1-63679-479-2)

Appalachian Awakening by Nance Sparks. The more Amber's and Leslie's paths cross, the more this hike of a lifetime begins to look like a love of a lifetime. (978-1-63679-527-0)

Dreamer by Kris Bryant. When life seems to be too good to be true and love is within reach, Sawyer and Macey discover the truth about the town of Ladybug Junction, and the cold light of reality tests the hearts of these dreamers. (978-1-63679-378-8)

Eyes on Her by Eden Darry. When increasingly violent acts of sabotage threaten to derail the opening of her glamping business, Callie Pope is sure her ex, Jules, has something to do with it. But Jules is dead…isn't she? (978-1-63679-214-9)

Head Over Heelflip by Sander Santiago. To secure the biggest prizes at the Colorado Amateur Street Sports Tour, Thomas Jefferson will do almost anything, even marrying his best friend and crush—Arturo "Uno" Ortiz. (978-1-63679-489-1)

Letters from Sarah by Joy Argento. A simple mistake brought them together, but Sarah must release past love to create a future with Lindsey she never dreamed possible. (978-1-63679-509-6)

Lost in the Wild by Kadyan. When their plane crash-lands, Allison and Mike face hunger, cold, a terrifying encounter with a bear, and feelings for each other neither expects. (978-1-63679-545-4)

Not Just Friends by Jordan Meadows. A tragedy leaves Jen struggling to figure out who she is and what is important to her. (978-1-63679-517-1)

Of Auras and Shadows by Jennifer Karter. Eryn and Rina's unexpected love may be exactly what the Community needs to heal the rot that comes not from the fetid Dark Lands that surround the Community but from within. (978-1-63679-541-6)

The Secret Duchess by Jane Walsh. A determined widow defies a duke and falls in love with a fashionable spinster in a fight for her rightful home. (978-1-63679-519-5)

Winter's Spell by Ursula Klein. When former college roommates reunite at a wedding in Provincetown, sparks fly, but can they find true love when evil sirens and trickster mermaids get in the way? (978-1-63679-503-4)

Coasting and Crashing by Ana Hartnett Reichardt. Life comes easy to Emma Wilson until Lake Palmer shows up at Alder University and derails her every plan. (978-1-63679-511-9)

Every Beat of Her Heart by KC Richardson. Piper and Gillian have their own fears about falling in love, but will they be able to overcome those feelings once they learn each other's secrets? (978-1-63679-515-7)

Grave Consequences by Sandra Barret. A decade after necromancy became licensed and legalized, can Tamar and Maddy overcome the lingering prejudice against their kind and their growing attraction to each other to uncover a plot that threatens both their lives? (978-1-63679-467-9)

Haunted by Myth by Barbara Ann Wright. When ghost-hunter Chloe seeks an answer to the current spectral epidemic, all clues point to one very famous face: Helen of Troy, whose motives are more complicated than history suggests and whose charms few can resist. (978-1-63679-461-7)

Invisible by Anna Larner. When medical school dropout Phoebe Frink falls for the shy costume shop assistant Violet Unwin, everything about their love feels certain, but can the same be said about their future? (978-1-63679-469-3)

Like They Do in the Movies by Nan Campbell. Celebrity gossip writer Fran Underhill becomes Chelsea Cartwright's personal assistant with the aim of taking the popular actress down, but neither of them anticipates the clash of their attraction. (978-1-63679-525-6)

Limelight by Gun Brooke. Liberty Bell and Palmer Elliston loathe each other. They clash every week on the hottest new TV show, until Liberty starts to sing and the impossible happens. (978-1-63679-192-0)

Playing with Matches by Georgia Beers. To help save Cori's store and help Liz survive her ex's wedding they strike a deal: a fake relationship, but just for one week. There's no way this will turn into the real deal. (978-1-63679-507-2)

The Memories of Marlie Rose by Morgan Lee Miller. Broadway legend Marlie Rose undergoes a procedure to erase all of her unwanted memories, but as she starts regretting her decision, she discovers that the only person who could help is the love she's trying to forget. (978-1-63679-347-4)

The Murders at Sugar Mill Farm by Ronica Black. A serial killer is on the loose in southern Louisiana and it's up to three women to solve the case while carefully dancing around feelings for each other. (978-1-63679-455-6)

Fire in the Sky by Radclyffe and Julie Cannon. Two women from different worlds have nothing in common and every reason to wish they'd never met—except for the attraction neither can deny. (978-1-63679-573-7)

A Talent Ignited by Suzanne Lenoir. When Evelyne is abducted and Annika believes she has been abandoned, they must risk everything to find each other again. (978-1-63679-483-9)

An Atlas to Forever by Krystina Rivers. Can Atlas, a difficult dog Ellie inherits after the death of her best friend, help the busy hopeless romantic find forever love with commitment-phobic animal behaviorist Hayden Brandt? (978-1-63679-451-8)

Bait and Witch by Clifford Mae Henderson. When Zeddi gets an unexpected inheritance from her client Mags, she discovers that Mags served as high priestess to a dwindling coven of old witches—who are positive that Mags was murdered. Zeddi owes it to her to uncover the truth. (978-1-63679-535-5)

Buried Secrets by Sheri Lewis Wohl. Tuesday and Addie, along with Tuesday's dog, Tripper, struggle to solve a twenty-five-year-old mystery while searching for love and redemption along the way. (978-1-63679-396-2)

Come Find Me in the Midnight Sun by Bailey Bridgewater. In Alaska, disappearing is the easy part. When two men go missing, state trooper Louisa Linebach must solve the case, and when she thinks she's coming close, she's wrong. (978-1-63679-566-9)

Death on the Water by CJ Birch. The Ocean Summit's authorities have ruled a death on board its inaugural cruise as a suicide, but Claire suspects murder and with the help of Assistant Cruise Director Moira, Claire conducts her own investigation. (978-1-63679-497-6)

Living For You by Jenny Frame. Can Sera Debrek face real and personal demons to help save the world from darkness and open her heart to love? (978-1-63679-491-4)

Mississippi River Mischief by Greg Herren. When a politician turns up dead and Scotty's client is the most obvious suspect, Scotty and his friends set out to prove his client's innocence. (978-1-63679-353-5)

Ride with Me by Jenna Jarvis. When Lucy's vacation to find herself becomes Emma's chance to remember herself, they realize that everything they're looking for might already be sitting right next to them—if they're willing to reach for it. (978-1-63679-499-0)

Whiskey and Wine by Kelly and Tana Fireside. Winemaker Tessa Williams and sex toy shop owner Lace Reynolds are both used to taking risks, but will they be willing to put their friendship on the line if it gives them a shot at finding forever love? (978-1-63679-531-7)